BOOKER – No Más

A Novel

Volume 5

By
John W. Mefford

Sugar Hill Publishing

ISBN-10:1943774048
ISBN-13: 978-1-943774-04-3

Interior book design by
Bob Houston eBook Formatting

To stay updated on John's latest releases, visit:
JohnWMefford.com/readers-group

One

My first mistake became vividly obvious two minutes after the taxi driver zipped out of Joaquin Balaguer International Airport. Without even tapping the brake, the bushy-haired driver barreled the hunk of metal into a herd of vehicles, leaning the rust-covered four-door so hard to the left we clipped the front fender of an open-bed truck carrying chicken coops. I slid across the glazed, plastic-covered backseat, slamming me against the door—which then flew open.

Clinging to the door, my momentum shoved me out into traffic, my ass nearly grazing the pavement at about fifty miles per hour. My eye caught the same black fender we'd just hit, only inches from the swinging door. Fighting a potent centrifugal force, I muscled up to where my hands had a solid grip of the window opening. Just as I torqued my torso to thrust my body into the backseat, the car tumbled over clumps of hay, sending me straight up, then back down.

Something popped at the hinge, and the door dropped a good six inches.

The shocks must have been made from sponges as metal scraped the pavement, sending sparks into my eyes. Sensing I was seconds away from tumbling into the chaotic traffic and ending up as road kill, I swung my right arm toward the frame of the car and grabbed it. Using my opposite arm to push off the flapping door, I hurled my body into the backseat. The second my butt hit plastic, the door snapped off the frame and cartwheeled down the road, splitting traffic in half.

At age thirty-two, I thought I'd just experienced my first heart attack.

But that was just in the first couple of miles when my heart palpitations hit meteoric highs.

Horns blared all around us. The driver simply saluted his fellow road warriors and pulled something out of his pocket and lit it up. He inhaled twice, then grinned, gazing into the cracked rearview. *"Bueno Focus."*

As my breathing motored like a jackrabbit, my eyes squinted against the remnants of hay fluttering into the car. "What?" I asked, realizing he probably couldn't speak a lick of English.

"Bueno Focus." He tapped the discolored yellow dashboard, showing off teeth the same color.

If I didn't know better, I'd say the amused cab driver was part of a movie set featuring the worst stunt drivers on the planet. I just then noticed the logo on the wheel and pieced together what he was trying to tell me. His Ford Focus was a good car.

I would have agreed, maybe about fifteen years ago.

The cab hit a patch of traffic, and we crawled along for a while, which only drew more stares. Scared eyes glanced at me as if I'd taken part in some atrocity. Releasing my clutch of the front passenger seat, I tried to ignore the shifting heads and beady eyes, and leaned against the plastic, finally able to take in a deep breath.

I smelled pot. I swatted the air under my nose, shooting an eye toward the driver, who instantly jerked the car onto the graveled shoulder and gunned the little four-banger. At the next opening, he veered left without so much as glancing in his mirrors. We nearly side-swiped a convertible sports car. I grabbed the front seat and promised myself not to let go until we reached our destination.

Twenty minutes later, Meat Head made a beeline toward a tiny opening in front of Hotel Don Juan—parallel parking apparently wasn't part of his driving test. He shoved the fourteen-foot car nose-first into a ten-foot space, popping the right front tire onto the curb.

For whatever reason, I chose not to slide out the open-aired side. Instead, I heaved myself out the right side, grabbing my brown leather duffel bag.

Which leads me back to my list of mistakes. The second one hit me in the wallet. I should have negotiated a price before I got in the car.

"*¿Usted me puede pagar 50 dólares? O lo podría llevar a una mala parte de la ciudad?*"

In so many words, I was able to piece together that I had to fork over fifty US dollars or he would keep driving me until he reached the bad part of the city.

Not willing to put my life on the line to save a few bucks in a country I knew nothing about—and realizing I could bill my new clients—I handed over three twenties and held out my hand through the driver's side door.

"*¿Diez?*" I wanted my ten bucks in change.

Cackling up a wet lung, his eyes hidden under wrinkled flesh, he popped the clutch, and the vehicle screeched away, barreling over my sandaled foot, leaving a plume of polluted smoke.

"Uggh!" I yelled out, hopping on one foot. I would have shot him the finger if I didn't think I'd draw the ire of his taxi-driver brethren hovered around me. Maybe he was in a hurry to go find his door. Or maybe he'd dump the car and use the fifty bucks I just gave him for an upgrade.

"Mother…" I said, under my breath, wiggling my toes to determine if the three thousand pounds of torque had displaced any of the hundreds of bones in my foot.

Out of the corner of my eye, I noticed a guy waving an arm. I turned my head while still leaning over and bending my toes, my leather duffel bag sitting next to me.

"Our Lady of Divine Providence." Eyes wide with reverence or fear—I wasn't sure—a kid crossed himself. "That is my church. I made a pledge to never curse, and to call out all others who do. There is a better place. And I can take you there."

He'd yet to blink once.

"Sorry if I offended you," I said, noticing peach fuzz above his lip. "It's just this ass…uh, almost killed me driving like a bat out of hell, then ripped me off, and ran over my frickin' foot. Welcome to Santo Domingo, I guess."

I turned my attention back to my foot, but a quick blur snapped my head right. The little heathen had stolen my bag—a very expensive bag at that.

"Fuck!" My patience meter was redlining as I darted off to catch the little shit. The way the locals were playing me, I must have had "Naive American" plastered on my forehead.

Weaving through people like slalom skiers, I wasn't gaining much ground, even though the kid didn't look a day older than thirteen. I caught the flash of his red shirt hurtling a small stone wall, the bag's straps draped over his back. He was a pro at this and probably knew exactly how to elude any tourist ballsy enough to chase after him.

Veering right, I took a sharper angle and leaped over the same stone wall farther down, just as he looked back.

That was his biggest mistake.

He didn't see the bellman crossing the path with a cart full of luggage. The kid went airborne.

"Mierdita. Debería de llamar a la policía para meter tu culo sin hogar en la cárcel," the bellman yelled at the kid, who appeared woozy just as I ran up.

I couldn't understand much of his rapid-fire Spanish rant, but I did get "police." Also, because of past experience with my Latin ex-fiancée, Eva, I knew that he'd called the kid a little shit.

Couldn't blame him.

I held out my hand for the kid. His lips drew a straight line as he glanced left and right, perhaps looking for a better option, wondering if I would lead the procession to the local precinct.

"Are you hurt?"

He brushed himself off, even though he'd landed on cushy luggage. "I'm good," he said. "Just seeing how fast you are."

"How old are you?"

"Old enough to drive in Santo Domingo." Crooked teeth split his face, and he lifted his arms wide, as if laying claim to the entire bustling city.

"Figures."

"You going to call *policía?*"

The bellman continued muttering phrases under his breath as he started reassembling his cart.

"Why don't you help him?"

The kid forced out a breath. "Not my *trabajo.*"

"Help him."

Forcing out a breath, the kid picked up the remaining bags and reloaded the cart. The man turned to me and said, *"Gracias, señor."*

"De nada."

I picked up my bag and tried to acquaint myself with the layout of the hotel grounds. Off in the distance, I spotted the aqua ripples and whitecaps of the Caribbean Ocean and started walking in that direction, quickly realizing my foot still hurt.

"Damn driver," I said to no one.

"You like that bag, don't you?"

Glancing down, the kid's bare feet smacked the stained concrete.

"You speak good English."

"The land of Dominican Republic is filled with many surprises. Welcome to my land," he said, taking a bow while walking.

"Yeah, thanks." I stopped in my tracks, holding up my hand so the kid wouldn't plow into an older couple walking across our path. They both wore wrap-around shades.

"Hip," the kid said, a smile escaping his face.

"What's your name?"

"I've been a called a lot of things in my life. I was told when I was younger that my parents named me Sebasten."

I shot him a look. He was playing the sympathy card. I immediately felt my pocket for my money clip.

"Usain Bolt."

"The fastest man in the world," the kid said, raising a dramatic arm to the blue sky.

"You're about as fast as a lightning bolt." I chuckled once, knowing the joke was on me.

"*Tornillo*. That's bolt in Spanish."

"You must run track in school?"

Shuffling his feet, I could hear them scratch against the hard surface. Callouses. He rested his smallish hands in his pockets, but his fingers poked through. Suddenly, I felt sorry for the little shit who tried to rob me.

"School's not my thing."

"You never told me how old you are."

"*Catorce*."

"Fourteen, huh?"

"You know Spanish," he said.

"*Un poco*."

He lifted his chin. "No worries. I know Spanish, English, even a little Italian and French."

"How did you learn all those languages if you're not in school?"

"I observe people. I listen to them, mimic them. Helps me understand what they want out of life. Then I know what to sell them."

I smacked my leg and cracked another chortle. "Bolt, you're too much. I don't need to be sold anything." I craned my neck over the crowd.

Flicking his hand against my shoulder, he said, "You're looking for someone. A special lady perhaps?" He shot me a wicked grin.

If he only knew how special she was. "Right now, I'm meeting someone at a place called Barra Océano Azul."

"The Blue Ocean Bar. It's not easy to find in this huge metropoli."

"You mean, metropolis?"

"*Sí*, that. Follow me. I can take you there. Anything you need in Santo Domingo, Seb…I mean, Bolt can get it for you. Anything."

Bolt wove through the crowd, following an endless maze of paths lined by lush vegetation, water features, and even a few more Bolts looking for patsies like me, it appeared. I'd let the kid stick around a while, but I knew not to turn my back on him.

In one hotel door, out another, then circling down a curved stone path, Bolt jumped into the sand and extended a hand. "I offer you Barra Azul Océano."

Typical seaside bar, thatch roof, or so it appeared, a few tables, patrons drinking fruity drinks with umbrellas, all of whom looked like clueless tourists. I glanced at Bolt, suddenly concerned I'd escorted the fox into the hen house. He flipped his longish hair out of his eyes, then stuck his hands back in his pockets. He looked slightly uncomfortable.

My eyes gravitated back to the ocean for a moment. It was calming, allowing me to reflect on why I made the two-thousand-mile trip from Dallas.

To hunt a cold-blooded killer—my ex-girlfriend.

"Are you hoping a beautiful mermaid appears?" Bolt's hands outlined an hourglass figure.

A flashing image of...*her* prancing across my condo floor dashed in and back out of my mind.

"There have been stories, that much I can tell you, mister. *Lo siento mucho.* What is your name?"

"*Me llamo Booker.*"

"Ahh. Mr. Booker."

"Nope. Just Booker."

A clanging bell just over my shoulder. Turning away from the ocean, a bartender swung a small rope, banging the little ball against a cast iron bell that had seen better days. Suddenly, a group of dancers, jugglers, and two men blowing whistles appeared at the end of the path. The patrons jumped from their chairs and started clapping their hands, shaking their hips. The group paraded through the bar area. Bolt smacked my arm, urging me to join in the revelry. I played along and clapped. Bolt nudged me again, pointing out I wasn't keeping the beat.

That just showed how much my mind had shifted to thinking about...*her*.

The parade marched away from the bar, and everyone applauded. A second later, I was being scrunched against the bar.

"Was that some type of signal?" I asked Bolt, withholding the urge to thrust my body backward and send three or four guys barreling into another table.

"Happy Hour. That's how a lot of these tourist hotels and bars show that it's time for Happy Hour."

Now I understood the rush of patrons. Pulling my phone from my shorts pocket, it showed straight-up five p.m. local time.

The same man who clanged the bell tossed down a napkin. "Drink for you?"

Glancing around, I thought, *Why not?* then pointed to a drink a few feet down the bar from me. "I'll have whatever that drink is with the red umbrella."

"Oh yes, our special, Ron de Fuego."

"Rum of fire?" I just wanted to stay lucid for my meeting. Surveying the area, I didn't see anyone matching my contact.

"*Haga dos bebidas, señor,*" Bolt said, bouncing his finger off the bar.

"Really? You thought I wouldn't notice?"

The bartender opened his arms, and I waved the kid off. "Just one. Gracias."

"But, Mr. Booker, I helped you find this bar. I can see you are here for a purpose. Do you not owe me one?" His voice pitched higher, finally cracking.

Bolt might act like he was twenty-something, but he was still a teenager. "I made sure the bellman didn't call the police after I chased you down when you stole my bag. Don't you owe me one?"

I gave him a smirk. He shrugged his shoulders, releasing a toothy grin.

"Can't blame a man for trying."

I popped his shoulder. "You're hardly a man. What's the drinking age in the Dominican Republic?"

"Sixteen," he said, placing his hand on the bar. "So, I'm really not that far away."

The bar man arrived with my drink, condensation dripping down the side. "It's eighteen. Don't listen to him." He shifted his eyes to Bolt, shaking his head while walking to help another customer.

"Nice one, Bolt. You think you can manipulate everyone to get what you want? That might work on some folks, but one of these days, you're going to con the wrong guy."

If anyone could spot manipulation, outright deception, it was me, given my recent history. And I wasn't thinking about the legitimate cases I'd worked since I started up my PI business eight months ago.

His eyes moved to the ocean over my shoulder, then he nodded. "You are right, Mr. Booker. I'll show you that I can be an honest person."

My first thought was that he wanted more time to figure out how to lull me into thinking he was harmless, and then I'd end up explaining to authorities my association with a known thief.

"We'll see."

I led us to a table at the edge of the bar area, less crowded, not as noisy. Just then, I noticed a man standing at the entrance, cleaning his sunglasses with the end of his aqua T-shirt. His shoulders didn't fill out his stained, white-linen jacket. Slipping his glasses back on, flesh drooped all over his face. A prominent, dark mustache was speckled with gray, which matched the color at his temples. He started walking our way, scanning the area.

Lifting from my seat, I felt my chest thump a little harder. I was about to finally hear the scoop on where I could find the murdering temptress who had rocked my world.

"Bolt, you need to go sit at another table for a while."

Two

No sooner had I sat down across from Tito Valdez, an old friend or relative swooped in and literally plucked the wiry detective from his chair, shaking him like a rag doll while laughing and hugging him at the same time.

While the reunion dragged on, I slurped another mouthful of Ron de Fuego, three types of rum soothing my nerves. I released an audible breath, partly wishing this trip was purely recreational.

The other part of me was ready to confront the seductive blonde who had killed two talented performers all because they had simply spoken to me. After assaulting my mom, she manipulated me one last time before using my own gun to knock me unconscious and leave town without a trace. A week later, I read a note she'd left me, where she admitted to teaming up with a terrorist who had created chaos across Dallas by setting off bombs, killing dozens. She used her seductive ways to convince the warped twerp to make a spectacle of her wedding with Ashton Cromwell, the young heir to the Cromwell billion-dollar empire…well, at least half of it, since he had a brother. Cromwell was blown up while hanging from the top of the Old Red Courthouse in downtown Dallas.

A sandy breeze blew my napkin off the table, but I snatched it midair. Sipping my drink again, I peered around Valdez and his boisterous friend, and spotted Bolt sitting at a table, drinking a carbonated beverage I'd purchased for him, yik-yaking away with a waiter. I had a feeling he was convincing the guy to dump all of his money into a timeshare Bolt was selling on the east side of the island in Punta Cana.

I wondered if Bolt's parents were still on the scene. He was independent, that much was certain. A survivor.

I thought about Ashton Cromwell's parents, Fulton and Muffin, the clients who'd hired me to hunt down their almost daughter-in-law. Just a week earlier, they'd called me to their estate off Strait Lane in North Dallas. They'd heard the same news that I'd been told the night before. Henry, my old college buddy and current Dallas County assistant district attorney, had interrupted the end of a friends-and-family summer party to tell me there were unconfirmed reports that she had been spotted in Santo Domingo. We'd heard similar news a few months earlier about her being seen in Hong Kong. The Cromwells said they couldn't take the uncertainty. They needed closure and would pay me anything it took to bring her to justice.

Watching their emotions churn into a boiling mess, I felt my gut implode, unleashing months of bitter resentment and anger, at...*her*, and myself for being duped. But if there was anything I'd learned while surviving the mean streets of South Dallas as a youngster, or working as a beat cop for the Dallas Police Department for seven years prior to starting Booker & Associates, it was to channel my disappointment and disgust into positive energy that would help me accomplish the goal: catch that conniving bitch.

"*Lo siento mucho acerca de la interrupción.*" Valdez waved to his friend while plopping back in his wooden chair.

"He doesn't know Spanish. Not that well."

Bolt had appeared out of nowhere.

"I thought you were enjoying your Sprite—"

"It's a 7UP."

"Whatever, 7UP. You need to be over there." I flicked a wrist.

"Are you the po-po?" a giggling Bolt asked Valdez.

"What is a po-po?" His saggy eyes thinned into slits.

"I've seen many American videos on YouTube, gangsta rap."

"He means the police. He's asking if you're a cop," I said to Valdez, then turning to the nosy teenager, "You need to go back to your corner of the world and find someone else to rope into your latest Ponzi scheme."

"I'm not a cop," Valdez said, locking his hands and setting them on the table.

"What?" I couldn't help but lean forward. "You are Tito Valdez, the detective for the Santo Domingo police force, right?"

"Tito? Were you named after the Jackson Five singer? Woo-hoo!" Bolt spun around and grabbed his crotch, adding a final hip thrust.

"Dude, you're killing me," I said, shaking my head.

Valdez rolled his eyes, then flicked a thumb at Bolt. *"Niños."*

I returned our focus to his identity. "Tell me I didn't travel over a thousand miles to talk to someone who wasn't even in law enforcement. Is this a sick prank of some kind?" I eyed Valdez and Bolt, wondering if somehow they could be partners.

Valdez held up his hands. "I'm a former cop. Was kicked off the force a month ago."

"Why?"

"They told me it was for drinking on the job. But I know that's a lie. I told them that." Perspiration bubbled near his thinning hairline. I could almost feel the heat radiating from the skinny former cop.

"I think we have something in common."

"What's that?"

"Working for corrupt cops."

"There's a story there," Bolt said, rubbing his hands together. He grabbed a chair and pulled it up to the table. "I'm all eyes."

"You mean to say 'I'm all ears.' Not right now. Tito and I need to talk about adult things. Go back to your 7UP. If you order another one, I'll even pay for it."

Bolt moped away, then quickly found a middle-aged couple to pester. I could hear the inflection of his voice, his hands a windmill of motion.

Picking up my drink, I sucked in the last few drops.

"You mind if I get one?" the former detective asked.

"Uh…sure." I spotted a waitress and held up my hand. A shapely woman approached the table and took his drink order— some type of rum straight up.

"I took on a security job at a local bank, but I haven't gotten paid yet," he said, opening an empty wallet.

"Sorry to hear about your job."

"Eh. It's probably better this way. At least I didn't get sucked in by the lure of dirty money."

The waitress dropped off his drink, and he didn't waste time taking a gulp. "I know you are anxious to know about this woman who is accused of murder back in Dallas, sí?"

"Yes. She admitted to it." I touched my jaw and recalled the throbbing pain from the gun's impact, something close to an infected root canal. "Do you know where I can find her?"

"Me? No. But I know someone who says he can."

This felt like a human shell game, and I slumped in my chair. "Where is this guy? Don't tell me, it's the cab driver who ran over my foot."

"Ha!" He chortled. "You Americans enjoy sarcasm. I do as well."

He grinned under an extra-long mustache.

"Can you bring me to him?"

"Mass starts in a few minutes. He will be busy the rest of the evening. I will take you there in the morning."

I chewed the inside of my cheek. "Did this guy's wife drag him to church on Wednesday night?"

Another quick laugh from Valdez. "Father Santiago. He's my priest."

Just what I needed—a confession.

Three

The last image my mind captured just before closing my eyes was a crested moon hooking into the backdrop, just next to the top of an enormous lighthouse. I recalled Bolt telling me that some of the remains of Christopher Columbus were kept inside the monument. For some reason, it made me think about King Tut, which then led to a memory of watching Steve Martin perform at the Meyerson Symphony Center in Dallas—positioned just down the street from Wylie Theatre. That instantly segued into the night of the first Arts District murder. A GSW to the forehead of Courtney Johnson. A professional hit if I'd ever seen one.

Little had I known that *she* was behind the professional hit.

Wrestling with the notion of regurgitating all the memories I'd tried to purge months ago, it felt like a rubber mallet was pounding a wide nail deep into my skull.

Unsure if I'd truly fallen asleep, I first caught a waft of sweet syrup mixed with a pungent odor. Sweat? Peeling my eyes open, I was staring at an old stone wall. Then something nudged my back, round and hard.

The barrel of a gun.

My pulse ignited, flashing alarm signals throughout my core. Somehow, I didn't move, pretending I was asleep.

"*Si te mueves, te voy a matar.*" A voice full of wet rocks spoke quietly.

I had no clue what he said, but it didn't sound like an invitation to dinner. Wait, *matarte*...back in the hood I'd been threatened with that phrase. Kill. He wanted to kill me.

My senses on high alert, I listened for a click. Another poke, this one just inside my shoulder blade. I had no idea who I was up against, how I could combat this would-be assassin.

"*Me voy a comer para el desayuno,*" he growled.

I think he said something about eating breakfast? Confusion racked my brain. The butt of a gun was inches away from lodging a bullet in my spine, and he was talking about breakfast and killing. Dammit, I wish I'd paid more attention to Eva's Spanish rants.

Unable to swallow or feel any liquid in my mouth, I knew I had one chance, and it wasn't a strong one at that.

Channeling the adrenaline that was already sending my pulse skyward, I flipped my blanket over my back while lunging out of bed. With the blanket now covering the gun, I grabbed for the barrel just as I swung a right cross to the chin of my attacker. The crack echoed in the barren room, and he staggered back, grunting in sudden gasps, muttering phrases I couldn't understand.

I still had a hold of the gun, but he was lumbering about four feet backward, and he took me with him. The blanket started sliding off just as the moon's radiant glow gave me enough light to see his features—pronounced belly, bearded face, moving like he was older, much older. I stopped my attack, then tossed the blanket to the side.

I was holding a metal cane missing its rubber tip.

We both let go of the cane at the same time, and it rattled off the concrete surface for at least ten seconds. I took a single step toward the man, his face now wedged in the corner of the room. I could see scraggily silver hair hanging down to his shoulders.

Just then, the door burst open, a light popped on, a single bulb dangling just above my head.

"Hector, Hector, why must you do this?" The woman I'd met earlier threw her arms up in the air, shaking her head at me while scooting up next to the grisly man. She started babbling all sorts of phrases, most of which I couldn't translate, but I was rather certain I didn't want to.

Seconds later, a weary-eyed Bolt darted into the room. "Mr. Booker, what happened?" He shot a glance in the corner.

"Hoy. Mr. Hector, Mr. Hector." Bolt now flailed his arms and walked to the corner.

I stayed put, feeling like I'd interrupted a family moment. I wiggled my toes on the cold concrete, waiting for someone to speak up and fill the awkward silence that wasn't contained in the corner of mumblers.

After I agreed to meet Valdez in the morning, hours earlier Bolt had convinced me he had the perfect place for me to stay— in the heart of the city, close to everywhere but still in a safe zone. Skeptical, I considered pulling up a hotel app on my phone and looking for a four- or five-star establishment downtown. With the Cromwells footing the bill, cost didn't enter the equation.

But that didn't account for Bolt's persuasive nature.

"Who wants to stay in a cold, impersonal high-rise where people only want your money when you can stay in a family-owned place that is comfortable, laid back, and takes care of the people like family?"

Call me a sucker, but I took the bait.

Upon our arrival, it didn't take long to see that describing the place as comfortable might have been a slight exaggeration— almost like calling the cab I'd taken from the airport a smooth ride.

I met the owner of the brownstone, Lupe, who initially came across as cordial, but quickly became a bit histrionic when two little kids ran by her desk squirting each other, and the rest of us in the vicinity, with water guns. In fact, she raised her arms and pointed to the heaven above, much like she did when she came into my room a few moments ago.

In addition to the clotheslines that crisscrossed the stairwell, kids running around in diapers, and the stench of urine lingering in the damp air, Lupe informed me they'd run out of "luxury" rooms, which is how I ended up in my current digs. She tried to be accommodating, but my room, with a single oval window, had the feel of a third-world-country prison rather than a third-world-country hotel.

The kicker came when I overheard Bolt negotiating a side deal with Lupe as we walked toward my room. In so many Spanish words, I was able to ascertain that he would be able to spend the night for free since he'd brought her a paying customer. She argued that she didn't have room, but he finally agreed to sleep in the laundry room. I didn't push it, since it was obvious that Bolt didn't have a home to sleep in, and I questioned if his parents were anywhere to be found.

As I waited not so patiently in the middle of the room, I thought about Samantha, my dimple-faced six-year-old. I hated being away from her, even if she had entered the phase of life where she could hardly utter a word without peppering me with umpteen questions, many of which I either had no knowledge of the answer or had no desire to answer. ("Daddy, why aren't you and Mommy married?")

"Mr. Booker, it is okay. Mr. Hector has…uh, these episodes."

The man pulled away from the wall, staggered a couple of steps, then righted himself as Lupe held tight to his arm. Bolt rushed over and held him up from the opposite side.

Strands of hair covered his face, although his eyes didn't appear to be open. He rested a free hand against his jaw.

"*Dile que lo sientes por amenazar su vida*," she said into his ear.

Bolt leaned toward me, cupping his hand so that only I could hear him. "She's asking him to say he's sorry for threatening your life."

I nodded. "Who is he?" I whispered.

"Lupe's *hermano*."

"Brother. Got it."

A few seconds clocked by and no one said a word, only a light hum resonating from the light bulb above us. Lupe leaned her head in, apparently trying to find his eyes.

Out of nowhere, a rooster went off in the distance, and my eyes suddenly grew heavy. It must have been close to dawn, and I hadn't slept more than hour all night.

A grumble from Mount Hector.

"Go ahead and say it, if you want to stay in my place," Lupe said in plain English.

"*Lo siento por interrumpir su sueño.*"

"That's all you're going to say to this man who thought he had a gun against his back?" Lupe picked up the cane and held it front and center. "You don't even need this thing…unless you're drunk."

I began to pick up a waft of booze. I wanted to swat the air in front of me, but I didn't want to interrupt the intervention.

"I am sorry for pretending I had a gun. It was just a joke." He tried to chuckle, but she swung an elbow into his ribs.

"Sebasten, can you help me take Hector to his room?" Lupe nodded at me. "Mr. Booker, I do apologize. Hector can't control himself when he has had too much to drink." They shuffled out of the room.

My body hit the bed before the door clicked shut. Seconds later, though, my favorite rooster announced the start of the day again, and I knew any type of peaceful sleep was a lost cause.

"Some of the best coffee in all the Caribbean," Valdez said, placing coins on the counter of a corner vendor set up near a bus stop.

People knocked me to and fro as if I was just an impediment on their way to get their morning coffee and newspaper.

"I'll take one. Anything to get some caffeine."

Valdez translated my order, including the extra sugar, as I watched another man behind the counter hand change back to a guy to my right, who had snapped a newspaper open. I tried to understand the forty-two-point headline across the front page.

"*Huelgas Cartel de espalda*," I said out loud, as Bolt nudged his way through the pack.

"Can I get a coffee?"

"You're too young. What does this headline mean?" I pointed at a newspaper resting on the counter.

"Cartel strikes back."

I took my coffee and wove through the crowd just in time to follow Valdez onto a bus. He sat in the outer seat opposite of me. Bolt tagged along, sitting diagonally from me, eager to visit what he called "my church." I had a feeling there was some angle to his proclamation.

Timing my sips in between the bus lurching in and out of potholes, the smooth taste of java filled my senses. I closed my eyes for a brief second, allowing the caffeine to infiltrate my arteries and boost my energy.

"The best, huh?" Valdez said, holding up his cup.

Booker nodded. "Dominican Republic might have the best coffee in the world. At least the world I've been exposed to."

Valdez leaned in and cupped his hand. "No one likes to admit it, but most of this coffee is imported from Columbia."

"Ah. Makes sense."

He put a finger to his mouth, as if I'd been sworn to secrecy.

"Do you know much about the growing drug cartel issues in the Dominican? I saw that headline."

I could see Bolt casually angle closer while his eyes peered out the window.

"Despite our own issues with corruption, in the last six months or so, the government initiated a task force to fight the flow of drugs through our beautiful country. The government claimed victory on many fronts. But like any good heavyweight...like your 'Iron' Mike Tyson, the drug cartels have fought back. I believe they want to prove how cruel and vile they really are. To scare the people. To scare our government."

"Is it working?"

"Yes," Bolt said assertively, leaning in the middle of our conversation. "I have friends who had no choice but to work for the cartel. They were killed and their bodies thrown into the sewer. No one cared because they didn't have parents, a family, or a home."

A wave of concern washed over me, wondering if Bolt had been swayed by the lack of food or shelter to do the dirty work for the dirtiest of people.

"I'm sorry, Bolt."

"We all have to go sometime," he said, glancing away. I wondered if he was hiding watery eyes.

The bus crossed Rio Ozama, moving west. After making two stops, we turned right on Calle Pepillo Salcedo and passed Estadio Quisqueya Juan Marichal. I recalled all the incredible baseball players from the Dominican, including Marichal, a Hall of Fame pitcher for the Giants back in the 1960s. I knew the names of countless other players who had learned the game on this island: Sosa, Ramirez, Pujols, Cano, Martinez.

Buildings grew taller, the roads had fewer potholes, and generally the vibe morphed into a more modern city the farther west we drove, the bus cutting in and out of smaller coves, its brakes squeaking at every stop.

"This is it," Valdez said, popping my arm while walking down the aisle.

Moments later, the three of us walked through the church's front door. I could see the modest sanctuary through another set of double doors, a couple of folks doing some work near the front.

"Let me get Father Santiago," Valdez said.

Bolt darted around us, saying, "He's my *padre*. I will get him."

It sounded strange, Bolt claiming the priest as his father. I had to assume he meant it in a Catholic way.

A few moments later, Bolt came out, one of his arms looking like he was conducting a symphony, followed by a man dressed in the typical priest garb, a long brown robe, white collar. He walked as if he was balancing a stack of books on his head, and his demeanor was just as even-keeled.

"You've come a long way to find this woman named Britney Love," Father Santiago said. He sat in the pew in front of me and Valdez, twisting around to look at us as he spoke. Bolt had read the tea leaves and said he needed to make a couple of important requests from the man upstairs, so he walked up and hung out near the altar.

"She personally killed at least one person, hired someone to kill two others."

"Allegedly," Valdez said, glancing at me.

I gave him a straight-faced response. "You still have the cop mindset. I lost that months ago. She committed the crimes; there's no question about it."

The Father offered me a knowing look, nodding his head. "You have personal investment in this woman. I can sense your emotion."

If he only knew. My stomach churned like a blender filled with nails, jagged memories wrenching my mind.

"Emotion is a broad term. The friends and family of the people she killed have emotion for their loved ones, and they have a different emotion toward...*her*. My clients are the parents of her former fiancé. He was blown to kingdom come the day they were supposed to get married."

A surge of bile tickled the back of my throat, as my chest lifted with every audible breath.

"Passion might be a more accurate term. Is your passion driven by love or resentment?" Silver-streaked hair outlined a face etched with a surplus of lines, his tranquil tone giving me pause, allowing the question to simmer.

"I don't love her. I can't love her. But I also haven't spent every waking moment of my life trying to plot retribution either. I'm at peace with it."

It sounded like the right thing to say, and saying it made it real. Maybe.

The Father shifted his eyes to Valdez, then nodded back at me.

"Okay, I might be exaggerating a bit. Let's put it this way. My life was going pretty darn well until the moment I heard she had landed in Dominican Republic. Honestly, even if the Cromwells hadn't hired me, I probably would have eaten the cost somehow and traveled to Santo Domingo to find her, bring her back."

For whatever reason, my mind flashed on an image of the last moment before Henry revealed the Dominican Republic information, interrupting an unexpectedly special moment. Connected at the hip as dusk enveloped our little party in the park, Alisa, my lone assistant/partner at Booker & Associates, and I had just shared a kiss. The kind that was soft, lingered an extra second, energy zipping between us, blurring friends and family who were playing soccer nearby.

Alisa and I shared a distant past, a one-night stand back in college. We crossed paths years later when my long-time running buddy, Justin, opened a bar and Alisa became his lead waitress. When I started the PI business, she, more or less, got sucked into the whole thing. Not because she was drawn to the intrigue and excitement. Instead, she became enthralled with research and the sense of accomplishment she felt from parsing through mounds of information to find that one nugget that would help us break open a case. In other words, she quickly became my most valuable asset. But romance had never entered the equation. She had her private life and I had mine.

Until a week ago.

Following Henry's disclosure, my mind entered a wind tunnel, and it was difficult to process everything until my butt hit the miniature seat on the MD-80. Even then, thoughts of Alisa were set aside, replaced by the volatile pings of emotion Father Santiago had detected.

"Mr. Booker, are you with us?" Valdez asked.

I'd been staring at the beams crossing the ceiling of the sanctuary. I quickly spotted Bolt speaking to two older women near the front of the sanctuary. "Just checking in on Bolt."

The Father chuckled. "Your concern for him is quite touching. But Sebasten has been on his own since he was a young kid, six or seven years old. He's more capable of taking care of himself than many adults I know." He raised an eyebrow, releasing a genuine smile.

Shifting in my seat, it reminded me of my younger life when Momma would pull me by the ear to church every Sunday. My bony ass and the pew were not a good mix. I looked like a Mexican jumping bean, I was so squirmy. A similar feeling of restlessness came over me.

"I've run into this woman you call Britney a few times. Just last week I spoke with her at the hospital," the Father said.

"Was she injured?" I said far too quickly.

"She was there aiding a little boy. She told me he had broken his collarbone while jumping down the stairs of her school."

I let that sink in a moment, recalling that she'd been accused of having an affair with one of her high school students in West Texas, according to reports that came out after she'd escaped.

"Father, you have to understand the type of person we're dealing with here. No one is safe around her. She will manipulate anyone to get what she wants. And if life doesn't go just the way she plans, she'll do anything to get her way. Including killing. Do you know what it takes to kill another person? Not in self-defense, but to conjure up the idea and then to follow through on the act. It takes one sick mother…"

"Fucker."

I looked to my left, and Bolt had slid into the pew, carrying a shit-eating grin. Then he realized the setting and our company. "Oh, forgive me, Father."

The Father nodded, resting a hand on Bolt's head.

"I understand your unease, Mr. Booker, given everything you experienced."

Unsure why everyone kept adding thirty years to my age by calling me Mr. Booker, I just rolled with it.

"I get the feeling you're not a believer," I said with a smirk playing on my lips.

His face stretched into a wide smile. "I like your play on words. I am a believer in the man upstairs, as you noted earlier. But I also believe in repentance and forgiveness."

While I knew the world was a better place because of people like Father Santiago, that didn't mean I was in the mood to present a full-blown prosecutor's case. That was Henry's job.

I tried to swallow, then realized the well had dried up. I smacked my lips a couple of times, attempting to drum up enough liquid to speak clearly.

"I'd rather not debate her innocence or guilt. All I'm asking is for you to share with me her whereabouts, and I'll take over from there."

"You need to know I'm not even certain it is her?"

I remember Henry using the term "unconfirmed reports." Was this what he meant by that?

"I'm all ears."

Twisting his head, he gave me a confused look, then glanced at Valdez and the kid, who had already heard too much.

"Feel free to share with me everything you know," I said, holding up a finger.

"*Sí*. I just saw a picture of this Britney Love person about two weeks ago while watching CNN Internacional. She had white skin, golden hair, styled like she was worth a billion pesos. She was attractive, but seemed a bit snobby. She had a distant look in her blue eyes."

"We heard earlier reports that she had changed her appearance. Not surprising that she's not a perfect match to the picture from her old life."

He cleared his throat. "It's strange, though. This woman from the hospital, she has some similarity to Britney Love, but it's not a close resemblance."

A tiny prick nibbled at the base of my skull. Was it a tinge of doubt to the outcome of this expedition? I hadn't given myself any other options. I'd known with a hundred-percent certainty that I would soon have her in my custody and would be working through the process of extraditing her back to Texas. The Father had poked a hole in my perfect little plan.

But I wasn't going to surrender my purpose that quickly.

"She would do anything to remain free, trolling on those she can manipulate. Including changing her appearance."

"Ana Sofia's skin color is much darker."

"Who?"

"*Lo siento mucho.* The woman I've seen who looks a little like Britney Love, her name is Ana Sofia."

I let it resonate inside, thinking of the girl now suspected to be Ana Sofia. Adding the unfamiliar name on top of the Father's doubt, the headache that had been temporarily cured by the Columbian coffee began to invade my frontal lobe.

"Where can I find...*her*?"

"Mr. Booker, why don't you say this woman's name?" Bolt tugged my T-shirt.

"Long story."

"I know she is a bad woman. Whether she is the same woman Father Santiago has seen, I can't say. But it doesn't change anything. I was told a long time ago to face my fears, even if it was the fear of the unknown."

"I wouldn't call it fear, Bolt. It's more like being so pissed off you can't see straight."

He giggled, nudging my arm.

"But I get what you're saying," I said, turning to the Father. "So, where can I find...Britney?" *There, I said it, dammit!*

"I've been to her school. I will take you."

His eyes narrowed a bit. Was he protecting this woman, thinking I might harm her? Being the island outsider, I realized I could only demand so much if I wanted any type of reciprocal assistance.

"Fine. How far is it?"

"I have some matters to attend to first. Plus, she must finish her school day."

I held back the urge to roll my eyes, thinking of...Britney leading a normal life, helping mold young minds. I literally feared for their safety. But I could wait a few more hours.

"I want to be there when the last school bell rings for the day."

On the offhand she catches wind of our arrival, I wasn't going to give her a single minute to slither away this time.

Four

Momma always told me that patience was a virtue—her way of suggesting that I needed to dial down my insistence on resolving everything without understanding the motivations and desires of others.

On that one count, even at age thirty-two, I hadn't made Momma proud.

Sipping a bottled water, I sat on the edge of my metal chair in an outdoor café about two miles from the church. I'd reluctantly agreed to wait until school ended before confronting Britney. My mind was already spinning with how to approach the situation, what to say, what she might do when she saw me, how I might feel when I laid eyes on her.

I also knew there was a risk in waiting an extra few hours. Father Santiago could be warning her as Valdez, Bolt, and I ate our casual lunch. Outside of alienating those who had helped me, I didn't see another option. Still, it was a risk, and that only added an extra twist in my knotted stomach.

Lip-smacking sounds came from my right.

"It's nice to see you're enjoying you lunch, Bolt."

He looked up while continuing to shovel the food in faster than he could chew.

"I...I usually don't get the chance to eat such *fantástico* food," Bolt said with chipmunk cheeks. "*¡La mejor comida de todo el mundo!*"

Unsure exactly what he said, I could see how important food was in his life. I was glad to help him out. It was the least I could do, despite him trying to steal my bag. I chuckled inwardly, knowing he'd quickly grown on me, even with his master sales skills. But more than anything, he was a survivor. That was something I could relate to, even three decades into my life.

"Mr. Booker, are you going to finish your meal?" Bolt said as food spewed through his lips.

I'd taken no more than a couple of bites.

"You do not like our authentic cuisine?" Valdez scrubbed his bushy mustache with his napkin.

He sounded slightly offended.

Holding up a hand, I said, "It's not that. The food is fine, and before I leave the island, I hope to truly enjoy one of these great meals. But—"

"Mr. Booker is worried about meeting this Britney woman again," Bolt said, gripping my plate while looking me in the eye.

"Go ahead and knock yourself out."

He turned his head, and I quickly realized I'd uttered another American phrase that probably made no sense.

I scooted the plate his way. "I meant to say, I'm not hungry. So feel free to eat my lunch."

"Gracias, Mr. Booker. You are the best."

A car backfired in the street, and I glanced upward. Suddenly, a ripple of screams came from just down the sidewalk. Then two motorcycles screamed in from the east, fishtailing in front of a small newspaper stand. Two men on each cycle, wearing all black.

I spotted an automatic rifle.

"Get down, now!" I grabbed Bolt's shoulder and shoved him under the table just as the crackle of bullets echoed off the buildings. Valdez lowered to one knee, reaching inside his jacket.

"Left my gun at home," he said.

People around us dove for the concrete, allowing me to better see the scene play out. One man with a backpack over his shoulder crumpled to the ground, both hands pressing against his protruding gut. I could see blood and anguish on his face.

More screams, including a hysterical lady behind me who had started crying and yelling in Spanish.

Staying low to the ground, I wove between two chairs and a table as the ambush continued. With all the reverberation, I couldn't determine how many shots had been fired.

A lady's head snapped back. She'd been shot in the skull. She tumbled against a metal trashcan and fell face first to the unforgiving surface.

Just then, I spotted a guy off the second cycle running to a bus that had stopped just before the gunfight. Was he going to mow down everyone on board?

My chest exploded. Instinct kicked in, and even with no weapon, I knew I had to stop the insanity.

Taking three giant steps, I leaped over a three-foot metal railing that surrounded the café patrons. Just as I landed, more gunshots rang out, and I dropped into a crouching position. The first gunman was still shooting at anything that moved on the north side of the street. Glancing right toward the bus, the second gunman had pulled out a can of spray paint and had just finished scrawling something in black. I could see people jumping over seats and each other in the bus, trying to move away from the side with the man in black. Squinting for a brief second, I couldn't tell what he'd written—letters, a symbol, who knew?

Just as he turned to race back to his ride, I darted out of my stance, making a beeline for the same motorcycle. Hoping like hell none of the assailants would spot me and shoot me down in the middle of the street, I closed quickly.

The driver jerked his head my way, his eyes hidden behind the tinted cover of his helmet. Revving the engine, he yelled something to his cohorts. Still on a dead run, I planted my left foot and dove headfirst. Out of nowhere, the graffiti guy leaped on the seat, wrapping his arms around the driver. Swinging my arm as the bike lurched forward, my finger hooked the passenger's T-shirt.

I dropped to the ground, my head bouncing off concrete. But I never released my grip. The man pulled right, forcing the motorcycle to wobble, but it kept surging forward, dragging me down the street, rocks and glass ripping away layers of my skin. Just as the two-wheeler clamored over a pothole, the T-shirt ripped, the guy flailing his arms against my fist.

The next few seconds happened in slow motion.

Screams mixed with whining engines filled my head. With my shoulder halfway out of its socket, the bike spun its back wheel, spinning a cloud of burned rubber. The sun's reflection pierced my vision for a brief second as the man swung his arm downward. Then I saw something silver, sharp and serrated. My brain told my hand to let go, but it wouldn't. Suddenly, the front wheel hit the road, propelling the bike while tearing the shirt some more. The blade missed my knuckle by an inch, slicing his shirt in half, dropping me to the pavement. The driver shaved more rubber, shooting pebbles into my face, as it finally gained traction and sped down the street. It hooked a right and disappeared before I could take another breath.

I finally heard my lungs take in air, and I realized I hadn't breathed since I'd leaped for the motorcycle. *What the hell was I thinking?*

The scent of blood pinched my nostrils as sirens bounced off the buildings and cries grew in intensity.

"Mr. Booker, Mr. Booker, how bad are you hurt?" Bolt grabbed my shirt and tugged, his breath spilling out in gasps, his voice pitched higher than usual.

"That's my bad arm," I grunted, rolling onto my side.

"Oh, I'm sorry. I see blood. Help! We need help over here!"

Valdez appeared. "What the hell were you thinking? They could have killed you."

"I wasn't. It was stupid. I was stupid."

A paramedic dropped next to me.

"I'm fine," I said before he said a word. "Go save the others."

He paused.

"*¡Ir a salvar a los demás que fueron fusilados, joder!*" Bolt yelled, a blue vein snaking down his temple.

I lifted to a sitting position as Bolt went and found a bottled water and gave it to me. For a few minutes we sat in silence. Paramedics engulfed the macabre scene, trying to help those who'd been gunned down. At least a hundred cops descended upon the area. Eventually, two got around to asking me what I saw. Again, my sanity was questioned.

I couldn't put up much of an argument.

Once all the gunshot victims were treated, I let them administer bacitracin and apply bandages to my wounds. Nothing serious enough to keep me from walking away.

An hour later, Bolt, Valdez, and I broke free from the gory gun-shooting scene, ambling toward a bus a few blocks down. We caught up with Father Santiago, who felt the need to quiz me further about my decision-making. Standing next to a man drinking a can of Dr. Pepper while scanning the newspaper, I responded with my own question, directed at Valdez.

"Four guys on motorcycles target a news stand in the middle of a restaurant district in the good part of town. Was someone sending a message?"

He pointed at the man's newspaper, where the same headline we'd seen earlier now had become far more personal. "It's got to be the cartel. They're flexing their muscles."

"Did you pick up what that guy painted on the bus?"

Valdez and Bolt both shook their heads.

"I couldn't tell if it was a symbol or letters. Regretfully, I'm not connected into the police investigations," Valdez said, removing a handkerchief and blotting his sweaty forehead. "Whoever is behind this, it is obvious they only mean to intimidate, like any other terrorist cell. Which means people will die. Who knows when it will end? If it will end. I'm afraid for our country. I'm afraid for our people and the kids who will find no other options than to work for these animals."

He glanced at Bolt, who for once had nothing to say. None of us did. Fighting back against a cartel or terrorist cell was like fending off an F-5 hurricane. Inevitably, the destruction would win out.

The bus squealed to a stop, a foul odor of exhaust replacing the smell of blood and death. I draped an arm over Bolt's shoulder as we stepped on board, ready to face another killer, knowing she might be more cold-blooded than the men I'd just encountered.

Five

Laboring up an inclined dirt road, Father Santiago held up a hand, then stopped and leaned against a tree, his chest rising in quick order.

"*Lo siento...mucho*," he said in gasps. Resting his hands on his knees, he let his head drop forward, as drops of perspiration trickled to the ground.

Part of me wanted to suggest that he loosen his collar. I wasn't Catholic, and I didn't understand the symbolism and rituals. But I had to respect his dedication to his faith.

"*Un momento*," he said.

I peered over a ridge and could see three one-story buildings carved into the hillside, each with front porches, the area enclosed by a wide-planked, white-painted fence. A wooden sign stood about ten feet off the grass.

"La Academia de Aprendizaje," I read out loud.

"The Learning Academy," Bolt said.

The Father finally got his breathing under control, and we finished the last leg of our hour-long trek. A beeping sound blared across the small campus, then kids of all ages poured out of the buildings, moving in an orderly fashion, all wearing a uniform: powder blue shirts and navy blue shorts. Some of the kids walked past us, just at the outside gate, others milled about between the buildings.

"Lots of happy kids. The future of Santo Domingo," the Father said proudly, a smile on his face.

Out of the corner of my eye, I spotted a woman exiting the center building holding the hand of a young girl, maybe five or six years old. Samantha's age. Cloaked by the porch's shadow, I could only see the woman's lean build and carefree but confident gait.

I swallowed a dry patch, my pulse thumping in my head.

Just then, she emerged into the sunlight, and it felt like the knife I'd seen earlier had punctured the wall of my gut and someone was twisting it. Britney, although she was a brunette, her hair chopped short.

As she angled away from the building, she caught sight of us and waved. Feeling like my sandals were nailed into the ground, I didn't move, unsure if I wanted to tackle her to the ground, or hug her and ask how she has been all this time we'd been apart.

She once took my breath away; now she stripped me of reason and action.

The Father waved back, then led our way through the gate. I followed behind Valdez and Bolt. I couldn't take my eyes off her, for all the wrong reasons, and because I'd known what she'd done.

Still fifty feet away from us, she stopped and spoke to two other kids, and I eyed her from head to toe. *What the hell? Who is this woman?*

Picking up the pace without trying, a toxic mixture of anxiety, disgust, and bewilderment chipped away at my stomach lining. At ten feet and closing, she lifted her head, and part of me wondered if she might finally notice me and take off running—if it was Britney. With the tentacles of a lethal box jellyfish, doubt crept into my mind.

"*Hola, Padre,*" she said far too casually, messing up the hair of a male student, who smiled in response. Even with cuts on my face, bandages on my elbows and knees, her vision swept right past me, as if I was a tourist, or even a tree.

"Ana Sofia, it's a great day to learn, is it not?" the Father said, leaning in and kissing her on the cheek.

"Every day is a great day to learn." She turned to the boy, placing a hand on his back. "Marco, please tell the visitors what we repeat every day."

Showing off two gaps in his front teeth, he leaned his shoulders back and barked out, "*Aprenda algo nuevo todos los días.*"

Bolt cupped a hand over his mouth and leaned toward me, whispering, "Learn something new every day."

"Got it," I said softly, my eyes still zeroed in on everything Britney, or a close resemblance to her.

Ana Sofia was the same height as Britney, although she looked a tad shorter because she wasn't wearing her usual designer heels. Ana Sofia looked like a schoolteacher, wearing a khaki skirt, just above the knees, and a white blouse that sported the school's logo. But it wasn't low-cut and see-through, like so many outfits I'd seen her...or Britney...wear.

Staring at her face, the cheekbones seemed like they'd shifted, her jawline a little less pronounced. Her eyes. Gone were the sparkling sapphires, replaced by a mesmerizing amber, which, as I just noticed, nearly matched her skin. I gave her figure another onceover. I'd never seen her with such a deep tan.

Bolt stuck an elbow in my rib, and I quickly realized Ana Sofia had extended her hand.

"Mr. Booker, are you going to shake the lady's hand?" the Father asked.

She gave me a quick shake and a quicker nod, turning to the boy, who said, "*La señorita Ana Sofía, tengo que ir a mi clase de matemáticas.*"

"Marco has a math lesson he needs to take," Bolt said in my ear.

The boy jogged to the far building, as the little girl held tight to two of Britney's fingers.

"What do you teach?" I asked, drawing looks from my traveling party, the pause of silence a bit too long.

"A little bit of everything," she said with a strong local accent.

"Ana Sofia is the head master and owner of La Academia de Aprendizaje," the Father said.

Wiping a layer of perspiration from my crumpled forehead, I gave the Father an irritated look. The experience was surreal, in the worst kind of way, and here he was putting on a sales job.

"I only want to help these kids gain knowledge, grow up to be engineers and doctors and writers, to contribute to society."

Shutting my eyes for a brief moment, I could feel sunrays against my face, the scent of grass clippings in the heavy air. Taking in a couple of breaths, I tried to make sense of everything I'd witnessed. I couldn't.

"Are you from Dominican Republic?" I asked directly.

"I moved here when I was twelve. My parents were rather nomadic when I was young, like little Maria here."

The little girl looked up at Ana Sofia and smiled, then she began to sway her head back and forth. "*Tengo sed, señorita Ana Sofia.*" Little Maria pushed out the F sound, reminding me a bit of Samantha a few months ago.

"She's thirsty," Bolt said.

"I had that one," I said.

"I'm so sorry for letting you melt in the sun. Please come inside. I'll let Maria help serve everyone some *limonada de hielo*."

"Ice lemonade," I said to Bolt.

"Great idea," the Father said as the congregation shuffled toward the porch. "Ana Sofia, you must show me your new digital library. You spoke about it when I last saw you at the hospital. By the way, how is that boy doing with his collarbone?"

"Pablo says he feels like a girl. He wants to remove the bra, as he calls it." She giggled and squeezed her eyes a bit. That was Britney, at least her behavior.

All along, I'd prepared myself for the unthinkable, realizing Britney would do anything to survive. But the longer I was around this person, it almost felt like an imposter had stolen some of the mannerisms and caring tone of Britney. How could that be?

I felt a tug on my T-shirt.

"*Aquí está su limonada, Señor Booker*," Maria said.

Lowering down to my knees, I took the drink from Maria, who curled a lock of straight hair around her ear. "*Gracias, Maria*." She smiled, rocking back and forth on her heels, then turned and ran back to the tray full of cups.

She quickly grabbed another lemonade, but just as she lunged a step, the plastic tumbler crashed to the floor, spilling the sticky substance all over the wood surface and Maria's sandaled feet. Instantly, the little girl burst out in tears. I walked over and offered some assistance.

"*Está bien, está bien*," I said, kneeling next to her.

She glanced at me, but then shut her eyes and squeezed more water from her eyes, her feet seemingly bolted to the floor. I'd felt the same way outside a few minutes earlier, minus the tears.

Spotting a sink off to my right, I unrolled a mound of paper towels and dampened them under the tap. Two seconds later I was cleaning her feet and sandals. *"Está bien."* It's okay, I said, and then she grew quiet, releasing a couple of gasping sniffles.

"Yo también quiero ayudar," she said, taking a wad of paper towels from my hand. She kneeled on her knees and began to soak up the sticky substance off the wood floor.

"All finished. *Muy bien,*" I said, smacking two hands together.

Maria smiled.

"Can you say thank you to Mr. Booker?" Ana Sofia leaned down at her waist toward the girl, her face no more than a foot from mine.

Without being obvious, I tried to swipe a glance at her skin. It was so smooth and velvety I wanted to touch it to see if it was real.

"Gracias, Mr. Booker," Maria said, then she ran over to a computer where Father Santiago and Bolt were standing. Valdez had made a trip to the bathroom, leaving the leggy brunette and me alone at the far end of the room.

My jaw opened, all sorts of phrases ready to spill out, some sweet and caring, others filled with vitriol.

"What part of America are you from?" she said, like we'd just been introduced at a social event.

Narrowing my eyes, I searched for the real Britney. For a moment, I thought I saw her, but it was difficult to look beyond the chopped hair and dark, magnetic eyes.

"I don't want to create a disturbance here at your...uh, school, but I need to ask you some questions."

"I see. Not in the mood for pleasant small talk." She interlaced her fingers, placing them in front of her body, then licked her lips...just a bit too slowly.

Was she screwing with me, whoever she was?

"Mr. Booker, come see how this computer works. I can look down from the sky and see the top of this building," Bolt said, sidling up next to me. He looked at Ana Sofia and shot her a quick wink.

Damn, that kid was a player.

"Give us one minute," she said, holding up a hand. He shrugged his shoulders and walked back to sit at the computer station.

Valdez had just ambled into the room, using his T-shirt to wipe his glasses.

"Mr. Booker, I do have something I'd like to speak with you about." Her volume had been cut in half. She held out a fist, then slid a small piece of paper between my fingers.

"I'd appreciate it if you came to our place for dinner this evening." She held her gaze, her tone serious. Grabbing the paper, I saw an address.

"Our?"

"My fiancé, Juan Ortiz, and I both live there. We have an important matter that we'd like to discuss with you."

I nodded for a good ten seconds, replaying her words. Did she somehow know I'd be at her school this afternoon?

The Father must have said something. I eased my neck around, wondering what else he'd relayed to her. I also wondered what kind of bullshit story she'd given him. Just because he was a man of the cloth didn't mean he wasn't also a man of cash.

"Give me a couple of hours to finish up here. You can join us at *seis*?"

Despite air conditioning smacking my face, I felt a line of perspiration at my hairline. Could she be sending me into some trap? Maybe she was biding time to make her ultimate escape, and she'd paid a group of local thugs to shank me. Clean and easy, at least for her.

Another thought hit me: how the hell did she get the money to run a frickin' school? I knew she bankrolled a fair amount from her future in-laws from the prenup agreement, but I was certain they'd stopped paying her monthly stipend months ago.

"*¿Tenemos una cita?*"

A nudge at my side. Bolt appeared, smiled at Ana Sofia, then flicked his hair to one side while leaning in to me. "You guys have a date?"

"It's not what you think. Just talking."

"I know there might be a history…but keep me in mind if things don't work out."

I wanted to remind him that if she was indeed Britney, his first date with her might finish with his neck sliced open. But I tried to remember our setting and her oddly normal demeanor.

"Thanks, Bolt. I'm sure I'll be back at the brownstone before your bedtime. Maybe I can read you a story."

His thick eyebrows met in the middle and gave me a playful shove. "Come on, dude."

I forced out a laugh. "Whatever, dude."

He ran his fingers through his hair, ensuring he had that Justin Bieber look. "I watched an American movie once at a small picture show. The actor said, 'Don't blame da player, blame da game. Boom."

Bolt's Rico Suave act aside, I prepared myself to be played by the biggest playa I'd ever known.

Six

Ten-foot stucco concrete walls surrounded the corner lot in the Los Rios section of Santo Domingo, a higher end area just west of the National Botanical Garden. While Bolt had informed me this morning that the line of social and economic affluence started at Rio Ozama and only increased moving further west through the city, that notion had already been shot to hell once today. Gunmen had sprayed a flurry of bullets into a harmless crowd, killing at least six, wounding many more, dragging me behind one of their motorcycles just for kicks.

Pretending to read a bulletin stapled to a light pole across the street—something about missing cats, *los gatos*—I watched a man wearing a ball cap slowly pace back and forth just inside the iron gate entrance into the compound.

If I was a smoker, I would have sucked in half a pack by now, my brain cranking through theories of what I was witnessing. This was Britney's house, or Ana Sofia's, depending on which side of my brain, or other body parts, were winning the blood infusion battle. I chewed the inside of my cheek and tried to fathom how Britney/Ana Sofia could afford to run a school and live in a Dominican Republic palace. The Britney I'd known had family roots from the flatlands of West Texas, not Caribbean royalty, if there was such a thing.

I took a final glance at the address on the piece of paper and stepped off the curb, paused for a moment to let two luxury sedans drive by, then walked toward the ornately designed iron gate. Halfway across the street I realized the intricate design highlighted the number thirty-five. Strange, since that wasn't the address.

A few steps away, the man in the cap turned and faced me, then pulled out his phone and spoke while keeping his eye on me. Seconds later, he pocketed the phone.

"I'm here to see Br...uh, Ana Sofia," I said, wondering if he'd understand the English. He adjusted the bill of his black cap, and I noticed the white cursive letters of NY on the front. Flipping a key into his palm, he unlocked a chain that roped through the two sides of the iron gate. "Señorita Campos is expecting you, Señor Booker," he said, enunciating each word in slow motion.

Father Santiago had never shared her last name. Ana Sofia Campos. It kind of rolled off the tongue. Maybe that's why she used the name...if she was Britney, somewhere under that darker complexion.

"The front door is just around the corner there," he said, extending an arm.

"Thank you," I said.

The view from inside the gate was stunning with pink, red, and yellow blossoms scattered throughout the lush landscaping, surrounded by exotic vines and shrubs outlining the home—white stucco with a mahogany trim. The detail and finish were topnotch, as good as I'd seen in Preston Hollow back in North Dallas. Angling right, the pavestone driveway poured into a side area, where a six-car garage hulked on one side of the surface, the home's entrance on the left. Craning my neck, I could see an Olympic-sized pool in the back and a separate area where water snaked down a formation of rocks, spilling into a smaller, kidney-shaped pool, the entire area enveloped by tropical vegetation. Somehow, the entire grounds gave off a vibe of tamed wildness.

A few months ago, I would have described Britney in similar fashion, at least when we…*Why am I even going there?*

I came close to knocking myself upside the head, then found the front door and stabbed the bell, taking in the sweet fragrance of yellow blossoms growing off the vines that lined the arched front entry, at least twenty-feet high. I took in two deep breaths and still had time to hear the end of the bell's elongated chime.

"Damn, this place is ostentatious," I said to myself. I could picture my business partner, Alisa, standing to my right, her eyes pulled so far in her head I would have thought she'd been bitten by a zombie.

I think I cracked a smile as the door to the palace opened.

"Mr. Booker, *buenas noches.*" Another man wearing an NY cap. This guy was shorter, as round as a basketball. I couldn't tell where his chin ended and his neck started.

"Señorita Campos is waiting for you in *la biblioteca.*"

"The library," I said, casting a gaze around the foyer, full of marble, bronze statues, and a chandelier that appeared larger than my Saab 9-3 back home.

The basketball waddled away, and I followed him through a living room, then down a hallway lined with pictures of athletes in uniform, mostly baseball players. We hooked a left, passing a bar, then a glass-enclosed wine cellar.

"Here you are," he said.

Entering the room with stained panel walls, I saw the back of her head as she looked out into the backyard the size of a football field.

"Mr. Booker, thank you for accommodating my wishes. I truly appreciate you coming," she said, finally turning to face me, her hands gathered in front of her skirt.

Part of me wanted to say, "Drop the bullshit acting," but I hesitated. Something about her seemed oddly familiar, yet foreign at the same time.

"Sure. I'm eager to understand what you'd like to discuss. I have something I'd also like to cover with you."

"Very well," she said, avoiding eye contact while walking to a small bar tucked in the corner of the room. "A drink? We have this new Chilean red I've wanted to try." She raised a bottle, the spiked corkscrew positioned in her other hand. It glared off the light spilling in through ten-foot windows.

I assumed the "we" included her fiancé, or maybe she was referring to her New York Yankees team of bodyguards.

Holding up a hand, I said, "I stick with the virgin drinks until I finish the business of the day. Bottled water will work."

Part of me wondered if she should have known that…known me.

Reaching up to remove a goblet from the rack of glasses, I couldn't help but catch her calf roll into a ball of muscle. A slideshow of images popped in my head, and I could practically feel the silky texture of her legs that used to make my heart pop an extra beat.

I just felt a quick flutter in my chest, and I forced my eyes upward. She turned her head, her lips pressed together, as if she were sealing them shut so they wouldn't release her true thoughts.

With her wine poured, she handed me the water, then she extended her glass, apparently waiting for me to return the toast. I paused, considering my options. I'd purchased a set of handcuffs on my way over with the hope and expectation she'd be in my custody by the end of the night, making our way to the American consulate.

"To the pursuit of happiness," she toasted.

"To life," I countered. "At least for those who still have the opportunity to breathe. Because we both know you can't attain happiness when you're six feet under."

No response.

A wave of heat rushed up my neck. I could feel my jaw muscle flex and I realized my entire body was rigid with intensity. Breaking the silence, hard-soled shoes clipped off the floors, heading in our direction—someone moving at a fast pace. My elbow flapped against my rib cage, my instincts seeking the protection of my Sig Sauer. But it was in a safe tucked away in my closet back in Dallas. I turned the angle of my body, ensuring I wouldn't be attacked without me seeing the thug Britney had hired to finally kill me...something she'd promised me in her final Dear John letter.

Rounding the last turn into the room, the man wearing cowboy boots quickly noticed my defensive posture, and he walked straight for me. At the last second, he held out his hand.

"You must be the man Ana Sofia has told me about. Mr. Booker T. Adams?" he asked with a strong Spanish flare. His grip was firm, his forearm oddly strong. He held his gaze, as if he was trying to affirm some predetermined assumptions about me. He appeared to be troubled. A blue vein scaled up both sides of face, dumping into pouches of baggy skin. One bag twitched randomly, which made his glassy, red-rimmed eyes less noticeable. But I noticed.

I nodded and reciprocated the handshake, noticing his Wrangler jeans, a black and white Western shirt with the sleeves rolled up to his elbows. The thirty-something man moved past me in quick order, walked over to Ana Sofia, rested a hand on her back and kissed her on the lips. I didn't feel any type of jealously or anger, but I found myself studying her every movement, still wondering if this was indeed Britney Love.

Just then, I spotted her nails digging into his rib cage.

I quickly recalled Britney leaving a trail of nail marks down my chest and across my back. We had that type of raw passion. Or was her emotion actually some type of sick, pent-up aggression at me or men in general?

"*Tenemos que discutir por qué trajimos al señor Booker a Santo Domingo,*" the man said, bringing a hand the size of mine to his stressed forehead.

"*Él acaba de llegar. Se piensa que es mejor que compartimos juntos para que pueda entender su dolor y nuestra urgencia,*" she responded, placing her hand against his chest.

Ana Sofia shifted her eyes to me, obviously wondering if I could understand their dialogue.

Outside of my name, I could only see that my presence had a purpose in their lives. And I didn't think they wanted to kill me, at least not right away. I uncorked the water, slurped another mouthful of water, eyeing the far wall, ceiling-to-floor shelves full of books. It even had one of those rolling ladders on a track. Damn, this place was Disney World.

"Mr. Booker, I do apologize for my rudeness," the man said. "I needed to discuss with Ana Sofia where we were in the process of acquiring your services. I believe—"

I choked on my water, then had to wipe my mouth with my bandaged arm.

"You want to hire me to help you?" I held out a finger as my mind tried to comprehend something I could have never predicted, at least not in the dozen other scenarios I'd thought were possible. "Am I supposed to start laughing now or have the cameras not started rolling yet?"

Ana Sofia lowered her head, while the man rested his hands just above his belt loops.

"I think we need to start from the beginning," she said, gently patting the man—her man—on his chest. "Let's have a seat and discuss. Please."

She extended her hand, and I obliged for now, plopping down in an overstuffed chair that molded to my body like it was custom made.

They sat on a sofa, barely an inch separating them. Ana Sofia placed a hand on his thigh and squeezed it.

We opened our mouths to speak at the same time. Then, "I'm sorry," we both said in unison.

"Go ahead," she said. "You're the guest."

I nodded twice, once again wondering if I should be reading between the lines on every phrase that left her perfectly shaped mouth. Looking at the man, I said, "For starters, I never got your name."

"Where is my head? I'm just out of it," he said.

"It's okay, honey. He'll know soon enough."

My eyes shifted between the two of them like a tennis match.

"I'm Juan Ortiz."

"That helps. Juan and..." I purposely withheld the second name.

She leaned forward just a tad, her lips almost mouthing the words to me. I let her hang for a good five seconds.

"Ana Sofia," she finally said, a hand against her chest. Then she turned and smiled at Juan, who seemed confused.

I kind of got a kick out of that exchange, which, by watching her squirm, immediately tilted my scale back to the Britney theory.

"Juan is a retired baseball player."

He couldn't be *that* Juan Ortiz, could he? Scratching my goatee, I envisioned him in pinstripes, the kind worn by the New York Yankees. Number thirty-five, the pitcher with the fastball that was once clocked at a hundred miles per hour. It made sense, the number on the front gate, the staff wearing Yankee baseball caps. The compound oozed money. If my memory served me correct, I believe he'd signed at least two contracts north of twelve million dollars each. And the money in baseball was all guaranteed.

I'd met a few celebrity athletes in my day, but it wasn't Juan who drew my attention. I eyed Ana Sofia, wondering what the hell she had planned for Juan Ortiz, or his millions in cash.

"Congratulations on your career. You were on the team that won the World Series title over the Phillies?"

His head bobbed just once, his lips straight, as if it was a struggle to think about those days.

"You boys can talk sports another time," Ana Sofia said. She inhaled, seeming to gather her thoughts, then continued. "Mr. Booker, we've had a traumatic incident occur within our family."

"You're married?"

Shaking her head briskly, she batted her eyelashes, which were void of makeup. "Not yet. We're engaged, but living in the same home, sharing our lives, it certainly feels like we're married. Juan's previous wife died in a car crash. They shared a very special boy, Esteban."

Juan brought a hand to his face, and he wiped away a round of tears. Anyone with kids would have felt empathy for the star athlete. I was no different, although with my background, I also became inquisitive.

"Your boy, is everything okay?"

He shook his head, his chin quivering, as more tears escaped his eyes, which appeared worn and distraught. He nudged Ana Sofia.

"You can't imagine how difficult this is for Juan. And for me," she said.

Inching up in my chair, I popped my fingers against each other. "I'm listening."

Another deep breath by Ana Sofia, the rise of her chest catching my eye for a second.

"Esteban has been kidnapped." Curling her lip, she glanced at her fiancé then dabbed the corner of her eye.

"When did this happen?" I asked.

"About two weeks ago."

"Fifteen days, almost exactly." Juan wiped his eyes and looked at his watch. "Sometime between nine and ten o'clock at night. He was on his way home from playing in a baseball game."

"Let me get you a glass of wine, honey," Ana Sofia said, rising from the couch. "It's that new Chilean wine we—"

Pinching the corners of his eyes, Juan said, "No quiero una copa de vino de lujo. Sólo dame una cerveza."

He wanted a beer. She seemed pained by his response, but quickly set aside the longer bottle and opened a mini-fridge under the granite countertop and pulled out a yellow bottle with a blue label. I read "Carib Lager" on the side.

"Here you go, honey."

The former major leaguer downed half the bottle like a professional. "Sorry if I was rude, dear. I'm just so stressed by everything that has happened with my Esteban."

She rested her hand on his thigh, a little higher this time. "He's *our* Esteban, don't forget that."

He nodded, then took another swig of his beer and stared at the bottle. It was nearly gone.

The glare of the western sun invaded the room, diverting my eyes for a moment. It allowed the last couple of minutes of conversation to resonate, my mind searching for the reason why *I* was sitting there.

It hit me like a wrecking ball slamming into a dilapidated building. Britney must have somehow planned to get me to Santo Domingo. Without taking the time to piece together the precise timeline and hold a few terse one-on-one conversations, I couldn't be certain how she'd pulled it off. But as I stared at the woman who looked like Britney's distant cousin, supposedly with different blood running through her veins, I couldn't think of a different scenario that made any sense at all.

She didn't want to harm me. She wasn't running from me. While she was using an assumed name and somehow had managed to change her appearance, Britney only wanted me to find her soon-to-be stepson.

Saying the theory to myself sounded absurd, on more levels than I could count.

I had to ask questions about whom she was and why she felt like she could trust me. I couldn't just sit here and pretend they were a normal client. Hell, I already had a client...to find Britney, bring her back to stand trial.

Mission accomplished, at least the first of the two goals. But had I essentially been baited into traveling to Santo Domingo to rescue the boy? Or was there more?

Eyeing Juan Ortiz, I could feel his suffering. I couldn't hijack the conversation just yet.

"I'm not saying I'll take on any case. I'm currently pretty booked in that department," I said, glancing at Ana Sofia. She quickly leaned forward and brought the glass of wine to her lips and took a sip, her eyes watching the wine swirl in glass.

"Ana Sofia has said you are the best private investigator in America. She did her research and read about you on American websites. Is this a lie?"

I released a single chortle. "I'm not aware of a national survey that shows me ranked in the top ten of American PIs, no. And I haven't made the cover of *Time* or *Newsweek*."

"I can see are you a modest man. I was humble when I played ball too. Then I would mow down the opponent with a fastball, high and tight, and then their knees would shake. That's how I got respect."

I nodded, thinking Juan and I might view the world through a similar lens, although his was platinum lined with diamonds. I was okay with a more practical version.

Then I looked at our other similarity. We'd both slept with the conniving, murderous bitch. I knew it, but he was obviously clueless. I took in a breath, realizing there was a possibility this person wasn't Britney. My mind continued to swing wildly between ninety percent Britney and ninety percent Ana Sofia.

"How much progress have local authorities made in trying to find your son?" I asked, sticking with the kidnapping angle for now.

They both looked at each other.

"Did I say something that upset you?"

"We haven't gone to the authorities," Juan said, fidgeting with the end of his jeans.

"We were told that if we went to the authorities, they would kill Esteban. We just couldn't take the chance," she interjected.

"There's more," Juan said, nudging his significant other. "Too many police and army members are corrupt. If they were involved in finding Esteban, they'd sell him out just like that." His fingers snapped louder than I'd ever heard. He had used his pitching hand. "I don't want to take that chance. I didn't know who to turn to, who could help. That's when Ana Sofia said she found you. You will help bring home my boy, won't you?"

I'd doubted that Juan Ortiz had ever had to plead to get what he wanted, at least since he started earning seven figures a year.

"Juan." The round man entered the room. "You have a visitor. Should I tell them to come back?"

"This must be about the money," Juan said, lifting from the chair. "Please excuse me for a brief minute. This is important."

He brushed by my chair so fast a breeze blew against my face. As his boots clopped off the hollow floors behind me, he left a wake of awkward silence in the library.

"He's meeting with his banker, although we're not sure if that will make a difference," she said, draining her glass and setting it on the coffee table.

"How much is the ransom?"

"There isn't one, at least not yet."

A dryness hit the back of my throat, the same I'd felt countless times before when I had sensed the worse outcome for the victim. And there was no worse crime than one committed against a kid.

"Have the kidnappers contacted Juan?" I realized I was leaning forward, my forearms planted on my knees.

Licking her lips, her eyes narrowed a bit. She glanced over my shoulder.

"Look, we don't have much time."

Her accent had evaporated.

"Britney?"

"I don't go by that name any more. Like I said, we don't have much time."

My pulse thumped my neck, but I didn't move a muscle.

"What did you do to yourself?"

"I can't talk about that now. Later. Maybe."

I could taste blood inside my mouth. I'd begun my chewing routine.

"Juan doesn't know who you are."

"He knows I love him. That's all that matters."

I couldn't help but shake my head. "How do you know what love is?"

"Booker, please. This isn't the time." She held out her hands as tears bubbled in her eyes.

I'd seen the act before.

"Is any of this real?"

"What? Of course. You know Juan Ortiz. He's an authentic person. We had a great life together, until his son was abducted. You can't fake that."

My mind was spinning, the Britney/Ana Sofia riddle now solved. Sort of.

"So what is all this about? Did you purposely lure me here?"

She nodded, again glancing over my shoulder while toying with her ear lobe. I noticed her hand free of any ring.

"To do what exactly?"

"Find Esteban and rescue him. That's all I want. That's all Juan wants. To get his boy back. I figured if anyone could understand the love of a child, it was you. I know you'd fight the greatest army in the world to save Samantha."

She knew she was hitting my soft spot. It was working, but I couldn't forget what she'd done.

"You killed at least three people. You should be in prison."

"Listen. Do you think I would have gotten you to Santo Domingo thinking we wouldn't have to deal with my past? I know I can't avoid it. But I had to reach out to you…for Juan."

A single tear rolled down her tanned face.

It felt like a torch had been lit against my head. I resumed popping my fingers against each other, my eyes trying to penetrate the real person sitting five feet from me.

"You never answered my question."

She closed her eyes for a brief moment, a tiny line forming between her eyes. I'd never once seen a line on her face. But I'd also never seen her so stressed.

"My head is spinning. What did you ask?" She picked up her wine glass, saw that it was empty, then quickly walked to the bar and poured another glass.

Once she turned to face me again, I said, "Have the kidnappers contacted Juan?"

"Yes, but not directly. They've contacted me just once."

"You! Why you?"

She held out her hand. "Please, we need to keep this quiet."

"Your fiancé doesn't know you've spoken to the kidnappers?" I dialed back my volume, but not my intensity.

"Yes." She held up a finger, then kicked back a huge gulp of red wine. "Do you really think I would keep that from him?"

My face drew a blank stare. "Juan doesn't know what you're capable of. I do. It's a logical question."

"Fine. I'll appease you. Juan knows they called me. I shared everything with him, and we made the decision together to contact you. He would never turn his back on me. We're a team."

She'd tried to poke my guilt button. Not a chance that was happening.

"I'm assuming you didn't tell him the method in which you got me here?" I arched an eyebrow.

"I've shared a great deal with Juan, and he with me. But we all have a past, don't we?" She returned the raised eyebrow, then sipped her wine while kicking her crossed leg.

"So you want me to find the kidnapper, rescue Esteban and bring him home…in a country I know nothing about?"

"You are resourceful and shrewd, and you understand the world is made up of many types of people," she said. "Booker, don't you realize how much notoriety you've received for solving the cases you have since you started your PI business? It truly is remarkable."

Now was she trying a different approach, stroking my ego. I let the thought end there.

"But I let one get away," I said, pursing my lips.

The sound of boots bounced off the hall walls. Juan was seconds away from entering the room.

"Please, do we have a deal?" she asked, her eyes, shifting between the doorway and me.

"I want to help find the kid. But where's the deal part?"

She closed her eyes. "I will never marry Juan, that much I know. After you return Esteban, I will not fight extradition. I will accompany you back to Dallas and deal with the repercussions of my actions. That is my promise."

I tried to run through my negotiation options. There weren't many, especially with Britney living behind a fortress. By running a school that appeared to have such a positive impact on the kids, she'd succeeded in weaving herself into the fabric of the community. If I had no leverage, she could drag out the extradition process for years, giving her time to find her next Sugar Daddy.

"You for the kid," I said.

Looking me straight in the eye, she said, "You have my word."

"Sorry about the delay," Juan said while brushing by me.

"Not a problem."

"Has Ana Sofia helped you understand how important Esteban is to us?" Juan's voice cracked just as his back hit the sofa.

Pausing, I could see his emotions swell once again. The correlation to my Samantha was obvious. For a brief moment, however, my thoughts turned to when I was teenager and my dad was AWOL. It didn't take two hands to count the number of times I recalled seeing him in my life, at the time I received my football scholarship to the University of Texas, and he made a cameo at high school graduation. And once, he took me to the park—I was just a little tike—and the entire time I played on the jungle gyms, he just sat off to the side on a bench, preoccupied with something he was reading.

His absence was a defining pillar of my life. I knew I had to be a better father than dear old dad. I became wired to set my adversities aside, even use his absence as a motivation at times. While I'd told myself he wasn't worth a two-second thought, let alone my love, deep inside I could feel an emptiness, as if my experiences were missing a key...pillar.

I nodded. "We've come to a mutual agreement on the terms of my work. That's the business part." I scooted the edge of my chair. "I understand this is your worst nightmare come true. I'm sure your head is spinning, you can't sleep, and you forget to breathe sometimes."

He brought his hands to his chin, swallowing back a round of tears.

"I'm going to ask you questions. Some will be normal. Others might sound irrelevant. But I need to know you'll be completely transparent."

He shot a confused look at Britney—his perfect little Ana Sofia. "Mr. Booker is just asking for us to tell him the complete truth. That will not be a problem," she said turning to me, the Spanish lilt in her voice magically flipped back on.

"Of course. We are an open book. Anything to bring Esteban home," Juan said.

And Britney to justice.

Seven

I needed the cover of night, that much I knew. Otherwise, I felt like a high school freshman thrust into the starting quarterback job for the Dallas Cowboys—unprepared to the point that I couldn't even predict the worst outcome.

Check that. The most brutal hit I took playing football two years into college resulted in a dislocated shoulder. I'd also suffered at least two concussions, a broken finger, and had my kidney bruised during my athletic tenure.

Tonight's operation had a better than even chance of me ending up eating lead for dinner.

Resting an arm on my backpack in the tiny backseat of a twelve-year-old Mini Cooper, the car's undercarriage slammed into a pothole, jarring the countless boxes of restaurant glasses stacked in the front passenger seat and next to me in the back. I'd questioned this method of transportation the moment I laid eyes on the car when the driver, Manuel, a fifty-something restaurant supply delivery man, had pulled the two-tone low-rider into the alley behind Valdez's favorite Santo Domingo eatery. A second cousin to Valdez's wife, Manuel had been arrested three months earlier for distributing what sounded like the Dominican version of moonshine. Valdez called in a favor and had the charges dropped, only because Manuel promised to walk the straight and narrow while also agreeing to any additional task Valdez asked of him.

"He owes me one. There will be no problems with him maintaining absolute secrecy about your trip outside of the city," Valdez had said a couple of hours ago, as a purple dusk gave way to a nighttime sky filled with glowing stars.

Given Manuel's moonshine background, I was half expecting to see a 1969 orange Dodge Charger fishtail into the alley, carom off a couple of barrels and take the car up on two wheels, then come to a screeching halt— à la the General Lee.

"What the hell kind of car is this?" Bolt brought both hands to the top of his head. "It looks like something out of a circus."

Manuel unfolded his lanky body from the front seat and leaned on the roof.

"Are there ten clowns inside too?" Bolt asked, maintaining a straight face while glaring through the windows.

"*El mejor paseo en toda la República Dominicana. No hay tarea demasiado grande para el Mini. Todo terreno, todo el tiempo, todo el tiempo.*" The man dressed in all white kissed the top of his car, releasing a snaggle-toothed smile that made me think he'd never seen a dentist.

"He thinks his car is the bomb." Bolt rolled his eyes and thrust his hands apart, as if he were Lebron creating a mushroom of dust before the start of a game.

Without wanting to risk my life and the secrecy of my mission, I ultimately opted to avoid the multitude of alternatives in the Santo Domingo taxi services. I'd just have to eat my knees for the duration of the one-hour drive.

Manuel used two hands to shut my car door, cramming my shoulders against the stack of boxes to my right. Once he crawled into the front seat, he said, "I know roads like back of my foot. I can get you there with no lights on *carro*, if that is what you hope."

His English was choppy, but I got the gist of what he was saying. "I just want to get there in one piece, without anyone stopping us and asking us where we are going. Do you think we can accomplish that?"

"*No hay problema*," he said, showing off his grill through the rearview.

Tapping my backpack, I tried to picture how a routine traffic stop might play out. Cops would ask why I was dressed like a mime and then, without cause, search my bag. That's when the reaction would turn volatile. Guns would be drawn and adrenaline would flow like a flooded Rio Ozama, leading to a jittery barrel flashing in my face.

The cops on the scene would shout into their shoulder radios, spitting out dramatic descriptions of a foreign terrorist with a bag full of weapons. Backup officers would be called, superiors would get on the horn and bark out more orders. And that's if I just sat there and didn't move. If I dared to attempt an explanation—which, admittedly, would be a bold-faced lie—they'd likely consider me a hostile perpetrator, and within their interpretation of the law they would have the right and authority to use any physical means possible to subdue me.

In other words, they'd probably beat the shit out of me. And if I were them, I'd probably be just as skittish...minus the unsolicited police brutality piece.

A quick image of what a Dominican jail cell might look and smell like shot into my head. Pigs in slop might have better conditions. And I'd be rolling around in there with them.

Adjusting my knees a good half-inch, I tried to live in the moment, not get too caught up in what could go wrong. Frankly, injecting law enforcement into this operation wouldn't be the worst thing that could happen.

There. I found my happy spot.

I hadn't seen anything more than a distant house light in the last twenty minutes, about the time pavement had turned into dusty red clay. The Mini's tires crunched across tiny pebbles, the sound of glass being put through a meat grinder. While my entire body felt every little bump and piece of gravel, it seemed that Manuel wasn't hell bent on putting our lives at risk, allowing me an opportunity to quickly replay the whirlwind from the last twenty-four hours.

Swearing Valdez and Bolt to secrecy, I shared my entire conversation with Juan and Ana Sofia, who turned out to be Britney. Even with Valdez and Bolt, I knew I was taking a chance. Were they part of the masquerade to land me in Britney and Juan's compound? While they'd known I had my doubts about Ana Sofia's legitimacy, they appeared genuinely shocked when I recounted how Ana Sofia had flipped a switch and turned into Britney at first opportunity.

I convinced myself that running into Bolt was no more planned than getting in that defective taxi at the airport. It was sheer luck. As for Valdez, it was difficult to completely dismiss the notion of his involvement. Having lost his job recently, he needed the money. He was the one who had gotten word back to the states. But he appeared to be harmless, nothing more than a conduit for Father Santiago, who had forged some type of relationship with Ana Sofia. For right now, the Father was on the outside of my Dominican inner circle.

Knowing we had less than no time—I'd told Juan and his Ana Sofia that Esteban's fifteen-day disappearance lowered the odds of him returning safely to a single-digit percentage—I met

Valdez and Bolt after I left the Ortiz compound at a small café near the brownstone just east of Rio Ozama.

While I offered to pay them a fee for any help they provided, each said they would have done the same without compensation. With two daughters of his own, Valdez said, "As a father, my greatest fear is someone taking our kids. With all of his money, many people think Juan has everything he wants. Well, he only had a bigger target on him and his family. I can't imagine what he's going through."

Bolt seemed a bit more reflective. "For someone like me, I idolized Juan Ortiz, not just because he was a legendary baseball player who made millions of dollars playing for the New York Yankees, but because he is a father to a boy who is my age. I dreamed of having a father just like him, the same athletic build. A man who commands respect. I want the kid, Esteban, to be able to go home to his father."

Speaking in hushed tones under a fluorescent light that blinked every few seconds, the three of us plotted our next move.

"Unfortunately, kidnapping has become all too common in Latin America, as a form of intimidation as well as securing a large payout, many times helping bankroll illegal drug operations. I've seen it happen occasionally here in the Caribbean," Valdez said, sipping a can of Coke. "But given how you described Britney's interaction with the people who have Esteban, authorities may not be aware of every kidnapping."

The waitress set down plates of *arepa* in front of each of us, a sweet dessert made with cornmeal and coconut cake. I glanced over my shoulder, ensuring she was out of eavesdropping range. "There is something strange about this kidnapping. In her one conversation with the kidnappers, Britney said they never demanded any money."

"Did they not ask for anything?" Valdez rubbed his thick mustache.

"According to Britney, they only said they would hold Esteban until they got what they wanted and that they would be in touch."

"Did Britney or Juan have any idea what they were referring to?"

"No. At least they said they didn't."

"You don't think they're telling you everything?"

I paused for a second, a fork of *arepa* halfway to my mouth. "Britney would lie, cheat, steal, and kill to eat her next meal. Thankfully, Juan isn't from the same gene pool."

"Pool? Swimming pool?" Bolt asked, flakes of cake spilling off his lips.

"Sorry, I should have said it's good they aren't related."

Bolt cocked his head, curious. "That would be illegal, no?"

"Ignore my use of American phrases. Let's just say that Juan seemed completely distraught. I think he would do anything to save his kid. And it appears he doesn't have any other options than for me—now us—to rescue Esteban."

Valdez removed his black-rimmed glasses and rubbed a thin layer of condensation off the lenses. Even late in the evening, I could feel a line of sweat tickle down my back. Humidity was a constant companion in the Dominican.

I set down my fork, then took a drink from my bottled water.

"To kidnap the son of a local legend, that would take some balls," I said without thinking.

"*Grandes testículos*," Bolt said, a smile on his face.

Valdez glanced at the teen and shook his head, perhaps hoping he'd be able to keep his daughters away from the likes of the kid with a lightning-quick brain...and feet.

"Mr. Booker, you are right. That is where we should start. Who would not flinch when plotting such a crime? Let me think a moment." He pulled out his phone and thumbed through pictures and contacts.

A few minutes passed, and we all finished our *arepa*.

"Ahh," Valdez finally said, again stroking the enormous mound of hair on top of his lip.

"Something got your attention. Who are you thinking is behind this?"

"Not sure."

"I thought you had this ah-ha moment."

His forehead crumpled. I tapped my head, disgusted at myself for being stupid enough to confuse my Dominican partners with another Americanism.

"A thought came to your mind. What was it?"

"I have general theories, but nothing solid."

My shoulders slumped a bit, and I leaned back in my chair and crossed my arms, frustration beginning to move its way up my esophagus. The canister of chalky Tums that usually saved me about now was tucked away in my car's glove compartment, two thousand miles away.

"But I do have a contact. An ex-con. Just got out of prison about a year ago."

"You know him well? He's a friend?" I asked, sitting up.

"I know him very well. I put him in prison."

Bolt had been chugging down his second can of Coke. He choked, then sprayed us with a layer of sticky soda.

"Nice, Bolt. Nice. Can I get some water over here please?" I asked a nearby waitress.

"*Dos aguas por favor*," Valdez said, holding up two fingers.

She brought the waters, which we used to wipe the goo off our arms and faces.

"Sorry," Bolt said. "But Tito Jackson said that he's friends with a guy he put in prison. How can we expect the person to help us?"

I gave Bolt one of those looks. "He's not a member of the Jackson Five."

Valdez shook his head, trying to ignore Bolt. "I arrested Alejandro twice in one week for selling bags of cocaine on a street corner. He cursed me when I told him he was going to prison. A month later, he sent me a letter at the police department, thanking me for saving his life. He admitted he was hooked on cocaine, and even with a wife and daughter, he could do nothing more than sell drugs every night to those more desperate than him."

"Makes you feel good, huh?"

"The pay has never been good, especially in a poor country. But, yes, reading his letter made me think I had made a small difference in at least one person's life." Valdez sipped his Coke. "Alejandro was small time, but he was connected."

"We need to meet him."

Valdez puffed out his cheeks. "Might be a tough conversation. His sentence was reduced because he turned state's evidence. He probably wants to keep a low profile. He doesn't want to be seen talking to a cop. Even an ex-cop," he said, placing a hand on his chest, his stretched T-shirt flapping like a wind-blown flag.

"He's our best chance, our only chance right now, at getting a lead, or at least another connection to someone who might know. It might take four or five connections. Who knows? We need to talk this guy, now."

Valdez had just tapped his phone. "Hold on." He rose from his chair and stepped outside. We watched through murky windows as he paced on the sidewalk, initially smiling and laughing, then his face turned serious. Finally, a head nod.

The metal frame door scraped the bottom plate as Valdez walked back to our corner table near the window.

"Just as I thought. Alejandro wants nothing to do with talking about his life of crime. It's ancient history," he said.

"Dammit. Give me the phone. Let me talk to him," I said.

Valdez chuckled. "Listening to the two of you speak would be like watching an American sitcom. You wouldn't understand what he was saying. But—"

"Where does he live?"

"Damn, you're aggressive."

"Esteban might already be dead. We don't have time to fuck around." I glanced at Bolt. "Sorry...again."

"Mr. Booker, I was trying to get to a point." Valdez lurched his chair forward a couple of inches. "I played the guilt paper. I reminded him how I helped turn his life around. He was still hesitant to meet with us. But then his daughter spoke in the background, and I asked what he would do if someone took her from him and his wife."

Bolt held up a fist. "Give me some skin, Tito!"

The unlikely pair bumped fists.

Two hours later, we crossed a street with a single light at the corner, bugs flocking around the yellow color as if it were their last food source. Beyond a bent chain-link fence, we turned into a small playground on the side of an elementary school. It was so dark from the sidewalk, I couldn't see the school's facade.

"He's supposed to meet us at the swing set," Valdez said, his head on a swivel.

Clouds had rolled in, eliminating even a soft glow from the nighttime sky.

"Crap!" I said in a loud whisper. My shin had just caromed off the bottom of a slide.

Something moved just ahead, and I put my arms in front of me.

"Alejandro?" Valdez asked, each of us shuffling forward as if we were crossing a minefield.

Three more steps, and my hand reached out, catching a swaying empty swing, Bolt a step behind. As we turned toward each other, I moved a hand toward my chest. I needed the comfort of my security blanket, my Sig Sauer.

"He was here," Bolt said. "Did he get scared and decide not to meet?"

Two hands at his waist, Valdez didn't respond while he scanned the area.

"Any chance he's been lured back to the crime life, and he just set us up?" I hunkered down to a couple of feet off the ground, trying to see movement.

Motion at ten o'clock. Pivoting left, I caught fluttering wings lifting a small bird off the top of a jungle gym. The small bird veered toward three other birds about the same size. They fell into formation and glided away.

Bolt shuffled two steps in front of me. Reaching ahead, I took his elbow and guided him back behind me. I spoke in a quiet whisper. "You're my eyes behind me. Nudge me if you see anything at all."

"Got it, Mr. Booker."

"Valdez, you packing?"

"I forgot my pistol again. I had no idea we'd be in danger. In the future, if you're around, I will always need my sidearm."

Edging beyond the swing set, the three of us paced our steps in unison. Objects came into focus, but they were inanimate—a lone car tire resting on its side with weeds poking through the donut hole, a rusted jungle gym, a roundabout with a single tennis shoe on top.

"Did you hear that, Mr. Booker?"

My breath caught in my throat. "Hear what, Bolt?"

A hand grabbed a fistful of my T-shirt.

"Valdez, hold on."

The three of us looked frozen like mimes in Klyde Warren Park back home.

"There it is again," Bolt whispered.

Hearing must get worse with age. I couldn't hear a damn thing, not even a distant car.

Suddenly, a dog barked.

"I heard that," I said.

"Could be someone running from the school," Valdez said.

"Or to the school," I added.

Taking in two more breaths, I waited for another audible or visual signal. Still dead as a ghost town. But I had a feeling someone was watching us, waiting for the right moment "Time to call the cops?" I asked Valdez.

Just then I heard a zipper, then shoes dragging a pebble against concrete. Flipping my body left, I was in a fighting position, knowing neither my fists nor my chest could stop a bullet. Even a knife, if used effectively, could take me down. A second away from taking an offensive tactic, I heard three words.

"*Yo soy Alejandro.*"

Still driven by a chugging pulse rate, I spotted a squatty guy emerge from the shadows near a school doorway.

"*¿Manuel? Usted nos ha asustado, hombre. Usted es el único?*"

"All alone," Alejandro said, his English choppy but understandable.

Despite jungle-forest weather conditions, Alejandro wore a dark hoodie, zipped in front, his face barely visible through a tiny hole.

He was scared.

Valdez engaged him in a quick conversation, mostly in Spanish, playing the interpreter when necessary.

"Have you convinced him I'm not with American DEA or any other law enforcement agency?"

Valdez chuckled, resting a hand on the shorter man. "He was skeptical at first. He's a hard one to convince. Right, *mi amigo*?"

"*Sí.*" Alejandro shuffled his feet, moving his head left and right.

Paranoid must be this guy's middle name.

"Why's he so jittery?"

More discussion in Spanish.

"The whole city is on edge," Bolt said as Valdez opened his jaw.

Valdez put a hand over Bolt's face, essentially claiming possession of Alejandro as his contact, his responsibility. "If anyone spots Alejandro talking to anyone who's not a close friend or relative, word will get back to his old associates. They'll assume he's a snitch. Then, it would only be a matter of time before they send someone to hurt him, or his family, or both."

I didn't want us to have an unexpected visit from any of his former thug buddies any more than he did.

"Let's not waste time then," I said, rolling my arm as if I just started a play clock.

Valdez nodded and turned back to Alejandro, who stared at his lips.

"*Necesitamos una lista de personas que tendrían las bolas para secuestrar al hijo de Juan Ortiz.*"

Alejandro wiped his face, and I could still see a sheen of sweat. He reached a hand into his hoodie pocket, and I jerked my hand outward, my body dropping lower.

"*Maldita sea, este tipo es un paranoico,*" Alejandro said, pulling a pack of cigarettes from his pocket. He chuckled and flicked his wrist toward Valdez.

"He thinks you are—"

"Paranoid. I got that part," I said, blowing out a breath.

The hooded ex-con flicked his lighter, illuminating our area for the first time since we arrived. I noticed two broken windows just to my right.

"Is this school shut down?"

"Sadly, public schools here face a difficult task. They try to educate our youth, to break the cycle of crime and poverty. But many who live in poverty end up stealing equipment and supplies, or even copper wire, from the very school that could teach them the skills to be productive in our society without breaking the law," Valdez explained.

"That's tough," I said, realizing how lucky my Samantha was with her school back in Dallas.

"That is why schools like the one Britney, er…Ana Sofia…whatever her name, teaches at are so important. It's funded by scholarships, private donations. People don't look at it as a government handout that they can pillage."

For many citizens, Ana Sofia was viewed as a savior of sorts. It was impossible to picture the Britney I knew filling the role of caretaker to hundreds of kids. While Ana Sofia was essentially the same person, my mind had witnessed her in that environment. I couldn't figure out the logic behind my thoughts, or what drove them exactly. Aside from the identity shell game, I still couldn't fathom how she was bankrolling this endeavor.

"*Hey, tipo.*" Alejandro had turned his back to us, his head bobbing up and down as he spoke on his cell phone.

I ticked my head toward Alejandro, asking Valdez who he was calling.

"A guy he knows. Supposedly does contract work for people with money. If this kidnapping really happened, his buddy will know. He guaranteed it."

A couple of minutes elapsed. He pivoted around to face us while using his shoe to snuff out his first cigarette. The second one was already in set-up mode.

Alejandro muttered something.

"He asked if he heard anything about Esteban's disappearance," Bolt said, whispering at my shoulder.

"And?" I asked.

"*Él sabe*," Alejandro said, looking right at me.

"What does he know?"

"Esteban was kidnapped," he said, blowing a plume of smoke into my face.

"Does he know who did it, or where they have Esteban?" Valdez jumped in.

Alejandro shrugged, shaking his head. "*No comprendo.*"

Bolt leaned in, using a hand to speak as if he was a politician. "*Tito está preguntando si su compañero sabe quien secuestró a Esteban y donde lo escondieron.*"

"He called me Tito again," Valdez said with a dry tone.

"Ahh." Alejandro inhaled another nicotine shot, then released two donut-hole breaths of smoke. "*Esta es una gran mierda de tiempo.*"

Valdez shifted his eyes to me, then back to Alejandro. "*Usted no va a estar implicado en esta búsqueda. Nunca vamos a mencionar su nombre, ahora, o despues que encontramos a las personas que hicieron esto.*"

Bolt cupped his hand against his mouth and translated. "He's telling him we must never share his name with anyone."

I nodded, as all eyes looked at me. "*Bueno.* I agree."

Alejandro began shuffling his feet, as if he'd taken some type of hyper pill or was trying to mimic a boxer.

"*No sé hombre. Si te doy este nombre, yo podría estar muerto antes de que salga el sol.*"

"He's worried that if he tells us anything, somehow they'll get to him and kill him before the sun rises in the morning."

Scratching the back of my head, I couldn't think of anything to say to ease his fears. My contacts at the Dallas county DA's office or at DPD or the FBI or any other American agency were about as worthless as a single peso in the Dominican Republic.

"Does he want money? *Dinero?*"

The shuffling ceased and white teeth glowed in the middle of his dark hoodie.

"Did I just speak his language?" I asked.

"I think you did."

"*Todo el mundo tiene necesidades monetarias. Quiero que mis hijas vayan a la universidad,*" Alejandro said.

"He wants his girls to go to college," I said.

"Are you going to pay for college for his two daughters?" Bolt asked.

"Hold on." This time I stepped away and made a call.

The other line picked up on my third ring, but no one spoke. "Hello?" I said.

It sounded as if the phone was brushing against clothing. "Hold on," the woman whispered.

I heard a door shut.

"Hi, Booker," Britney said without a Spanish accent.

I still couldn't wrap my mind around her dual lives.

"I have—"

"Do you remember the times we'd have phone sex?" she asked with a quiet giggle.

I fought back a suppressed image, chiding myself for even going there. "Now's not the time."

"Oh, that's not why you called? I was hoping we could relive old times. I'm wearing—"

"Britney, stop." And this is the woman who told me she loved her fiancé? I shouldn't have been surprised.

"You don't want to play?" Another giggle, this one filled with a mocking dose of disrespect.

"I have information about Esteban."

She didn't respond for a good five seconds. "Where is he?" Her voice was subdued, but serious.

"I've made a contact with someone who I'm hoping will tell us, but I need a favor from you to make this guy comfortable with the arrangement."

Britney listened intently, then she offered just what I needed to seal the deal with Alejandro. Thankfully, she managed to avoid further conversation about sex and phones and old times.

Through Valdez, I explained the offer to Alejandro: if he would reveal all the information about Esteban's kidnapping, his girls would have the opportunity to finish the rest of their schooling at La Academia de Aprendizaje free of charge.

Alejandro crossed himself, then shook my hand nonstop for a minute. *"Muchas gracias, Señor Booker. Usted ha levantado un gran peso de mis hombros."*

"I think you have an *amigo* for life," Bolt said.

My stomach first felt the absence of gravity for a split-second. That was quickly followed by a thunderous bounce off the bottom of a pothole large enough to swallow the Mini Cooper. I felt the thud collapse my spine just before I rebounded upward and banged my head off the Mini's roof. Another blow to my vertebrae, but from the opposite end.

On reflex, I tossed out an expletive or two as I tried to brace my arms against the window on one side and a flimsy box of glasses on the other.

Reaching for my sore neck and back, I stopped halfway when I heard the noise. It sounded like a rubber propeller flapping against the wheel well. My sarcastic side wondered if the pothole had carved a hole into the bottom of the tin can.

"*Pedazo de mierda carreteras.*" Banging his steering wheel, Manuel cursed the roads, which were probably used more by horses than horsepower.

Manuel tapped the brakes, and the noise mercifully ceased. Throwing the door open, I toppled out of the car, spilling onto my hands and knees.

"I know the road like back of my foot, but not the damn potholes. Mother fucker!"

Kneeling down at the left wheel well, Manuel shined his cell phone flashlight on the damage. The tire was gutted, ripped to shreds.

"You got a spare?" I asked, turning back to the tree-covered mountain, wondering how far we had yet to go on our four-wheeled journey.

Without answering, Manuel pulled out the spare, tossed the tools on the red clay.

"Seems like I had to change a tire every month when I was younger. We'll knock this out in ten minutes, maybe less."

Eight minutes later, we stood next to the car, staring at a half-empty spare. But that wasn't the worst of it.

"I can't believe a pothole dented the rim. We're screwed," Manuel said.

"That's what happens when you drive a tin can."

He shrugged his shoulders, then tossed the tools back in the car.

"This is going to cost me a boatload of money."

"Don't worry. I'll make sure my client pays you back."

"Really? Do you think they'd spring for a full set of new tires, shocks and struts, and a new suspension? This road is a bitch," he said, running his fingers through his thick mane.

He made me chuckle. "I'll see what I can do."

Over the next couples of minutes, Manuel attempted to use a map app and his memory of the narrow path to provide me enough guidance to reach my destination on foot.

"Just remember, there are two forks. Go left at first one, then right. Wait...hold on." Touching his fingertips to each temple, he appeared to be meditating. "It's the opposite. First fork, go right. Second fork, go left."

"Right, then left. Got it," I said, pulling a shoulder holster out of my backpack and snapping it into place.

"Yeah...uh, that's right, I mean correct."

Manuel gave me a bro hug and wished me luck.

"I don't know much about your mission, but I've heard stories about who is on the other side of that mountain. Are you scared for your life?"

"Thanks for asking. I'll be fine. It's dark outside. No one will know I'm there. Just doing a little observing, that's all."

"Yeah, right," he said, turning the ignition of his Mini Cooper. He slipped the tin can into drive, curled around to face east, and puttered along at about ten miles per hour.

He waved out of his window. "Later, my man."

Checking my phone, I still had a single bar. I fired off a text to Britney—something I never imagined would happen just a day earlier—asking for her and Juan to pay for Manuel's repairs to his Mini Cooper. They could afford it.

I hoisted my backpack onto my shoulders and continued the journey on foot. A half mile later, I hit the big hill Manuel had told me about, a good forty-five degree incline that had a hairpin turn at the top. It didn't slow my pace. Swinging my arms with my knees bent slightly, I made good time. But I was sweating like a barbequed pig, which smeared the dark makeup I'd applied to my face in the early part of my trip. My nearly black face matched my gear—black long-sleeved T-shirt, black hiking pants, black boots. The outdoor store we visited had run out of camouflage, but going all black was the smarter choice with the night operation. The outfit essentially served as a personal sauna, steam practically rising out of the neckline. Given what I'd heard about Dominican spiders and other oversized bugs, sweating off five pounds was an easy sacrifice. Plus, I knew I'd likely have to spend time up in tree or crawling along the ground. Anything to get eyes on who held Esteban.

At the top of the hill, I climbed over a throng of fallen trees, the incline not as severe. I pulled out my bottled water and took a quick swig. I'd need to conserve the water, ensure I had enough to last all night, if necessary.

I reached the first fork in the road. "Right first," I said out loud. The road instantly turned into a bumpy walking path. I also had to weave through a myriad of tall trees and brush, slowing my progress. The stars and moon cast shadows all around me, playing tricks on my eyes at least a couple of times. Once I became more accustomed to the surroundings, I relaxed a bit, allowing my mind to veer just slightly off its single-minded focus of finding evidence that Esteban was alive.

Without direct knowledge of the kidnapping, Alejandro's contact said the target plus the timing of the abduction had the characteristics of a Dominican drug cartel that had grown exponentially in the last couple of years, run by a guy named Miguel Amador. The contact didn't know much about him or his operation, other than he was ruthless and treated everyone who wasn't part of his operation the same—killing wasn't just a necessary evil to maintain a smooth operation, it was the cost of doing business.

The contact had provided pretty good details in describing the whereabouts of the Amador crew's home base. The cartel worked in the mountains, but our contact was almost positive certain government officials were aware of that location—and were bribed into protecting Amador. At least that was his running theory.

Coated with a double layer of sweaty clay, my body was still strong and chugging on eight cylinders. My regular workout routine at home had done me well, even at the ripe old age of thirty-two.

The topography changed dramatically over a hundred-yard section. Hiking at a forty-five-degree angle up the steep hill, I took the rough path around clusters of boulders and patches of dense trees packed in so tight they concealed almost every bit of light from the starry sky.

I came upon a group of trees that together formed the shape of an S. Pausing a moment, I took a quick drink of water, then pulled out my phone, opened the map application, and found my GPS location. It appeared I was close to the camp's location, maybe thirty minutes away by foot. Hard to know exactly, especially without knowing the terrain. With that knowledge, I pocketed the phone, my senses amped up to a heightened level of awareness.

Something moved off to my right. I hunkered down, setting a hand on a boulder in front of me as I flipped my backpack off my shoulders. Squinting, my eyes begged for a flicker of light to catch a glimpse of who or what was at the top end of the S. I unzipped my pack as quietly as possible, pulling out my 9 mm Luger, a Kel-Tech P-11 I'd picked up at the secondhand outdoors store. I was all but certain I was holding a stolen gun, but earlier I had few choices if I wanted to wrap up the sale without drawing attention to the fact I was a foreign visitor.

With a barrel length of three inches and a weight just under a pound, the Luger didn't pack the punch of my regular sidearm, a Sig Sauer P226 X-5. It would have to do.

Both hands wrapped the polymer grip, my fists resting on top of the smooth boulder. Perspiration cascaded off my face. I took in even breaths, attempting to curb the rush of adrenaline zipping through my core. I didn't want to use the gun, knowing the sound alone could elicit a response that would rival a kicked fire ant mound, flooding the forest with hidden enemies.

But I also realized I could be surrounded at this very moment. My thumping pulse reverberated in my ear, and that was all I could detect for seconds, maybe a minute.

I felt pressure against my thigh. Catching my breath in my throat, I realized the pressure wasn't just in one spot. It moved, pulsating around my leg, then pushing up against and around my other leg.

It was a fucking snake. I hate snakes. Ever since my third-grade class visited the Dallas Zoo and a boa constrictor was placed on my shoulders, I wanted no part of a snake unless it was behind glass or on a pair of boots. The red-shaded, scaly skin crawled on my bare arms, and I could still remember cringing, my face a contorted prune. But that was nothing compared to what the creature did a few seconds later. The snake, called Barney, inched up my shoulder and I turned my head, my eyes drawn to the teardrop burgundy color under its piercing eyes. Suddenly, its jaw opened and a skinny tongue slithered out, sliding into my ear. I almost peed myself.

Now wasn't much different—though my hydration was low, so at least I kept my drawers dry. And I had a feeling that this snake, living in the wild, wasn't accustomed to interacting with people. My eyes glanced up, searching for movement through the thicket of trees and cloak of darkness. More pressure hugging my thighs, and I could sense this snake was stout. I couldn't help but look down. I could barely make out the shape, but I had no idea on the length. Too many stones and crevices around me, and not enough light.

Swallowing back a dry patch, sweat rolled off me like a waterfall. I'm sure it was peppering the snake. My instinct wanted me to jump to the side, or fling it away from me, and pound the crap out of it with the butt of my gun, or better yet, plant a bullet in its body. I tried like hell not to tense up. Five seconds later, my left thigh was free, and a few seconds after that, I felt a final surge pressure against my other thigh, and then it was gone.

I emptied my lungs, my shoulders dropping a tad. I rubbed my wrist across my brow, easing the flow of sweat burning my eyes, which still only saw outlines of objects anything farther than ten feet or so.

Just then I heard a sound, in the general area of the earlier movement. Someone taking steps. Short, choppy steps through brush, leaves. Was it two people? I glanced left, then right, then over my shoulder to ensure I wasn't being ambushed at this exact moment, as my heart clocked faster and faster.

The steps moved closer. I steadied my gun on the boulder, my eyes peering straight ahead. I didn't want to shoot blindly into darkness. Muscles were tight up my forearms, into my shoulders, no matter how I breathed. I knew my shot could be off, and that only added to my tension, but it also made me bear down, focus. I could feel the sides of my temple thumping, more sweat flooding off my face, my shirt soaked.

The steps picked up—a galloping set of clops. It was a four-legged creature, substantial weight by the thud against the ground. It was charging me.

At ten feet, it came into sight, and I could hear the panting grunts—a wild boar making a beeline right for me.

I had just a couple of seconds. With one hand on the gun, my other scooted across the landscape and found a rock the size of a softball. I hurled a fastball, releasing a guttural growl at the same time.

Bullseye. The boar winced and whined at the same time. I think the rock connected to his face. He veered left. I grabbed another rock and fired it. This one thumped off his side. The disgusting beast cut even harder left, opposite of my position, and ran off into the dense woods.

Pivoting on my knee, I propped my back against the boulder, my chest surging from heavy breaths. The Dominican wild and I had not exactly bonded.

Muttering a slur of expletives to myself, I pushed up to my feet, took another swig of water, then slipped my backpack over my shoulder and forged ahead.

I plodded another hundred yards before I found a small cone of light breaking through the umbrella of trees. I felt slightly less confined, but unless I could don a red cape and soar through the opening, it only served as a reminder of the time of day. A quick thought of my buddy, Justin, swept through my mind. He always gave me shit about one of my high school football victories eliciting a newspaper headline the next day that referenced me as Superman. It didn't mean much to me. I had a pretty good sense of my athletic ability, and Superman I was not. Not even close. But that's what friends are for, I'd learned. To give you shit about your most embarrassing moments. I'd returned the favor ten-fold to Justin.

Up ahead, I could see more spears of light penetrating the canopy, which gave me hope that I'd be able to detect what, or who, was around me. I'd been in more than a few scrapes, some that almost took my life. But I'd never felt such a sense of isolation. If I couldn't protect myself and stay out of harm's way, my life would end in the middle of nowhere. End of story. On top of that, a fourteen-year-old boy would likely be shot to death, his body serving as a gruesome piece of propaganda by the Amador Cartel to warn off any potential threats.

With the terrain not as hilly, I picked up my speed and covered a lot of ground over the next ten minutes, my eyes still scanning the area for all breathing creatures, with two or four legs. To elude detection, I avoided the spears of light. They were that dangerous to my short- and long-term health.

At the apex of the mountain, I paused for a moment near a small cave opening. Attempting to look down the mountain, all I found were trees and more trees. Who knew how many wild boars were traipsing around the wilderness looking for an easy kill like me? I crammed that memory, and my all-too-intimate experience with the slithering snake, into a lock box that had no key.

A quick check of my phone showed I should practically be sitting on top of the cartel's camp. Questioning everything and everyone now, I tried to imagine the ex-con, Alejandro, setting me up. Or maybe his so-called inside contact had given him bad information, if for no other reason than he enjoyed the notion of me slogging across a mountain all night while the Dominican wild devoured me. Scanning the area right around me, I was reminded how far away from society I was. No human could survive out here long, not without a well-established supply chain that brought in all the necessities to live—or operate an illegal drug-smuggling operation.

Just as I slipped the pack over my shoulders, I heard a quick pop echo in the distance, as if it was the fourth of July back in the states and someone had inadvertently released a single firecracker.

But it wasn't the fourthy of July, and it sure as hell wasn't Texas or any other state represented by a star on the US flag.

That was the sound of a gun. It could just be a regular everyday hunter. Or it could be a member of the cartel killing something that had blood running through its veins, for reasons I'd yet to learn. But that was at least part of my mission—figure out who was involved, how many were between me and a kid I hoped was still alive.

Crouching to a more athletic position, I plodded along at a slower pace, my eyes attempting to pierce the cloaked darkness. I flanked about thirty degrees right from where I thought I'd heard the gunshot, knowing all too well my calculated guess could land me right in the crossfire of some nefarious act.

What little light that existed at the top the mountain had now been swallowed by the trees. The landscape was challenging, the thicket even tougher to navigate. I couldn't move quickly even if I wanted to. Branches and vines zigzagged across my path. I felt restricted, as if I was stuck in a cornfield labyrinth with a ceiling about seven feet off the ground.

Lifting my knees as high as three feet to get past swatting limbs, rotted trees, and rocks larger than the Mini, I got the sense I was funneling into the web of a Godzilla-sized tarantula.

"Holy Mother of Jesus!" I said involuntarily. For some reason I'd incited a phrase I'd heard my mom use a thousand times. Leaves and coarse branches found their ways into my mouth and both ears. I ducked my head to avoid a vine, and a prickly branch dug a hole in my skin just to the left of my nose. I almost lost an eye on that one. Swiping away a slow ooze of blood, I climbed over another dead tree, taking an extra hop to right my balance.

I froze. Something taut and thin pressed against both my legs. My gut told me it wasn't a stubborn vine tangled amongst the swarm of branches. I swallowed, eliciting a crack in my eardrum, then I slowly reached down and touched a single finger to the object—it was a thin piece of string. I encircled the string between my finger and thumb, then brought down my other hand and did the same. I extended my arms outward and the string went beyond my reach.

What the hell was this, some type of tripwire?

Keeping my weight even, not adding or removing pressure off the string, I pondered my options. Secluded from anyone who could help, I realized I had only two ways to go with this. Lunge forward and try to dodge whatever might come flying at me, or leap back and hope like hell I could avoid the weapon. What if this triggered some type of trap door, almost like an underground lion cage…or maybe a wild boar cage?

Was I overthinking this? Maybe someone had left the twine as nothing more than a joke?

I wasn't laughing.

A few seconds later, I essentially flipped a mental coin: fall backward while covering my face and head with my arms.

With my knees bent at a forty-five-degree angle, my leg muscles had begun to feel the effects. I could last another thirty minutes, but by then they'd be shaking like the tail of a rattlesnake. Flexing my toes inside my boots, I prepped my body to drop and thrust back with every fiber of strength I could muster. I coiled my hands into fists, my arms bent at my waist.

I blew out a slow, even breath, raised my arms slightly, then…

Before I knew what was happening, a rag was stuffed into my face, covering my nose and mouth. A sweet, pungent odor flooded my senses. I knew exactly what it was: chloroform. Even with the surprise attack, I fought back the urge to inhale, but I could already feel the effects. My legs began to give out, my shoulders slumped. Suddenly, a beast of a man grabbed me from behind at just about the time I felt a sharp prick at my left kidney.

I could hear boots shuffling in the brush just behind me, but the man didn't say a word. I couldn't fight back. The pressure of the rag against my face wasn't of this world. Struggling to stay conscious, I tried to yell out, to say anything. Nothing came out, and I knew it didn't matter anyway.

The tarantula had lured me into its web, and there would be no escape.

My body almost totally limp, a haze engulfed my brain, quickly stealing my vision. The sound of rustling boots faded into oblivion.

I followed seconds later.

Eight

Another sweet smell woke me from a slumbering sleep. I quickly sensed that I was horizontal, as blood filled my brain.

That was a good sign.

Peeling open my heavy eyes, I realized I was lying on some type of table or cot. I felt fabric with my fingers, a cold, metal bar against my face. It was a cot.

I blinked a couple of times, as motes of light flickered around me. Were they real or the aftereffects of whatever drug was injected into my system?

I attempted to swallow but couldn't complete the task. I had sandpaper mouth and didn't feel like forcing a mouthful of broken glass down my throat—or so it felt.

Out of nowhere, I felt an insatiable urge to scratch my lower back. That's where I felt the prick. It must have been a shot of something debilitating...on top of the chloroform rag stuffed down my throat.

The itch from hell wasn't going away. I moved...*wait*. I couldn't shift my arms. Lowering my head, I blinked twice and yanked my arms. They were locked in place by a pair of metal cuffs.

Fuck!

I popped the cork on my adrenaline and without thinking shook my arms violently, metal clanging off more metal. I might as well have been trying to slice through thick vines and branches with a butter knife. It was a waste of time and energy.

My head grew woozy, and my stomach wasn't far behind. Attempting to shift off my right side onto my back, I could only get so far. The restraints kept me from moving more than a foot.

A wave of organic clarity washed across my mind. One more squeeze of the eyelids, and I finally took in my surroundings.

A wall to my left, made of rusted metal. The room was rectangular, a concrete floor with something sticking out a few feet away. I couldn't get a read on what it was. A counter in the far corner. I couldn't detect the surface, but I did see curtains hanging underneath, some type of purple floral pattern.

I spotted the handle of a skillet. Then I caught another waft of the sweet smell—this one far more pleasant than the one that turned out my lights.

A window on the other side came into focus, a dark, ugly curtain covering it up. Was it day or night? It felt like I'd been sleeping a while. My sweat had long since dried. Where was I?

Who had me? It had to be members of the Amador Cartel.

Suddenly, I heard boots clopping off the hard surface, moving closer. My body tensed. I slammed my eyes shut, but I couldn't keep from sneaking a peak. A curtain flung open on the wall to my left, and my heart skipped a beat. A large man emerged, dressed in camouflage and military boots, walking in long strides. Was he holding…another skillet?

With his back to me, he torqued the pan and something tossed into the air. Then he set it down on the counter. The sweet smell had turned tangy. Grabbing a spatula, he scraped a plastic bowl and poured a gooey substance into the first skillet.

The itch returned with a vengeance, and I couldn't help but flinch, my face contorting like a coiled snake, knowing I couldn't reach the irritation.

But I'd also just blown my cover of sleep. He knew I was awake. Turning my eyes back to the makeshift kitchen, I half-expected to see his ugly grill a foot from my face while tossing a three-foot machete back and forth between his hands.

I only saw his back.

"The shot I gave you is giving you the itching sensation," he said with a flat accent. "Just give me a second here and I'll take those cuffs off."

I replayed the words three times before I admitted to myself what I'd just heard.

He was trying to play the role of the good guy, or least the best of the bad guys. Or was he playing me, just like everyone else had since I landed on the island?

A metal skillet clanged against metal. It must have hit a burner of some kind. Then I saw boots and camouflage trousers walk toward the cot. The man leaned down, and I could hear his nasal passages forcing out breaths. He either had a cold or a broken nose.

As he fuddled with a small key chain, I caught a glimpse of his neck, the skin slightly pliable. Was that a scar blending in with one of the creases? He twisted his head a bit, and the discolored skin disappeared.

His hair was an odd combination of blond and chestnut, with a few visible streaks of gray, a bit of a curl at the ends, almost like a baby's.

This guy was some old fart. I'd take him down in seconds. He just needed to un-cuff my hands, and then I'd figure something out. My neurotransmitters weren't firing like they should. Connecting thoughts and memories were coming in short bursts.

One wrist became free, then he pulled off the second cuff and tossed the pair and the keys on the cot.

"Feel better now?"

I wasn't sure how to answer that question; the itch from hell roared back, and I scratched like a dog covered in mosquitoes.

"You look like a dog going after a mosquito invasion. If you had a tail, it would be waggin'," he said, releasing a slight chuckle.

Sitting up on an elbow, I hesitated, wiping my rubbery face. The phrase he used sounded similar to what I'd just thought. He wasn't native to the Dominican Republic. I'd guess east coast of the United States, nothing south of the Mason Dixon line. Something didn't add up here.

Unless I was being set up. But why? For what? By whom?

His chuckle echoed in my mind. Staring at a swath of concrete, I searched my memory database, trying to connect sound to a saved image. Something was there, but an association was murky, making me think it was an illusion, brought on by the drug combination, possibly the fatigue and stress of my wilderness adventures.

"You need hydration right now. Drink up," he said, sticking a glass in front of me. Damn, he was good at sneaking up on me.

Then again, with my current limited faculties, King Kong could scamper up next to me and I'd hardly notice.

Swirling the water for a moment, I brought the glass to my lips and paused.

"Are you just trying to drug me again?"

"Ha. Ever the cynic, aren't you?" he said with his back to me.

His voice was garbled a bit, but was sounding more familiar. Another quick reflection, but I couldn't connect it with anyone I'd met. Or so I thought. Trusting my memory and cognitive ability was a dangerous proposition, mostly for my well-being.

Without much thought, I downed the glass of water so fast the last third dripped down my wrist, spilling onto my face.

"Nice," I said, stretching my shirt to soak up the liquid.

Swinging my legs over the side, I sat up and instantly felt a wave of queasiness.

"That fentanyl will make you sicker than a dog. We're starting to see a trend here, you and a dog." He chortled once again, then started whistling like it was a lazy Sunday morning and he was cooking breakfast for the family.

Bringing both hands to my face, I pinched the corners of my eyes, somehow distracting my rumbling gut.

I lifted my eyes without shifting my neck. The man was vulnerable right now, absorbed in his cooking and whistling a tune that might have reminded him of when he was thirty years younger. Or maybe it reminded him of the last time he abducted a person and always kept drugs flowing through that person's system.

But what was his angle, if he wasn't a member of Amador's drug police?

Maybe he'd gone rogue and wanted to hold me for ransom to fund his own drug-smuggling operation. Or possibly he was part of Amador's gang, was given the role of playing friendly, but was nothing more than a mole. It would be the perfect cover, using a guy who spoke English, acted like he was American, warming up to me, slowly gaining my confidence and trust.

What was next, him offering up to help me on my mission?

"Once you're able to put two sentences together without slurring your words, I want to talk about why you're here. Maybe I can help."

Was this guy a fucking mind reader?

Peeking between my fingers, I watched as the man never stopped moving. He pulled two fold-out chairs from behind the magical gray curtain, flipped each one open and plopped them down on the concrete. Then he kicked over a round, plastic table, fluorescent green...like I might find in Samantha's bedroom in the future, although hers would have to be purple.

Staring back at the long curtain, I wondered who or what was behind it. Two guys pointing sawed-off shotguns right at me, salivating, waiting to get the green light to pump me full of lead? Was it more of a closet that spilled into a bottomless staircase? His little playground to experiment on all the poor souls stupid enough to be traipsing around the mountain in the thick of night?

"You still don't know what happened. I can fill you in." He reset the folded chair, scraping the legs on the concrete. Just as I glanced up, he turned away and went back to assembling his food items.

"I'm not sure I can stand up," I said, pissed at my inability to overcome the effects of the drugs.

"You'll get there. Just gotta fight through it."

"Easy for you to say. You're the asshole who drugged me. Why, I still don't know."

He ignored my comment.

I watched him peel back the purple-flowered fabric under the counter, open a small fridge, and pull out a carafe of what appeared to be orange juice.

"Join me for a bite. Your system needs some food." He set down two small plates and two glasses of orange juice.

He could have easily slipped a couple of Roofies in my juice.

Damn, I was questioning everything. I was a cynic. At least today I was.

Leaning back, I thrust my weight forward and pushed myself to a standing position. Head rush. Dizziness clouded my equilibrium, my calves bumping against the cot. Waving my arms, I couldn't help but fall back right where I started.

"Tell me you did that on purpose," the man said with more than a hint of sarcasm. "Kind of reminded me of a Conan skit.

Next thing you know you're going to pretend to use puppet strings to pull up each side of your body. You've seen that, right?"

This dipshit was trying to act like we were old friends, yet I still had the faculties of a two-year-old.

I blew out a breath, closing my eyes for a brief second.

"Conan the comedian? The rebel who wouldn't let NBC screw him over? My kinda guy," the man said, clearing his throat.

His voice sounded like it was perpetually gargling. Maybe he'd recently lost his voice or had a throat cold.

"I know who he is." I sounded like an old curmudgeon, maybe a hint of Uncle Charlie in me.

Suddenly, a honking noise came from outside. I could hear the whine of an engine pulling up just on the other side of the flimsy wall. The man marched behind the curtain. Before it settled, he flipped back through the opening. He wore a shoulder holster, with a gun tucked in the pocket.

"Who is it?" I asked just as his hand touched the knob on the door.

He turned his head halfway, and a quick shot of adrenaline zinged my chest.

Maybe he heard me gasp, but he paused, then swung the door open and slammed it shut.

Rubbing my eyes with the butt of my palm, I knew I couldn't trust any of my senses. They felt an odd combination of hyperactive and imbalance.

Loud voices jarred my attention. More than one person, speaking Spanish quickly, like auctioneer fast.

The man barked back, battling for supremacy over a rumbling engine. I couldn't decipher much with his croaky tone. Just a few phrases. Tilting my head toward the metal wall, I made out a "pay you," then "*hombres*," and finally a "keep it quiet."

I had no clue in what context he had used those terms.

The engine revved, and in a few seconds, I could smell the sickening exhaust. The place was definitely not well insulated.

Crack!

A gunshot. I flinched, a jolt pinging the base of my skull. I wondered if the man was being attacked. What the hell was going on? A drug deal gone bad?

I lunged to my feet, releasing a grunt. Spreading my legs, I righted my balance. I plodded toward the door, reaching first for the flimsy chair. It buckled under my weight but served its purpose. My legs stiff as board, I focused on the next step, and then the next, a waft of that tangy sweet smell brushing under my nose.

Pop-pop!

Two more quick gunshots. My heart cracked my chest wall, wondering if the man who had ambushed me hours earlier was face down on the ground outside being force-fed his own blood. Why did I feel compelled to help or even check on him? Why the hell didn't I go through the door with the curtain? I could have found a weapon or maybe a way out that wouldn't cross paths with the thugs who'd shot the man with a garbled voice.

Ignoring my own indecision, I lunged forward two more steps, falling toward the doorknob. I turned it, but it didn't budge. Setting myself, I cocked my forearm, putting more weight into it. It seemed to be pushing back. I tried again and felt the same response.

I was trapped inside. Without hesitation, I flipped on my heels, setting course for the gray curtain. Just then, the doorknob turned as an engine revved and tires squealed. Spanish voices hollered. I turned and took a step back to the door, wondering if one of them was coming inside to take me out. I saw a boot but didn't wait to see anything else. Pushing off my back foot, I threw my shoulder into the door, crunching the person against the doorframe.

"Ahh!"

The man's throaty yell. He was alive.

I grabbed the door and pulled it away from his body just as he took a step in my direction. We locked eyes, a foot away from each other.

My gut erupted into my back of my throat.

His pale blue eyes twitched ever so slightly, but he didn't look away this time. A thousand images flooded my frontal lobe, some of the man, some of me all alone cursing his absence, even a few of me as a five-year-old crying myself to sleep. Ten, no, twelve years had clocked by and nothing in return. It was like he was dead.

"Hiya, Booker. It's been a while." His lips tried to turn up at the corners.

My pulse redlined. "Not long enough. Dad."

Nine

"I've grown to love the greats in the world of jazz and R&B," Sean Adams said, a hand on his knee while he snapped off a piece of bacon. "From Duke Ellington to Stevie Wonder, Marvin Gaye. Most came out of Motown. Doesn't get any better than that. Your mom got me going on that music years ago. Just can't stop whistling the classics."

He released a guttural cough, as if attempting to dislodge a ball of fur. I wondered if he'd acquired a rare jungle disease while prowling around the dark landscape searching for people to mug.

Crossing my arms, I sat six feet from a man I hadn't seen since I was a sophomore in college. He had shown up to a Longhorns football game, even got to see me warm up on the sideline. I think he saw me as a possible future meal ticket, ride my football coattails, as it were. He probably wanted to join me on stage, shake the hand of the commish, share stories with other parents about how they supported their kids through years of tribulation and helped them overcome so many obstacles to allow them to be drafted into the National Football League.

But that sure as hell didn't materialize. Not that I didn't dream of it when I was going to Madison High School in South Dallas. But dear old Dad never supported any of my goals or dreams. The more I thought about it, the more I realized I used his absence as motivation to show the world what I could do without a father.

I realized it drove me to this very day.

That night in Austin was the closest I ever came to taking the field in a live college football game, which is probably why Sean Adams never appeared again in my life. Not a postcard or phone call, text message or email. *Nada*. He'd missed everything that ever mattered to me, including the first six years of Samantha's life—his granddaughter. Irreplaceable moments.

But I'm not bitter. I would have laughed out loud, had I not wanted to deal with his annoying questions.

"You going to tell me who those gun-toting thugs were outside?"

With his head leaning over his plate, he shoveled in a mouthful of syrupy pancakes. I'd yet to touch my food.

"You don't want to talk about Duke or Stevie, huh? I get it. We'll have plenty of time for small talk." He coughed again, attempting to clear a throat that seemed like it was coated with hardening wood glue.

"I don't know about you, but I'm responsible for people's lives. I don't have time to sit around and shoot the breeze," I said, palming my eyes again. "Just need a little more time to clear my mental cobwebs, then I'm outta here." I glanced at the door, wishing like hell I was already outside walking to anywhere, my focus back on the case that impacted a young boy's life.

"You do important work."

"Is that a question?" I asked.

He opened his mouth.

"Forget I said that. You're prying into my life. The life I created without a bit of help from you." I realized I'd been stabbing the air with my finger.

He crunched through more bacon, then wiped a napkin across his mouth. I just noticed how different he looked. Age had something to do with it. He must have been close to sixty years old. His hair had some type of coloration issue going on, but his face was different. And then there was his voice.

"I deserved that. And more." He sipped his orange juice, then forked another chunk of goopy pancakes.

Somewhat surprised to hear him admit to any wrongdoing, I could hear my stomach rumbling.

"I don't get the chance to eat like this very often. That's why I'm being rude and stuffing the food in without waiting for you to start. I apologize." He glanced at me, then returned his focus to his food.

Sean appeared to be in decent shape, especially for his age. No visible underbelly or extra tire around this guy. I noticed a couple of veins snaking down his arms. He'd matched my strength on the other side of the doorknob earlier. Well, my strength when sapped by a drug that could knock out an elephant.

Another tangy waft caught in my nostrils. Inhaling, I could feel a void of core energy, even with my brain clearing up.

"What the hell," I said, reaching over and snatching a piece of bacon off my plate.

A few seconds later, I'd finished off another piece of bacon and taken two heaping bites of pancake.

"How do you like the recipe?"

"Eh," I said. "You got any fruit?"

Lifting from his chair, he chuckled and walked to the counter. He reached under the counter and pulled out a red bowl.

"Pineapple, banana, or orange?"

"My body needs some vitamin C. An orange will work."

He picked up an orange and inspected it, like he was checking a baseball for a grease mark. He even tossed it in the air once. Then, without looking at me, he hurled the fruit on a frozen rope over my head.

My instincts took over, and I leaped out of my chair, lunged a step and snatched it about nine feet off the ground. I felt a click in my right shoulder, and I moved it around.

"Did you hurt that shoulder of yours again?" he asked, sitting back down opposite me.

I'd been rubbing my upper arm, hoping I hadn't partially separated it...again. It had been an issue since I'd been blindsided in a high school football game.

My eyes pinched together. "How did you know I ever hurt it?"

He nodded, a slow smile parting his lips. "We've got lots to talk about, Booker. While you were sleeping off your injection, I came to the realization that this was fate, you showing up in my life in the Dominican. It's time to share everything with you."

I could feel my pulse surging for no particular reason. When I'd crammed my body into the Mini Cooper hours earlier, I mentally prepared myself for everything I could imagine, mostly involving tortuous, inventive ways to get me to talk, if I'd been abducted by the same cartel who had Esteban. But I wasn't equipped to deal with revisiting my entire life, not in the Dominican forest and not while I was accountable for bringing home a kidnapped boy to his father...and my murderous ex-fiancée.

"I don't feel like listening to you giving me one pathetic excuse after another."

Using my knife, I sliced my orange in four equal parts and chewed on a wedge, the natural juice infusing my body with a jolt of energy and focus.

I felt eyes on me.

"Can I get you more bacon or pancakes?" he asked, removing his glare, walking toward the kitchen area.

"I'm good. I don't usually eat like a cow."

"I could see you're still in great shape. Always were a pretty driven kid."

"How would you know?" My voice was laced with venom.

He paused for a second. "Sounds like you developed a lot of discipline too. Must have been the police academy that gave you that."

Twisting in my chair, I just shook my head. "Did you find my life story on Wikipedia? Anything to make it appear like you'd been in my life the last thirty-odd years?"

Sean kept his back to me, flipped the faucet, and began washing dishes.

Even with the white noise, I could sense a lack of resolution lingering in the air. I picked up dishes and brought them to the counter.

"Thanks," he said.

"Sure."

I walked around the main room, my balance and brain both stable. Nothing stood out. No real personal items. A few canteens hung from pegs, a couple of chests, stacks of sheets and blankets, a backpack.

The water shut off.

"Hey, look out!" he shouted.

I stopped in my tracks. I looked down, then kneeled and touched the end of a piece of rebar. That must have been what I'd spotted from the cot, when I could hardly speak without spitting on myself.

"Special features on new Dominican homes?"

"Yeah right. Actually, this shack was built on a preexisting slab, along with three other homes and a garage behind us. Apparently, someone had started building a nice-sized home, then abandoned the project not even halfway through it. Squatters took over and built these....um, designer, makeshift homes. People in third-world countries will do anything to survive. And anything to make a buck."

"Wow," I said.

"It's kind of sad in some ways. But I admire the survival instinct."

My thigh muscles pushed me upward, and my head didn't spin. Progress. "I wonder if the people who left this unfinished house lost their money in the last economic downturn."

"The Dominican economy is a ripple in the ocean compared to the US economy, but it works off a different cycle. The weather plays a bigger role. It's actually called the breadbasket of the Caribbean because it grows, farms, and catches almost everything that's served for breakfast, lunch, and dinner."

"Didn't know that," I said, continuing my stroll through Sean's tiny home. "Sounds like you know this country pretty well. Still can't figure out why someone would just up and leave a piece of property without selling it off."

He wiped down the counter with a wet sponge. "Hard to say exactly in a country like this. Could have been someone in the drug-smuggling business. Tons of cash one day, then it's stolen or his drugs are hijacked the next. Tough business."

I scratched my scruff, wondering how much bullshit Sean was throwing my way.

"You never told me who those guys were outside."

He ran his fingers through his hair, and I could see he noticed my eyes checking out his odd hair color.

"Lots to share. I'm not even sure where to start." He tossed a torn, discolored towel to the counter.

"I'm not looking for an Oprah moment." Connecting Oprah to Sean almost made me chuckle.

"Let's sit," he said.

I had to do the opposite. "I'll stand, thanks. Need to get my gears and engine working in tandem."

He folded the chairs, leaned them against the far wall, and scooted the mini-table off to the side.

"Those guys are a few of my local contacts. You probably thought I was involved in something illegal. A drug deal possibly? Wait, is that why you were at the door? Did you think I'd been shot?" He held up a finger, his voice raspy.

I scratched the back of my head, glancing down at the rebar sticking out of the concrete floor. "It was pure instinct...and not because your DNA matches mine, supposedly."

"Ha!"

As much as I wish I could reverse-engineer my DNA, I knew he was my dad. He nearly matched my six-foot-three height, we had the same basic build: broad shoulders, smaller waist. While he was rather pale under a smattering of fatigue face paint, our facial structure had similarities...although something had changed.

"You look different," I said bluntly.

"I'm fifty-seven. Life happens."

I shrugged my shoulders.

He released a breath. "A herd of camels trampled my face. Took reconstructive surgery to piece me back together."

Was he serious or just telling me more lies to solicit some sympathy from his cynical son?

"You're chewing the inside of your cheek, just like your mom," he said. "You don't believe me. I can understand your doubt."

My stomach had begun doing flips, just what I'd been hoping to avoid. *Damn him!*

"Okay, I'll be the sucker. What were you doing to get caught in the middle of a herd of camels?"

He set his feet apart and raised both hands. "Booker, I'm going to share some stuff with you that...could be tough to hear.

Frankly, I'm breaking protocol by telling you anything. But I'm willing to take the risk. Finally."

My feet felt nailed to the surface, so I propped an elbow on my crossed arm and nervously rubbed my chin.

He sucked in more air, as if summoning up a dose of courage.

"For starters, I got my new face because my cover had been blown. I was running for my life in the middle of a desert. I stuck my foot in a ditch and went to the ground. I sprained my ankle, couldn't move. A bunch of herders came my way, and camels pummeled me. I don't think they ever saw me."

I felt my forehead crumple. "What cover?"

"I posed as a peasant in a tiny village near Kandahar. Word circulated that I was connected to the US government. A local chief sent a gang door to door looking for me. They'd put a bounty on my head."

"What branch of the government, legislative or judicial?" I deadpanned, purposely downplaying an incident that could have killed Sean.

He smiled. "Neither. I was a 'contractor.'"

"You're not a salesman and never have been; is that the story you're trying to tell me?"

Shaking his head, he pursed his lips.

"Booker, it's—"

"Complicated, right. Why didn't you tell me the truth? Didn't you think I was worth that?"

He sucked in another breath, his eyes blinking a couple of times. "You're a grown man now. You've seen how the world works, at least part of it. In my career, you can't tell anyone what you do. It's not safe. It might be hard for you to comprehend this, but I didn't tell you or your mother because I wanted to keep you safe. I know I wasn't much of a father or a significant other. The only thing I could do was protect you."

A tattered loveseat sat to my right. I leaned on it, then rubbed my face, still trying to process everything.

"Momma hates the ground you walk on," I said.

"I know. And I know you've probably cursed me a hundred times as you've fallen asleep at night. All I can say is I'm sorry."

I couldn't let the apology sink in. "You've been a contractor all these years?"

"Yep."

"For who?"

I had my theories, but I needed to hear him tell me the truth.

He glanced away. "This is tough. I haven't shared my real background with anyone since I was recruited coming out of college."

I twisted my head.

"The CIA. Mostly," he said.

"Another gray answer."

"Lots to share. But I'm an open book. I'm finally ready to tell you everything."

So many questions ripped through my brain, many going back to when I was just a boy. That led me into thinking about Esteban.

"I've got some shit to share with you too. A boy's life hangs in the balance."

His eyes found the corner of the dilapidated main room. "He's why you were roaming around in the jungle in the middle of the night?"

"A contact shared with us—"

"Us?" Sean straightened his stance.

"A couple of locals who've offered to lend me a hand on the two cases I'm running with."

"Two cases. There's more than just finding this boy whose life is in danger?"

"It's complicated."

We both released a chuckle at the exact same time.

"Opening up isn't all that easy," he said.

I nodded, essentially admitting I shared a trait with Sean, my father. That had never happened before.

"You were saying something about a lead?"

"Right. Actually, it was a buddy of a contact who believes Esteban was kidnapped by members of the Amador drug cartel. According to the source, that group is based just on the other side of the mountain, real near where you— By the way, why did you mug me?"

I held out two arms, my mind finally getting around to asking what should have been my first question.

"Like every other decision I've made. To keep you safe."

"Couldn't you have tapped me on the shoulder, even called out my name?"

"I'd only seen you from a distance—"

"How could you see anything out there?"

"Night vision goggles. Surprised?"

"I shouldn't be."

"I'd been tracking you for just a couple of minutes, then you stopped between those two large trees. Your legs were bent at an odd angle. I was almost certain you'd found one of the tripwires. You knew you couldn't move, and I knew it, too. If I'd called out your name or tapped you on the shoulder, do you think you could have remained completely still?"

He had a point. "I hear ya."

Sean pulled out a cell phone, checked something on the screen. It looked like a model from five years ago.

"Got somewhere to be? A camel to hunt down, a country to save?"

I didn't mind throwing on a double dose of sarcasm. It was my coping mechanism.

"Need to file my report in six minutes," he said in monotone while pocketing his phone. "See, right there. I'm sharing more than I should." The last few words were barely audible, nothing more than wet rocks tossing in a blender. He coughed twice, then filled a glass with water and drank half of it.

I took a step toward Sean, extending a hand. "You okay?"

He nodded while clearing his throat. It sounded like he was cranking a lawn mower.

"You don't have some crazy disease from one of the enormous bugs I've seen around here, do you? I got welts on me the size of a goose egg."

I reached up to my neck and scratched one such bump.

His chest still lifting from his coughing fit, he raised his chin and pointed at a crease in his neck.

"You see it?"

Another step closer, then I saw the raised, discolored skin I thought I'd noticed earlier.

"Courtesy of the Taliban. I was in a group of four, trying to blend in with some herders moving across a mountain between Afghanistan and Pakistan," he said, pulling the lawn mower rope again. "At a makeshift check point set up by the Taliban, one of the guys questioned my paperwork. He stabbed me in the throat while I had my back to him. A gunfight erupted around me while I lay on the ground, blood pooling in the dirt around me. One of the few times I didn't think I'd live to see this day."

Sean's role in the world slowly began to take shape.

"How did you escape?"

"A couple of Apache helicopters were close by. They came in and cleared the zone, brought me back to camp Bagram. Doctors did a helluva job saving my life. I suffered major damage to my voice box, but given the odds, I was happy with the tradeoff."

"You were lucky," I said.

"It's my Irish blood," he said with a blue-eyed wink and a smirk.

"I've got some of that Irish blood in me, I guess," I said more to myself, thinking back on the few months since I'd left the DPD to start my own business. "I've got my own PI business, which connects to the original reason why I flew to the Dominican."

"I know," he said.

"What?"

"Well, I'm not aware of your original case, why you came to the Dominican, but I knew about your PI business. You've done some great work, helped a lot of people. From a distance, I've never been more proud."

Silence fell upon the room until both of us shuffled our boots on the smooth concrete surface.

"You've been watching me?" I wasn't sure if I was flattered or felt like I'd been stalked.

"Some of it I just found online, reading stories like anyone else. But I've got friends and contacts in agencies all over the world, even a few in Dallas. Let's just say you've made an impression."

My grin was short-lived as more doubt pinged my mind.

"You've traveled the world taking part in operations most people never hear about. It's a thankless job, I'm sure."

He nodded, but I could see he knew I had a point to make.

"Even though you felt like you had to lie about your career, you couldn't pick up the phone and call? You couldn't have visited more often?"

His lips drew a straight line, and he glanced at the floor.

"I recall one time when I was five or six. You dropped by Momma's place and picked me up. She had to tell me that you were my dad. You took me to the park, and I played on the jungle gym."

His eyes narrowed, as if searching his memory banks.

I could feel a swell of emotion catch my voice. "You just sat on the bench, reading, talking into some shoebox-looking thing."

When I finished speaking, the breaths came out in rapid burst. I hardly cared about his answer, but I'd wanted to tell him that for years.

"I had my head up my ass," he said bluntly. "What else can I say? I thought I had a higher purpose, more important work to finish. You seemed well adjusted. Your mother took good care of you. Looking back, I can see I didn't make the best decisions. But life goes on. You've turned out pretty good."

I wasn't sure my ex-fiancée, Eva, would agree. "Eh," is all I could muster.

He shook a long finger. "I recall that day now. It was late fall, chilly outside. You had on a Cowboys sweatshirt. Snot was running down your nose. Every time I tried to wipe it off, more would replace it."

Astonished to hear him recite that kind of detail, I just stared at this complicated man.

"Not that it matters," he said, "but that shoebox you think you saw, it was one of the early wireless phone devices. I had to carry around a battery pack as big as a shoebox. Bleeding edge technology."

I laughed for a quick second. "Can I get a drink of water? I'm not used to a carb fest for breakfast."

"My son, the workout fiend. Sure, let me get you a bottle of our coldest." He opened his mini-fridge and tossed me a bottle, then glanced at his phone. "Follow me."

He flipped back the gray curtain, and we entered a tiny rectangular room. A laptop sat on a small table, a bathroom with yellowish tile and no door to the right.

"I guess you don't host much company," I said.

He gave me the eye, both of us acknowledging our mutual dry humor.

The overhead light blinked. I glanced up and saw dried-up bug carcasses piled inside a cloudy light fixture.

"Damn, I thought the city of Dallas had funding issues for the police department."

He tapped a few keys on his laptop, then hit enter.

"Encrypted laptop to send out your reports?"

He squinted for a second.

"You need readers, don't you?"

"Just know I can kick anyone's ass out there, including yours if I have to." Lifting his eyes, he shot me a wink. "I'm just checking the forecast. The weather here can turn in a heartbeat. And if you're out in the middle of nowhere, it can be dangerous."

Staring at him mousing around the weather website on a laptop whose engine sounded louder than my Saab back home, a tinge of doubt crossed my mind. His mouse had a wire connected to it, and he pounded sticky keys with his forefinger. Not only did he appear to be a computer neophyte, his whole story seemed contrived—all for my benefit, it seemed.

Was I allowing my thirty years of built-up resentment to cloud my judgment? Possibly. Who wouldn't? But his crappy home, camo outfit, and stories of daring escapes and brushes with death made him seem larger than life, enabling him to remain clean of the murky minutia of where he'd been all my life. All it would take was an active imagination, perhaps facilitated by some of Tom Clancy's best work, and Sean Adams could deliver his best sales pitch ever. On his son.

Just the thought of it made me gnash my teeth, my hands curling into fists.

"Got a storm rolling in, according to this radar screen," Sean said, tapping his chin.

I glanced at the screen, noticed lots of forest green. Perhaps dear old dad used to be weatherman in Pocatello, Idaho, selling advertising just to keep the three-employee TV station open. Then he knocked up the cashier at the corner drugstore before taking all the money he'd stolen from all of his sales scams, and fled the country. He eventually found a cheap, unlicensed doctor in a third-world country, who sliced and diced his face until he was unrecognizable even to his own flesh and blood.

There couldn't be a connection to Britney, right? Her performance had been Oscar worthy, up until she admitted needing my services to bring Esteban back to his father. The more I thought about it, Sean's two-bit acting job bordered on ludicrous. I could only imagine how Momma would be ripping into him right now. He'd be lucky to make it out of this place alive. Knowing Sean, though, he'd think of some excuse or distraction, allowing him just enough time to hightail it out of this shack. We'd never hear from him again.

Is that what I really wanted?

I pushed out an annoyed breath. "Where's your top-secret passcode that gives you access to your CIA handler?"

"If I told you that, I'd have to kill you," he said, monotone.

I shifted my eyes his way.

"I'm just kidding ya, Booker. Dude, lighten up." He reached up and flicked his fingers against my bicep.

"You got my bag around this dump? I need to make a call, have someone pick me up, and get back to work on finding that boy. His dad would do anything for him."

"Ooh. Shot across the bow," he said, readjusting his position in the chair, his eyes still studying weather patterns and barometer pressure—shit that didn't matter. "Sure, I got your backpack. I hid it, just to be safe. Never know when someone might bust in unannounced."

I shook my head without him seeing me. I felt like I was playing pretend with my plastic army figures as a kid. What's next, him firing off Uzi rounds with his finger?

This guy must think I'm either naïve as hell or the dumbest guy in the Caribbean.

"Look…" I paused, trying to pull back my pulse just a tad. "I don't know what the hell you've been doing the last three decades, acting in two-bit plays, running from the law, knocking up women in every port and abandoning them and their kids. Who knows? Right now, I don't give a shit about your make-believe stories. Give me my bag, and I'm gone."

Placing two hands on his scarred desk, he pushed his metal chair back, scraping concrete. He lifted from the chair, flipped the curtain to the side, and walked toward the kitchen corner.

Maybe he'd hidden my bag right next to the bowl of fruit.

He bent down shuffled some things around, then stood upright, turning on his heels. He held a thick metal beam, about six-feet long. He gave me a quick glance, pushed one end up. *That sucker must weight fifty pounds, if not more.*

He walked to the front door and rested the beam inside two supports on either side of the door. I'd not noticed those before.

Was this guy a psycho? Maybe he wasn't my father after all, just some lonely pervert.

"Dude…" I put my hands in front of me—an automatic self-defense mechanism.

"Follow me," he said, brushing my shoulder.

I considered running to the door, lifting the steel pole, and bolting out the door. My curiosity won out.

I closed the distance between us in a couple of quick steps as he reentered the tiny back room. Walking past the computer setup, he approached a built-in bookcase. On the third shelf up, he shifted a stack of magazines to his right, then pressed two fingers into the side of the wood frame. I heard a soft knocking sound.

Then he pushed forward, and the entire bookcase swung inward. He flipped a light switch as I stretched my neck to look inside.

"Come on in," he said with a wave.

I paused at the askew bookcase, my eyes still processing what I was seeing on top of the conclusions I'd made about Sean the last few minutes.

"This is my safe room. Secure computer, a sixty-inch flat screen. Access to almost any information I need, either through what I can personally touch or my handler."

"Don't tell me you have a code name," I said, not believing the words escaped my mouth.

His lips drew a straight line. Perhaps he wasn't ready to share his deepest secrets—if all of this wasn't the greatest ruse since *The Sting*.

The space wasn't that large, maybe eight-by-ten. Organization was the major theme. Anchored under a narrow, polished metal stand-up desk sat a laptop, another twenty-four inch monitor just to the right. From my angle, I could just make out images on the screen.

"Are you playing a loop of Jack Ryan movies? What's that one where they go back in time when he's young and start kicking everyone's ass?" I took a couple of steps into the room, my head on swivel.

"*Shadow Recruit*. It's pure fiction, but not a bad watch if you just want a good laugh," Sean said.

Eyeing the monitor on the narrow desk, I could see the screen divided into six boxes.

"Those are real people on there. Do you have cameras feeding video into your...safe haven?"

"I call it Bermuda. It allows me to think about retirement some day in the future." His eyes drifted, and mine did as well. The lighting seemed like it was installed by a designer. A soft glow illuminated the area just above the cabinets, bouncing off the ceiling, making the room feel a little less restricted.

"I've got eight cameras set up; that's why you see the screens rotating. Three are positioned around this house, mainly for safety." He pointed to the box in the lower left corner. "That's a truck driving just to the north of our place here. If he turns into our alley, then I know he's either visiting the two older ladies that live next door, he's got to take a piss, or he's looking for something. Or someone."

My eyes didn't blink as I watched the truck turn right and putter down the alley toward the camera. A guy wearing a baseball cap threw the truck into park, slid out the door, glancing all around. Then he stood facing a wall, right next to a rusted garage door with vines growing all over it.

"He's a pisser," Sean said. "Just to give you some perspective, that garage is on the other side of this wall." He leaned back and smacked wooden board on the wall behind him. "Reinforced steel around the room."

"But if he or someone wanted to get in here, couldn't they just open the garage and see a room at the other end, with all this steel and fiber-optic cables?"

"If they could see it, yes. Inside the garage is a 1977 Monte Carlo, chocolate brown, with tan vinyl seats. The tires are missing. The car is up on blocks, covered with an inch of grime. I think small animals are living inside. The place is a dump. This room blends in with the back end of the garage. It looks perfectly normal. We're safer in here than the president is in the White House. Because we're basically invisible."

"You mean your boss." I raised an eyebrow.

He gave me a quizzical look.

"You know, the Commander In Chief, the head of the armed forces of the free world. That guy."

He chuckled, placing both hands on the desk as if it were a lectern and he was giving a political speech. "I really never thought of it that way. The CIA isn't in the policy business, despite what many have read or seen. But I'm an employee of no one. Remember, I'm a contractor."

"A contractor." I tapped my foot, letting that sink in a bit, my eyes still doing the room tour. My head popped back a few inches. A rack of clothes hung from the wall bordering the garage. Some of the items were normal Army-issued T-shirts, fatigue green and black the dominant colors. I touched a blue, tattered coat.

"The pay is that bad?"

He shook his head. "I have a number of disguises I can use, depending on what I'm trying to accomplish. Usually, it's a lot of surveillance."

"I've done some of that in my PI gig. But my main outfit is an old gray sweatshirt"

"In those two drawers under the rack, you'll find makeup, fake noses, ears, hair coloring—"

"Is that why part of your hair is almost as dark as mine?" I touched my tight fro.

"Yep." He coughed into his fist, his eyes shutting briefly, then he pointed back to the monitor on his desk. "I've got three more cameras positioned near a house in a nicer section of western Santo Domingo."

"Is that your mission here?"

"Hardly. The CIA wouldn't pick up the bill for all this if I was only doing recon on a single house."

"So what—"

He jumped in before I could repeat my question. "This is kind of cool over here."

Pushing a button that blended in with the metal frame of his desk, a cot unfolded from the wall, about waist high, all metal.

"So this is where you sleep if you don't feel safe in the main room."

He nodded as I held up a finger. "The mattress. Yes, I use a mattress, but this cot serves two purposes. I organize my travel bags, clean, assemble and load my weapons, and even apply makeup." He pulled a small lever above the cot and a foam mattress plopped down, revealing a small mirror.

"What about food or water if you're stuck in here a while?"

He pointed to the far corner. I went over and opened an eight-foot door, revealing a cadre of handguns, rifles, knives, rope, ammo.

"Damn."

"I meant the other cabinet."

"You expecting to fight a war?"

Shifting his eyes away from me, he walked back around to the computer. "Thanks to the rest of the world catching up to our technology, I'm able to stream in video off the satellite. Here you go, a nice afternoon game between the Cubs and Cardinals."

The big screen lit up, showing a slow-motion replay of the Cubs' centerfielder frantically searching for the baseball hidden in the labyrinth of the infamous ivy-covered brick wall.

"This proves I don't work twenty-four hours a day. It's my only chance to kick back and lose myself in something meaningless. Sometimes I find myself talking to the TV, as if the players or coaches can hear me."

"Or if you're a Cowboys fan, you'd be screaming at the owner."

He laughed, snuffing out a cough before it materialized into a full-fledged typhoon.

Taking in a breath, I padded around the room, my brain finally breaking free of the mental fog from my forced sedation. "You've been dodging my question."

"Which one is that?"

I glanced over my shoulder at him, then turned and counted the boxes of ammo on a shelf inside the weapon cabinet.

"Okay, okay. I told you I'm an open book, and I meant it. But you need to know this is not just highly classified; it's dangerous as hell. You mention this to anyone, especially in the middle of my zone, it could get you killed. Me too. Maybe others, like your new friends."

I turned and widened my stance, flipping my hand in a circular motion, essentially asking him to spill it already. "I'm a big boy."

He rubbed the back of his neck, shifting his eyes between me and his computer screen. "For some reason, this is difficult for me."

I didn't flinch, and I could hear his breath exhale in patterned bursts.

"My mission is to take out the leader of the group who is training South American terrorists."

I nodded, realizing Sean had probably killed people in his life.

"I guess this isn't your first assignment of this type?"

Two quick head shakes. "While I've had a lot of different missions, many turn out to be…this type."

"So essentially, you're a CIA assassin?"

"I wouldn't put it that way, for at least a couple of reasons," he said. "I have a conscience. I'm not a robot. They don't ask me to eliminate the head of the PTA at Samantha's school."

A breath caught in my throat. "You know her name?"

"Of course. That's what I really want us to talk about. Back to the job first," he said. "And just to be transparent, I have done work for other governments."

"Anti-US?"

"No, nothing like that. I think the agency actually prefers I'm a contractor. Less to clean up, so to speak. But they can also recommend me to carry out missions that might align with their goals. I've worked with the Israeli Mossad, the Saudi GIP, the Jordanian GID, the French DRM, and the British MI6. I guess I'm pretty good at what I do. At least they keep telling me that."

"Damn. Not sure what to say."

"I know it's a lot to take in, Booker. Hell, we just got reintroduced to each other after twelve years or so."

Staring at the floor, I let all the information swirl in my mind. A few minutes earlier, I had concluded that Sean Adams was a fraud, possibly delusional. Now, I was supposed to believe he was an international spy who specialized in the art of assassination.

I massaged one of my temples. Sean took a couple of steps in my direction, then placed his hand on my shoulder.

"I didn't mean to stress you out," he said quietly.

I twisted my neck, staring at his hand. He pulled it away.

"I got a lot on my mind, and that doesn't include everything that's happened to me since you ambushed me in the forest."

"The boy."

"Yeah. Esteban and the person who hired me. She...it's a long story."

"It might help if you share with me more details about Esteban's kidnapping," he said. "I might have some experience to share."

Was he doing all of this to bond with me? I couldn't even go there.

"Okay. Whatever. I haven't made a great deal of progress, though. Hunches and theories right now. I was just trying to prove out one of those theories when you grabbed me."

"Before a bed of nails plowed into your brain."

"Yeah, then." A smirk crossed my face. "I guess I should say thanks for saving my ass."

"I guess I should say that's what fathers are for. But I know I haven't earned that title. So, I'll just say, no problem, any time. And you owe me one."

He glanced at his computer screen.

"What's up?"

"I need to check in with my handler in two minutes. Just watching the time," he said. "So, you were saying earlier this contact of yours believes the cartel kidnapped the boy. Why?"

"It was bold. They took him right off the street. The kid was coming home from his baseball game. He plays baseball just like his dad."

His eyes narrowed. "His dad play in the big leagues?"

"I thought I'd told you. Esteban's dad is Juan Ortiz."

"The Yankees pitcher. He made millions. What's the ransom?"

"That was my first thought too. But they haven't asked…according to my client."

"You sound skeptical."

"Part of the bigger story," I said. "Do you know another way I can get information out of the cartel?"

He huffed out a breath, which unplugged two gurgling coughs. "There was one piece of my mission I didn't share earlier."

"We got distracted by…all of this," I said looking around. "You've got my attention now. Does it connect to Esteban's kidnapping?"

"Not sure."

"What am I missing?"

"The leader of the group training South American terrorists is Miguel Amador. The man who runs the drug cartel."

Ten

A procession of kids shot through the swinging door, screaming at a decibel level that must have rivaled a jet on takeoff.

Valdez, in the middle of readjusting his glasses, nearly poked himself in the eye at the sudden entry. Within seconds, the brownstone's dining room turned into a battlefield, girls on one side of our rectangular wooden table, boys on the other, all of whom were slinging spitballs—wadded up pieces of paper that they were throwing in their mouths, then hurling at their enemies.

Apparently, the quality of their shots wasn't nearly as important as the quantity. Aided by a cache of what appeared to be homemade slingshots, the kids propelled spitballs at a rate equal to semi-automatic weapons.

Splat!

A massive wet wad smacked Valdez in the forehead, sticking like it had suction cups.

Valdez opened his mouth, his face a wrinkled ball of torment. Just then, a pebble-sized wad slung on a rope pinged the side of his oversized schnoz, and he instantly covered his face with both hands while yelling something undecipherable, at least to me.

A booming thud and I lifted my eyes to see Lupe standing at the door, hands at her considerable hips. The kids must have felt her scowl, and they ran out of there faster than the blink of an eye. All but one.

Valdez jumped out from his position on the other side of the table, darting around the man with the gray ponytail in pursuit of the munchkin. Lupe marched around the other side. They had the boy cut off, as the rest of us sat motionless.

Just as the two agitated adults launched for the kid, he dropped to the floor and scooted under the table quicker than a jackrabbit. Popping up on the other side, the kid turned his head—a grin closing off access to his eyes—and stuck out his tongue. Then he ran out of the room.

"That kid will be washing dishes for the next five years of his life," Lupe said, raising a finger to the ceiling as she walked out of the room.

Back in his seat, Valdez grabbed a paper towel and wiped off his head and face, then stroked his mustache like it was a pet. I could see how kids might get creeped out.

"Wild hooligans," Valdez muttered.

"Okay," I said. "Let's try to put the entertainment aside and focus on our main problem. Finding Esteban Ortiz."

I glanced over at Bolt, whose eyes were scanning the room, mostly finding the man in the ponytail.

"Do I have everyone's attention?" Two heads nodded, but Bolt was too busy glaring at the opposite end of the table to hear me.

"What?" he asked, his eyes still looking straight ahead. He leaned closer to me.

"Your friend hasn't said a word since he showed up. He hardly budged when the little brats were firing spit wads all over the room. Is he a little...coo-coo?"

"No more than you," I whispered with a serious look. "Just joking. He's a little shy. He'll warm up; just give him a minute."

Turning back around, I could see Sean shift a dark pair of eyes in my direction. Earlier, at his humble shack, he'd convinced me that he wanted to do anything within his power to help bring Esteban home safely. I assumed a guilty conscience played a significant part in his decision, but I kept that comment to myself—one of the few I'd withheld since my reintroduction to him.

Sean had his own set of issues to deal with as a CIA contractor, specifically "eliminating" one of the most dangerous men in this hemisphere. That's where our worlds overlapped. He had an assignment that he couldn't ignore, and saving Juan Ortiz's kid's life was my top priority. Even though Esteban's life would be used as a bargaining chip to bring Britney back to the states to face prosecution on three murder charges, the teenager wasn't a pawn in this game, at least not to me.

But now I knew saving Esteban had nothing to do with my life or Sean.

A thought just crossed my mind. Was Sean Adams even his real name? There was still so much I didn't know about him. But I'd have to wait until we were alone to continue peeling back the mystical layers of my newly found relative—the one wearing a disguise that made him look like a Hispanic hippie without a care in the world.

"Before we brainstorm new ideas on how to get Esteban back safely to his father, you never told us what stopped you last night?" Valdez asked.

I cleared my throat, and my thoughts.

"He was being shot at by some hunters," the hippie uttered, his gravelly voice causing Bolt to wince a bit. "Damn poachers are trying to kill every last one of the wild boars left on the island. I have a place up on the side of the hill. I gave him safe haven for the night."

Nodding along with the fiction spilling from Sean's mouth, I glanced at the other two. I wasn't a fan of lying to two people whom I tended to trust—Bolt's initial grab-and-go strategy notwithstanding—but keeping Sean's identity and purpose a secret couldn't be compromised. His life, and possibly theirs, would be at serious risk if word spread about Sean's clandestine mission.

"Before I was run off, I found the camp off in the distance, but the outer perimeter is lined with booby traps. It would take a tank to get through there unscathed," I said, trying to sit more upright in the hoopty chair. "But we can't waste any more time. We need a new plan, today. Now."

Valdez brought his hands to his face, his eyes focused on the scarred table, as if he were willing it to give him an answer.

He said, "While my contact, Alejandro, was able to provide insight into the kidnapping, how do we really know the boy is in that camp? Booker has already risked his life once to get there. Dammit, I just wish there was an agency like the American FBI or CIA in the Dominican that we could trust." He lightly tapped his fist on the table.

I withheld the urge to glance at Sean, as Valdez continued, "I fear that this is a death march. And we don't have two hundred troops to bring in. I have run out of options." He dropped back against the chair, a look of disgust on his paper-sack face.

Suddenly, Sean released an ear-splitting cough, finishing with his typical gargling sound, as if his throat would be never be clear. Valdez brought a hand to his ear, and Bolt covered both ears, his eyes unblinking.

"Sorry, I've got a throat cold," Sean said, putting a fist to his chest.

We all stared at him a few seconds, giving my mind ample opportunity to create a scene in the Afghanistan mountains, imagining the exact moment when Sean felt someone stick a knife in his neck. I wondered if any specific thoughts crossed his mind as he lay on the ground bleeding out, gunfire all around him. Did he think about his family from years ago? His existence seemed very lonely, and for the first time in forever, a tinge of sympathy crept into my thoughts.

Another guttural surge from Sean, then he placed a hand on the table. "There's a truck that takes young kids in and out of the camp almost every day. Not exactly sure what they do there, although I have a guess."

Bolt snapped his fingers, leaning forward on his elbows. "That is our plan. I will figure out a way to join that group, go into the camp, and at least make sure Esteban is there and alive."

I locked eyes with Sean, then turned back to Bolt. "Not a good idea."

"Why not? Just because it came from a fourteen-year-old young man? I'll be fifteen in just three months." He sat even taller in his chair, flipping his hair out of his face Justin Bieber-style.

"It's dangerous. Didn't we already establish that?" I looked at everyone.

"But you tried to sneak into the camp, at night in the dark," Valdez explained. "What if someone got into the camp who was invited, basically?"

"I understand the theory." I scratched my scruff, now going on two days without shaving, even more for my goatee. "If it was me you were talking about, I'd be fine with it. The difference is age and experience."

Bolt raised higher from his knees, popping his finger off the table. "This is age discriminatory—"

"Discrimination," I jumped in.

"Age discrimination. I'm just as capable as the next person. I just don't carry a badge or haven't been to a fancy school."

I could sense Sean's eyes on me. I turned his way, and he gave me a half-shrug of his shoulders.

"See, even your hippie friend agrees with me," Bolt implored, his voice pitching higher. "By the way, you never shared your name."

Sean scratched the back of his head. I bet those wigs were uncomfortable.

"Most people just call me Jorge."

George. He'd probably used a thousand alias names. But was Sean Adams one of them? I really wanted to know if his last name was legitimate. Could it have been created by an analyst sitting in a cube in Langley, Virginia?

"You're not Dominican, I can see that in your skin color," Bolt said, his eyes closing slightly as his head turned a bit.

Sean chuckled once. "You're damn observant for being just fourteen." Sean shot me a quick glare. "I was born in San Juan, spent some in the US living around Miami. I guess you could say I'm a bit of a nomad."

"No-mad?" Bolt repeated, a big question mark covering his face.

"That just means I move around a lot."

If they only knew, I thought, but managed to keep a straight face.

"So how do you know about this truck going in and out of the cartel's camp?" Valdez asked.

"I told you guys earlier he has some experience in this type of situation," I said before Sean could jump in.

"Experience. He used to be part of Amador's cartel?" Valdez wagged his head, his sagging skin wiggling a step behind.

"He's not a cartel member. Never was."

"So why do you not tell us how you know this information? Are you a member of a Dominican task force?"

"No. I'm just a guy who wants to help return Esteban to his father," Sean said, pleading his case. "We're getting thrown off track of what is important here."

"I can vouch for...Jorge. He's a loner, a bit eccentric, but we can trust him."

I added a chuckle at the end, attempting to lighten the mood, then my eyes shifted to Sean, my gut coiling into a knot. My logical, PI side knew I had to say those words, to protect everyone in the room. But the other side of my brain, the one who'd only learned a few hours earlier the real reason behind Sean's ghost-like existence, hadn't been able to take that giant leap of faith or forgiveness or whatever it was. At least not yet.

"You are a former police officer, and a man who has saved lives, fought against evil as a private investigator. I trust you, Mr. Booker. And if I trust you, then I have to trust your friend," Valdez said, raising his hands toward me and then Sean.

My shoulders dropped an inch.

"So, it's all set?" Bolt said with a sly grin, rubbing his hands together.

"Trusting Jorge has nothing to do with you putting your life in the hands of a murdering drug cartel leader," I said.

"I cannot take this...disrespect," Bolt said.

I almost laughed.

"I can't allow a fourteen-year-old to risk his life," I said.

"What other options do we have to quickly get a person in that camp and give us intelligence? None, I tell you," Valdez said.

"If Bolt doesn't go in, another fourteen-year-old is as good as dead. You know that as much as I do," Sean said, staring me down.

I twisted my head. "You're taking up for him? He's a kid. Aren't adults supposed to protect kids, not use them to fix all the fucked-up situations adults create?" I looked at Bolt and winced at my foul language. "Sorry," I said to him.

"Shit, fuck, damn," Bolt spit out. "I can cuss like anyone. You don't know what I've had to deal with since I've been on my own. I may not be as big as you, but I've survived a tough life. I'm more of an adult than many people twice my age."

Bolt thumped his chest, his stature solid.

I forced air out of my lungs and scratched the back of my head.

"There's got to be another way," I said.

Sean tapped his wrist. "Remember, I've been around situations like this. Putting a human in the zone is no easy feat. Even if we had other possibilities, time is our enemy."

"Mr. Booker, I have no family. Esteban has a father, someone who would do anything to get him back. I want to do this... I *have* to do this for Esteban and for his father."

Pressure built in my frontal lobe. Everything about this place seemed misguided, seemingly turned upside down, from how the people viewed Britney/Ana Sofia, to the revelation about Sean's life, and now watching a teenager convince me he's ready to enter a combat zone, with the urging of Valdez and my newly found relative.

"What time do the trucks leave and get back?" I asked Sean.

"Next one leaves in an hour. I bet he'd be back before dark. They're just looking for kids who want to make a buck. It will be easy. Get in and get out," Sean said, obviously wearing his CIA hat.

Nothing about this trip had been easy thus far. But I let the majority rule on this one.

Eleven

"You're going to chew a hole through the side of your face if you're not careful."

Lifting my eyes from my phone, I gave Sean a stoic look. "He's ten minutes late."

"This isn't the Metro subway in DC. We're talking about a drug cartel in a third-world country," Sean said, sipping bottled water. "Don't get me wrong. Most of these operations are run like a company...well, more like an oppressive dictatorship. But, there are employees, layers of management and responsibility. Anything to keep the wheels of profit moving. And if they needed an extra incentive, they'd use physical intimidation."

"Exactly my point in not wanting Bolt to go in there. He's a boy," I said with a blunt tone.

"I know this isn't going to help much, but this isn't Dallas or DC or Chicago. We can't get resources at a moment's notice. We're in a foreign country, operating outside of the jurisdiction of the local police and every other law enforcement agency. We could be put in jail for any number of reasons. The number one reason might be that Amador has paid off half the force. Who knows? We can't trust them, that's all I know. If that kid, Esteban, is still alive—and that's a big if—then this is really our only chance to verify his location, given the tip you guys received."

I let the notion stir in my mind a bit. "It just doesn't feel right."

"It shouldn't. When it does, call me. I'll pay for you to see a counselor." He smirked, and I matched it.

I grabbed my bottled water and drained the last few drops, glad to see the line of shade pass over our outdoor table

Sean raised his hand. "*Otra de agua por favor*," he said to a nearby waiter.

"Not a bad accent. Sounds authentic, almost."

"Funny. I speak six different languages fluently."

"They teach you that in CIA school?" I whispered.

"Hardly," he said, looking down a second. "Remember, I'm a contractor. Most everything I've had to do, I figured out on my own, including how to speak a non-English language. It's a little about supply and demand. If they can't find an agent with the right skills, then the price goes up. That's where I come in."

"You trying to say you're loaded?" I thought about Momma going to school at night while she worked during the day. Meanwhile, Sean was drinking champagne in Champagne, France?

"I can still see doubt on your face," he said.

"Who wouldn't? You know Momma worked her tail off just to make ends meet. And she went to school at night to get her nursing degree."

I paused for a second as the waiter dropped off the water, and I cracked the lid and downed another gulp.

"Look, it's pretty obvious that you had other priorities. I get it. Well, I may not understand it completely, but the whole duty-to-serve thing, I'm familiar with the feeling," I said. "But if you had money, why couldn't you have sent it along with a note? Just to let us know you cared?"

"Booker, I can't undo the past." He cleared his throat, then drank from his bottled water. "The few times I did interact with you or your mother, I was putting you in danger. I realized I was being selfish. And that's why I stopped."

My chest lurched a bit. "I thought you saw me as your meal ticket, when you came to watch me at UT."

"I was proud of you, and yes, I wanted you to show them everything you had. I still think you had the talent to start at UT and even in the NFL. Maybe that's the father in me talking. But life happens for many reasons. And here you are."

"You're here too," I said.

He nodded, glancing down the street. I followed his eyes, but didn't see Bolt.

"I wasn't going to tell you this."

"Why not? And what is this?"

"What I'm about to say."

I paused, wondering what the hell he was about to share.

"You have another family in some other city?" I asked with a mocking tone.

He shook his head.

"Two other families, including one in Eastern Europe?"

"I was there recently, but no, I have no other family or kids."

"You're an open book, right?"

He toyed with the water cap for a moment. "I don't want you to think that I'm trying to win you over...to make you think I'm a saint and I haven't done anything wrong."

"Can't undo the past. Isn't that what you told me?"

He nodded. "I swore your Uncle Charlie to secrecy."

"About what?" I asked, arching my back.

"We had a deal that whenever I sent him money, he could keep a couple hundred for himself and then he'd give the rest to your mom. It wasn't a lot, but I think it helped put a few clothes on your back."

A swell of emotion came over me, and a lot of it felt like anger. I had no idea why, but part of me wanted to jump across the table, grab him by the hippie shirt, and shake him.

Flexing my jaw, I pushed breath through my nostrils.

"That pissed you off."

"It shouldn't."

"But it did. That's okay. I've thrown a lot at ya."

"Hell yes, you have," I said, pinching the bridge of my nose. "Uncle Charlie knew about your double life?"

"Not exactly. He knew your mother hated me, wouldn't speak to me, and certainly wouldn't take my money. Too much pride, that woman," he said. "She's a live wire. No offense."

I smirked. "She's not bashful, that's for sure. But she helped me grow up, helped me become who I am. Not that I'm all that, but she took on the burden of raising me by herself, and that's worth something."

"It's worth a whole lot more than the money I funneled to her through your uncle."

"I thought Uncle Charlie told me everything," I said more to myself.

"I'm glad he didn't. You would have only had more questions. Hell, you might have gone out on your own and searched for me."

"I know, it would have put me in danger," I said, like I'd heard it thousand times.

"You've always been inquisitive. I could see at a young age that you wanted to do the right thing, protecting your friends and family was at the top of that list."

I wanted to ask how the hell he knew, but I kept it to myself. Resentment would take a while to dissolve, apparently.

"Did your mom ever tell you how we met?"

Memory Lane. I was too intrigued to stop it.

"No. And I could tell she never wanted me to."

"This very same island, the other side."

"Haiti?"

"She was there on a humanitarian mission after a hurricane, and I was there...well, to try to keep the government from imploding, although she thought I was there to build homes. There was an instant attraction on so many levels," he said, staring off a bit.

"Remember who I am. Not sure I want to know the gory details."

"Mr. Booker."

I turned and saw Bolt holding up a hand, explaining to the waiter that he was with us and should allow him through the iron gate surrounding the café.

I lifted from my chair as he approached the table and put my hand on his shoulder. "Glad you're safe. Damn glad," I said, offering a wink.

"Hell yes, I'm safe," he showed some teeth while taking a chair.

"Now you're cussing like a sailor."

"Sailors cuss? Then yes, I'm a sailor, dammit."

"Seriously, you had me worried. Twenty minutes late," I said while glancing at my phone.

"I couldn't exactly tip the driver to hurry it up. If I had any money, they would have taken it from me. They searched everyone before we got on the truck and again once we arrived in the camp."

"What did you find out?"

"I will tell you everything I learned, but can a man get a drink around here?"

"The men already have a drink, but I'll have the waiter bring you a water."

"Make it two, please. They didn't give us shit during the whole trip."

"Hungry?"

"Always."

"Can we have two waters and a menu?" I asked a man with confused eyes. "I mean, *dos aguas* and a menu?" I didn't know the Spanish for "menu," so I mimed it as best I could, pretending to read a book.

"*Sí*," he said, and walked away.

Both Sean and I rested our elbows on the round table, Bolt sitting between us. I gave Bolt a head nod.

"What? Just another day at the drug-dealing office," he said with far too much sarcasm while scratching his chin as if he had a heavy beard.

"Seriously?"

The waiter's arm leaned in and set two bottled waters on the table and handed Bolt the menu. He ignored the menu, twisted the cap off a water, and chugged the first one without pulling up for air.

"Ahh." He used his T-shirt to wipe his mouth. "Long story short, I don't think Esteban is at the camp," he said reaching for the second water.

"What? Why not?" I asked.

"I got to know one of the little generals a bit. He knows everything that's going on around there, even things he shouldn't know."

"Little general?"

"*Generalillos*. That's what they call the older kids who oversee the rest of the kids who are working in three different stations."

"Stations of…?"

"Repackaging the cocaine mainly. First, the cocaine is delivered on a truck, already packaged up. Never found out where it comes from. Then, a group of kids empty the cocaine into the large pans. From there, the adults in white coats mix something in. I had no idea what it was, but they measured everything very carefully. Then the kids create different-sized packages, including some in little baggies. That's how they offered to pay us, with a baggie of coke. Can you believe it?"

"Did you take it?"

"Hell no. I'm a cash man." The waiter came by, and Bolt put in his order, handing over the menu.

"I see. You were telling us about this little general who gave you information about Esteban…"

"Not exactly. Esteban's name never came up. I couldn't just ask, 'Where are they holding the son of the famous baseball player?'"

"Good. Glad you played it smart," I said.

"Would you expect anything less?"

"From you, Bolt, no. You were saying?"

"This little general, Julio, who is a few years older than me, said he's been moving up the ranks in the cartel. Said Amador once recognized him for ramming the butt of his rifle into a kid working the assembly line. The kid had just spilled some product on the floor. Amador gripped his shoulder and told Julio that he'd be rewarded if he continued fighting for the cause, putting the cartel first in his life."

"Sounds like a religious fanatic."

"There's only one thing Amador bows down to: money. Well, that and a good-looking woman. If he has a blind spot, it's of the female variety," Sean said.

"Julio continued sharing his success story?" I asked Bolt, my mind still churning on Sean's insight of the ruthless cartel leader.

"I knew how to work him, how to make him feel important."

"You've got experience in that field."

"I felt like his skunk."

"You mean, shrink?"

"*Sí*, shrink. Julio told me everything about their operation. Even told me about their main rival."

"Who's that?"

"Someone named El Jefe."

"I haven't heard that name," Sean interjected, his faux gray-colored eyebrows scrunching together.

"We can get back to that in a moment," I said, my eyes on Bolt. "Let's focus on Esteban. Julio convinced you that Esteban wasn't located in the camp. How?"

"Julio's brain is like a…..uh…" Bolt glanced at other tables, then pointed as a waiter cleaned off a table. "A wet rag."

"I think you mean a sponge. But I get what you're saying."

"Right. Julio remembers the time of day when each task takes place. Part of that relates to his job, but he's driven to move up in the cartel ranks."

I gestured with my hand for Bolt to keep talking.

"We all worked in portable trailers. Guards with guns were posted both inside and outside the trailer. When we were leaving, Julio saw that I was looking beyond another row of trailers, through a cluster of trees. I heard gunshots; at least I thought I did." Bolt took a swig of water. "Where is my food?"

"It's on the way. Julio didn't get upset with you?"

"Not at all. He started bragging about how he got to train in the boot camp next door, and how he learned all types of fighting and torture techniques. He had a big smile on his face."

"The terrorist training camp," Sean said.

"They train terrorists?" Bolt's eyes appeared to be locked open.

I put a finger to my lips and hushed Bolt. "Yes."

"I suppose I can't help but tell you now, but Amador's group has diversified their business," Sean said. "Given their remote location in the middle of the jungle, being on an island, and basically being overlooked by anyone who tracks these types of things, Amador has a team of former terrorists who live and work at the camp. He makes a good chunk of change and knows he's protected from almost any group who wants to take him out. Now I wasn't aware of a rival gang moving in on his turf. You said it was run by a guy called El Jefe?"

"Terrorists," Bolt said, staring off, ignoring Sean's question. "Where do they come from?"

"Good question." I said, then nodded at Sean. "Jorge, you wanna answer?"

"They're called L-FARC."

"Wait. I've heard of a group called FARC. Fuerzas Armadas Revolucionarias de Colombia," Bolt said. "People throw their newspapers aside every day. Not as many newspapers these days since everyone has a fancy device, but I manage to catch up on the news."

"Then you should know that FARC has been negotiating some type of peace and amnesty agreement with the Columbian government." Sean shifted his eyes to me. "This is a splinter group, similar to what we saw when the IRA tried to become more of a political movement in Ireland years ago."

I nodded, impressed by Sean's knowledge. Then again, as he'd noted earlier, this is his day job, and if he wasn't keenly aware of every bit of information about the target, then his ass would be in danger. "What does the L stand for?"

"Loyalist. Meaning, if you're not part of our group, then you're not loyal to the cause. That's how they coerce more of the mainstream into the group."

"Sounds typical of many terrorist organizations, I would think. Feeding fear, and even guilt, on many levels."

Out of the corner of my eye, I could see Bolt studying Sean, then glancing back to me.

"You two know each other well." Bolt pointed a finger at both of us. "Friends for a long time?"

"Off and on," I said, hoping it would end right there.

"We go way back, just lost touch for a while," Sean said.

Bolt nodded, his eyes still examining us.

"I need to know more about this rival group to Amador, El Jefe. What did Julio tell you about El Jefe?"

"The name stands for The Boss or The Chief," Bolt said.

"I know Spanish, at least when people aren't speaking a hundred miles an hour," Sean added. "What did Julio share with you about El Jefe? Is the El Jefe cartel a threat to Amador's operation? Does he know what type of product they're pushing? Are they possibly looking to take the terrorist training away from Amador?"

Bolt held up his hands. "Whoa. So many questions. Why are you so curious about another cartel? Esteban was kidnapped by Amador's team, no?"

I held up a finger, saving Sean from his fixation on the Amador spider web. "We think so. That's what Alejandro's contact shared with us. If he was telling us the truth."

"You are right. We don't know, do we?" Bolt said.

"Given what Julio told you, or didn't…"

"I forgot to tell you that Julio bragged about helping kidnap the daughter of one of Amador's top lieutenants. Apparently, the lieutenant had tried to start his own operation on the side. Amador found out and ordered his daughter to be kidnapped."

"What did they do with her?"

Blowing out an audible breath, Bolt stuck a finger in the corner of his eye. "He was like a sick hyena laughing when he told me that he tortured her and raped her. They used a dull machete to chop off each finger and toe and mailed them to her parents."

"Jesus."

"It gets worse."

"How?"

"Julio brought her naked, bloody body out into the middle of the camp and said the kid who had the guts to put a bullet through her head would instantly be promoted to a little general."

"Someone volunteered?"

"According to Julio, five kids jumped at the chance. One was a girl. And he gave her the honors."

Shaking my head, I let the brutality sink in. "I'm just glad you got out of there with your life, Bolt. I don't know what I was thinking in letting you go."

A smile cracked his face. "I'm lightning quick, remember?"

"Oh, I remember."

"So what makes you think Julio wasn't involved in Esteban's abduction?" Sean asked.

"I guess I don't know for certain. But the way he talked, he acted like nothing happened around that place without him knowing."

"That kid has some problems," I said.

"I'm assuming that Amador's lieutenant was killed as well?"

"Julio said that Amador predicted he'd come to the camp begging for his life and his wife's life. He did, and then Amador had the newest little general shoot him point blank, dropping his body on top of his naked daughter's body."

"Demented," I said.

"Ruthless," Sean added, as we locked eyes. "But it appears they're more of an equal-opportunity cartel, given the consideration they gave the girl general."

Bolt shook his head. "Not so much. The girl who killed them was proud of her work and started boasting. Amador said he had to teach her a lesson in humility, and he took her inside his home and…"

The sun had dropped behind the low-rise building across the street, but I still felt a ring of warm air radiating off my body. Esteban wasn't the only soul who needed to be rescued, I thought. Countless other kids were caught in this pit from hell, likely too scared to break away, or perhaps addicted to the drug they helped package. But I was sure Amador and his lieutenants set up the operation that way—anything to create a reliance on the home cell.

The waiter brought Bolt's plate as I replayed an earlier comment from Sean. I took out my wallet and threw down enough cash to cover our bill, plus a sizable tip.

"Can we get this food to go?"

Another strange look from the waiter.

"*Comida, vamos?*" I pretended to spoon food in my mouth.

"Go? I need to eat. I've been working my ass off," Bolt said.

"Don't say ass."

"You know what I'm saying," he said, scarfing down another bite of something that resembled roasted meat.

Sean tilted his head, as if trying to read my next move.

I pulled out my phone, scrolling through my contacts. "I have a date to make."

Twelve

By the time the waiter brought the bag of leftovers from Bolt's food, the corner streetlights—at least those that were functioning—had turned on. We exited the gated café and walked down the sidewalk, moving west past a buzzing streetlight that acted as a bug magnet. I had to press my lips shut to ensure I didn't swallow a wayward bug.

Bolt had found a deflated soccer ball at the edge of a street sewage drain and was dribbling it down the sidewalk, occasionally jumping into the street to retrieve the ball. He never bothered to lift his head to check for traffic, but he had this odd awareness of when to dip in and out of the street without getting hit.

"What's your idea?" Sean asked, matching me stride for stride.

"Amador's weakness. Women."

"You plan on using one of my outfits, or do you want to create your own drag queen look?" Sean raised one of his fake eyebrows.

"Given what Bolt experienced, what he learned from that sick little general, we have no idea where Esteban is being held, if he's not already in a makeshift grave." I could feel my jaw tighten. "The time element is eating at me. It's hard for me to imagine what has happened to Juan's son. But I can't give up hope until we know something."

I hooked a quick left onto 4th Street, catching a waft of trash, something spicy mixed in. Sean caught up quickly, while Bolt continued kicking the ball around. The street was narrow, bordered by the walls of worn, brick buildings. A lone boy booted a can at the far end. Other than that, the road was barren of people and cars. I heard a dog bark bounce off the brick edifice, but with the echo I couldn't determine where it had originated.

"You're thinking a seductive woman might be able to pull information out of Amador without him knowing, am I right?" Sean asked.

"Bullseye. But what I don't know is how a woman would get close to Amador."

Bolt jumped over the sloped curb and hopped between us, juggling the ball on his knees.

"Not bad, Ronaldo."

Bolt just laughed and kept juggling the ball on his knees.

"You think you can find a real woman who's willing to take the risk?" Sean asked.

"If you can get us an opportunity, I'll take care of the woman part."

The corners of Sean's mouth turned upward.

"What?" I asked.

"Nothing. Well, there is something."

"I'm waiting."

"Amador doesn't leave the camp much, unless he's traveling outside of the country to spend his money or going to a club here in the city. I've tracked him numerous times, and he's only gone out on Saturday nights, and it's one club in particular—a club owned by his cousin, Club de Python."

"Snakes, really?" I shook my head. "My nemesis."

"Clubs don't bite."

"Good," I said, tapping a number in my recent call list. "Because this girl just might."

Stopping in my tracks, I turned my back from Sean and the distraction known as Bolt.

Two minutes later, I ended the call. "We're changing our route. Need to take a right up here. Then three blocks and another left. She'll buzz us in once we get to her apartment."

"Whose apartment?"

"Britney...the reason I flew into the Dominican."

"That's right, you never told me much about your original case."

"She's the one. My former girlfriend. She killed three people back in Dallas. The parents of her ex-fiancé paid me to find her."

"You found her."

"It didn't take a lot of work. But she's now engaged to Juan Ortiz. She convinced me that if I can bring Esteban back to his father, then she will not fight extradition and will go back to Dallas with me and face the charges against her."

"Why would Juan get mixed up with her? Don't tell me it's because she's drop-dead gorgeous."

"He doesn't know about her past. She's created a new life, a new identity. She runs a private school; people love her here," I said, turning my head his way. "She goes by the name Ana Sofia Campos. She looks completely different. Her skin is darker, hair is darker and chopped off. She's even done one of your tricks. Had some facial surgery, and it wasn't to tuck away any wrinkles."

"Wish that could have been my excuse. Then again, I am looking a little older these days," he joked, then released another wet cough.

Out of nowhere, something metal slammed into my rib cage, and I doubled over.

My knees hit pavement, as motes of pain flickered across my vision.

"*¡Meta su culo en el callejón. Ahora!*"

Spanish voices yelled above my head. Peering an eye open, I spotted three guys shuffling around in sandals, holding automatic rifles like they were batons. One poked Sean in the back of the neck, who raised his hands and walked past me.

"Get off ass," a thug said in broken English. He followed the order with another thrust of his gun into my gut, emptying my lungs of all air.

"Stop it, Julio!"

Bolt, with desperation in his voice.

Setting my hands under my body, I pushed upward. Bolt's legs flailed off to my right. I turned my head and found a guy dragging my little buddy by his shaggy hair like a wild cat. Bolt yelled, but it wasn't loud.

I only caught a glimpse of his eyes, but they were wide with fear.

We must have been followed since we left the café.

Up on one knee, I lifted to my feet and immediately felt a jab in my back.

"*Vaya, antes de que alguien nos vea.*" The guy behind me poked my spine with the edge of his rifle. That much I could handle. I was more concerned about his spastic movements and what would happen to my spine if he accidentally pulled the trigger.

Stumbling over a crack on the sidewalk, my side felt like someone was digging a fence post between two of my ribs.

Halfway down the alley, the sky almost completely dark, the three of us huddled against a greasy stucco wall, a flickering light off to my left. I finally had a chance to size up our assailants. They looked young. Teenagers, maybe seventeen or eighteen years old. Lean. Muscles rippled off their bare arms and shoulders, their hands constantly re-gripping their guns. They spoke amongst themselves, the one in the middle laughing while glancing at Sean. All three had teeth so white they glowed in the dark.

I sneaked a peek down both ends of the alley. Not a living soul to be found, not even the lone barking dog.

"Sebasten, I thought you wanted to learn more about our business, how I made my mark so that you could follow my path. But that isn't why you asked me so many questions, is it, Sebasten?" The guy I assumed was Julio flipped his gun over his shoulder and ambled toward Bolt, who stood in between Sean and me.

Standing almost my height, Julio drew closer, and I could smell booze in the air. Not a good sign. He dropped his gun on Bolt's shoulder, and my little buddy winced just a bit.

"You are just a little boy, aren't you? You've come back to tell your two daddies all about your trip to Disneyland."

Julio turned and shared a chuckle with his cohorts, then swung his fist around and connected with Bolt's jaw, bouncing his head off the stucco.

Both Sean and I took a step forward, the pain in my ribs a distant memory. In just seconds, we had rifles buried under our chins.

Julio turned to me as his buddy holding the gun against my face jumped up and down. "First, you're going to tell us who you work for, and then you're going to die. And I'll tell you right now, it won't be a quick death. It will be slow and painful, and you will beg me to save your life. And I will, for just a few more minutes." He chuckled and slapped his bare leg.

His bark cut through the air, the smell of booze undeniable. If I could have lit a match, the entire alley would have been a ball of fire.

"Sebasten, do you want to watch your daddies cry? I will make them cry, I promise you. And then you will sob as you watch blood pour from their souls. I will drink it, and it will give me energy and power!"

His booming voice caught the wave of a stiff breeze, and it seemed to carry forever. But there was no counter-sound, no response to his maniacal rant. It felt like we were on an uninhabited island, not in a city of more than a million people.

"Leave them alone. They are my friends. I'm the one you want to hurt." Bolt arched his back, defiance digging stress lines on his face.

I felt like strangling Bolt myself. Dammit, this wasn't the time to bring out the bold, rebellious attitude.

Julio just started laughing and popped each of his buddies on the arm, who followed their fearless leader into an outright laugh fest. They laughed so hard their bodies shook. The thug in front of me couldn't stop quivering, and his rifle tapped the bottom of my chin, almost like it was sending off Morse code. The chin music I didn't care much about. My sights zeroed in on his trigger finger, which ignited my pulse. If he jerked the rifle too quickly, I would never know, unless the bullet somehow would just graze my throat. Then I'd likely drown in my own blood—similar to what Sean experienced in Afghanistan.

"Why do you laugh at me?" Bolt continued.

It took everything I had not to put my hand over his face.

"Because…because, you silly little boy." Julio's snickering almost made him topple over as he wiped tears from his eyes. I didn't see the humor, only pathetic bullies who'd been brainwashed to the point where they wouldn't hesitate in torturing or killing all of us.

Julio steadied himself and gripped Bolt's shoulder. "Back at the camp, you thought you were playing me, asking me all sorts of questions. But I knew what you were doing all along."

He leaned down, his face barely an inch from Bolt's. "You think you are so smart. But it is I, Julio, who has the brilliant mind."

Suddenly, Julio rammed his head into Bolt's, who fell against the wall.

"Bolt!" I shouted.

He righted himself, brought a hand to his forehead. Blood squeezed between his fingers. His chest lifted in quick gasps, his unwavering stature washed away. I wondered if he might start crying, like a normal fourteen-year-old boy.

"You're from here, I'm surprised you don't know," Julio spat.

"What?" Bolt said meekly.

"You cannot fuck with Julio. You cannot fuck with the Amador cartel."

The little general started laughing again, spit flying out of his mouth.

Shifting my eyes right, I could see Sean, his arms hanging by his side, but slightly bent at the elbow. While his face almost looked catatonic, I could sense he was preparing to launch a surprise attack. But I had no idea when or how I needed to respond. I knew he probably had experience in life-threatening situations just like this—I'd been in similar scraps—but we weren't partners. We didn't know squat about each other's signals, let alone each other's strengths and weaknesses.

"Before we begin torturing you and your friends," Julio covered his mouth for a moment, "we need to know a few things. Or should we start by making an example of the old man here?"

Julio gritted his teeth, jabbing his rifle into Sean's ribs. For a second, I thought he was going to pull the trigger.

"No, stop!" Bolt yelled, reaching for the gun.

"Don't," I said, grabbing Bolt's arm.

It was too late. Julio backhanded Bolt across the jaw, flipping his head back to me. A mixture of blood and spit flew across my face. Bolt dropped to a knee, but used a hand to keep his balance.

"*Hijo de puta.*" Bolt cursed under his breath, his growl now filled more with anger, not fear.

I rested my hand on the top of his neck.

"You think you can protect this little shit?"

Julio scooted across the rocky pavement, bumping up against his partner, who still had his rifle tucked under my chin. "Your little friend is nothing more than a traitor to the people of the Dominican Republic. An embarrassment. Maybe his parents knew that, and that's why they left him."

Bolt sprung out of his stance, flailing his fists. I grabbed the collar of his shirt just as my personal thug rammed the butt of his rifle into the exact same spot on my rib cage.

Falling back against the wall, not an ounce of air left in my lungs, I managed to keep my grip of Bolt's shirt, yanking him back just in time. A Julio roundhouse right whiffed just an inch in front of Bolt's face.

"Ahh!" Julio yelled in disgust as he started pounding his foot into Bolt's head.

I threw my body on top of Bolt and quickly felt five, six, seven kicks and punches.

"Stop, please stop!"

Sean.

"We'll tell you whatever you want to know, but you have to promise us that you'll let the kid go."

The beating ended, and all attention turned to Julio bowing up against Sean.

"The old man speaks. I thought you were a mute."

Julio got so close I figured he'd be able to see Sean's fake eyebrows and mustache, and his wig.

"I...I am not well. I've been sick, and it's left me weak," he said, bringing a hand to his chest.

I could see where he was going, and it gave me hope. I moved to one knee and noticed the guns had dropped to their sides. Julio even took a step back from Sean.

"What do you have, old man? Is it contagious? Did you just spread your filthy germs on us?"

"I was bitten by an assassin bug six months ago in the Amazon in Brazil." Suddenly, his body threw out one of his gurgling, wet coughs. The armed bandits took another step back, instantly using their arms to cover their mouths.

Two of them started ranting and cussing in ultra-quick Spanish.

"*Cállate. Voy a decidir qué hacer.*" Julio said to his partners.

I only knew he told them to shut up.

"I have Chagas disease. It's parasitic. And since I can't afford insurance or any of the special medications, doctors say I don't have much longer to live." Another shorter cough, but Sean ended with the back of his hand against his lips, his eyes closed, as if he was saving his precious breaths.

Julio's eyes scanned Sean up and down, his face not quite as defiant.

"You're going to die anyway. I will still get my answers and then kill you and your friends. It will put you out of your misery. I will be doing you a favor."

"These two don't know a damn thing," Sean said, flicking a hand in our direction. "I've been using them since I met them a few days ago. I was only trying to find some cheap weed to deal with the pain from the disease."

Grabbing Bolt's arm, Julio spun him in closer and stuck the end of his rifle into Bolt's ear.

"So you shouldn't mind if I spill his brains all over this filthy alley. *Sí?*"

"Just because I'm about to die doesn't mean an innocent kid should die too." Sean held his gaze, his voice even, but not threatening.

"I'm sick and tired of playing games. You are all going to die, but first someone will tell me who sent you and what you were trying to find," Julio said, shifting his white eyes to each of us.

Sean unleashed a torrent of coughs. If I didn't know better, I would have thought he'd caught some type of funky tropical disease.

I took a purposeful step back.

"You never told us about this bloodsucking assassin bug, or that you had Chagas disease or whatever in the hell it's called." I raised a pointed finger at Sean, my voice rising in volume and intensity. "You only said that you had a bad cold. You lied to us all this time. You knew you were infecting us. You were going let us die. You're no better than any of them. Just a low-life killer."

I took two steps toward Sean, who raised his arms, fear in his eyes.

We were both on the same page.

One of the thugs jumped in front of me, shoving his gun against my chest.

"*¡Muevase p'atrás, regresen ahora!*" he shouted.

I kept pushing forward, trying to bait at least one more of the bandits toward me.

"I'll tell you who sent us; just stop hurting them," Sean said.

I glanced at him, but he kept his eyes off me. What was he doing? Couldn't he see that our plan was working?

A quick chortle from Julio, as he took a step toward Sean, but then backed up, drawing his arm closer over his mouth. "The old man is also smart. Maybe I will spare them. Tell me who sent you."

"El Jefe," he said.

"I should have known. Amador told us to be on the lookout for spies from the El Jefe clan," Julio said.

"I was paid two hundred dollars US to find a way—"

Julio jumped in. "Two hundred dollars isn't much to risk your life. Or in this case, little Sebasten's life. You're old and stupid."

"I only did it to raise money, hoping, somehow, I could find a way to pay for the medicine I need to...to keep living." Sean's shoulders slumped, his chin pressed against his chest.

"I need to know the identity of El Jefe."

"I never saw him. Word got around that I was desperate for money. A kid even younger than Sebasten ran up to me on the street, handed me a phone number. I called it and talked to a person who said he worked for El Jefe. Said they needed more information on the Amador cartel."

Damn, Sean was convincing.

"Give me that number," Julio held out his hand, then brought it back to his person. "Drop it on the ground and let me see it."

"I was told to throw it away."

Julio lowered his stance, studying Sean. "You are lying."

Sean held up his hands. "I don't have it on me, but I recall the number."

"Tell me. Now, quickly."

Julio barked instructions to his sidekick, who pulled a cracked cell phone from his pocket.

"What is the number?"

Sean rattled off nine digits as if it was his home number.

All heads turned to the thug with the phone pressed against his ear, his mouth hanging open.

I heard a high-pitched ring. The teen pulled the phone away and shook his head.

"That number didn't work," Julio said, turning back to Sean. "You playing a game with us? Do I need to put a bullet in the boy's head to get you to give me that number? I will do it."

"Don't you know?" Sean said.

"Know what?"

"They used a burn phone."

Julio's eyes glanced into the darkening sky.

"A burn phone is like a tissue. You use it and throw it away. That's how they work."

Julio looked down, as if pondering what all of this meant.

"I don't know El Jefe, but why is his group a threat to the Amador cartel. I thought your cartel controlled every drug moving through this island?" Sean opened his arms.

"We do," Julio barked. "Well, we did until the last few months."

"What happened?"

Sean was trying to pull information out of Julio, anything about this El Jefe character. He must be wondering if the new gang of smugglers was a threat to take down Amador without his intervention. Perhaps he was questioning whether they might try to get into the terrorist training business. Who knew? I just hoped his Q&A session wouldn't ruin our chances of surviving this mugging.

"One of our main suppliers has changed his alliances to the El Jefe organization. Another one is negotiating with Señor Amador, trying to screw us," Julio said, the rifle now resting over his shoulder and his voice more reflective. "We were on top of the world. Invincible."

Sean nodded.

"The biggest blow came when one of our shipments was hijacked just off the northern coast. It was like they knew the details of our operation."

I almost had to force my jaw shut. Somehow, Sean had reversed the tide without Julio knowing any better. I glanced down at Bolt, on one hand and a knee, blood smeared across his face, but he was as still as a statue.

"Who is this El Jefe character?" Sean prodded.

"There are rumors," Julio said, shuffling his feet.

Sean didn't respond, apparently allowing Julio to decide when to speak. Shifting my eyes, I could see the two thugs turning their heads toward the discussion, their rifles dangling off their hands. The mentioning of El Jefe scared them.

"Is everything okay back here?"

Flipping my head to the left, I saw that Father Santiago had glided into the alley. Julio and his henchmen jerked around to face him, lifting their rifles into firing position.

"Stop!" Julio barked as his brethren yelled something in Spanish.

In a split second, the scene had moved from calm to tense.

"Whatever you think you are doing, it will not serve you well," the Father said in his usual composed tone.

I wanted to yell at him to turn and run away, but I knew that would only escalate the situation.

The Father kept walking in our direction, seemingly unfazed by three rifles aimed straight at him. I turned to the thug nearest me, his nervous feet dancing like he was in a boxing ring. His neck began twitching.

The three thugs yelled at each other, I think fighting over whether they should kill the Father right there.

"*Mucha gente. Hay que matar al Padre, matar a todos ellos, y salir de aquí.*"

Something about killing the Father, maybe all of us. The Father was now only twenty feet away.

Just as I shifted my sights to Sean, Bolt...bolted, lunging toward Julio.

Our timing be damned! I leaped two steps toward the thug directly in front of me, took hold of the rifle just as he swung my way. The automatic weapon rattled off ten, maybe twenty quick shots. Bullets whizzed by my ear, over my head, pinging the wall behind me, who knew what else. With my adrenaline spigot wide open, I yanked the thug off balance, using his rifle to spin him around. He began to fall, but his finger was caught in the trigger mechanism. He cried out just as his body hit the ground. Lifting my shoe, I started to kick in his teeth, then I spotted a bone popping out of his finger. Yanking on the rifle, his mangled bone wouldn't give.

"Leave him alone!"

Looking over my shoulder, I could see the Father helplessly pawing at Julio, who was trying to kick Bolt off his leg. I ran in that direction, while quickly glancing over to Sean and his thug. The rifle had been discarded somewhere I couldn't see. The young combatant wielded a blade, his white teeth glowing in the darkened alley. They were circling each other, and I spotted blood on Sean's hands.

For now he was on his own.

Two steps before impact, I lowered my shoulder, gritted my teeth. Suddenly, another gun appeared. A handgun. Julio raised his arm as I plowed into him. The gun went off next to my ear, shooting a high-pitched spear into my brain. Someone yelled out.

"Asshole!" I yelled at Julio as we barreled into two trashcans, spilling our bodies and all sorts of shit to the soiled pavement.

I fought to grab his wrist with the gun, but he went spastic on me, gyrating his whole body, flailing his free arm and legs.

"Fuck."

His knee had found my nuts, my body flushed of all energy in a nanosecond. Before I could take a breath, hoping to recover even ten percent of my power, Julio was on top of me, knocking my hands out of the way, trying to bring the gun downward.

"You are going back to America in a body bag," he grunted, as if he knew my pathetic response was useless.

I swung wildly, my reserves still hovering near empty, connecting a couple shots to his jaw, but they merely bounced off. That only seemed to give Julio a boost, and he started to chuckle even in the middle of a claw-your-eyes-out fight.

Suddenly, the barrel penetrated my flailing arms. I could see his teeth flashing in front of me, another waft of liquor invading my senses.

"Noooo!" Bolt screamed.

Julio turned his head, then decided to swing his gun around. He was going to shoot my young friend who had the guts of a gladiator, even if he still looked like a fourteen-year-old kid. From somewhere deep inside, a tidal wave of adrenaline flooded my veins. Flipping my body left, I knocked Julio off balance, and the gun fired into the sky. Roaring with energy, I torqued my body upward, gripping his wrist that held the gun while connecting my fist to his jaw.

I heard a crack.

I popped my legs out and lifted his torso with my knee and right arm. With leverage on my side, I raised him up in the air and slammed his back down to the unforgiving concrete. He released a gasping breath, the gun sliding off to the side.

I rolled twice and stretched for the gun. My hand touched metal, then another hand pounced on top of mine.

"It's all yours, Booker."

Looking right, I found Sean staring at me three feet away, a wry grin on his face.

"Thanks," I said, pulling myself up and assessing our situation.

All three of the assailants were on the ground, writhing in pain. Sean's thug was the only one speaking, although he was curled up in a pool of blood.

"Casi se me cortó la polla."

"He's saying I almost cut off his...uh, manhood." Sean shrugged his shoulders.

"Did you?"

"I think it only grazed him."

"Mr. Booker, come quick!"

Bolt waved me over to the other side of a small dumpster.

"Father!"

The priest leaned against the rusted metal, his face sweating. He gripped his opposite upper arm, a deep crimson seeping into his brown robe.

"I don't cuss, but this might be my first time," he said through gritted teeth.

"Where's the nearest hospital?" I asked.

"Uh...I think a mile or so that way." Bolt pointed west, diagonally from the alley. I paused for a second, noticing his fat lip and blood on his chin, his shirt splattered with red like some type of modern painting. Sean's face looked like it had been dragged through the gravel, but his blood was contained to his hands.

"I'll be fine. It's okay. God was looking after me, that much I know."

Sean leaned past me, flipping the blade open, dried blood coating the sides. "I'm going to check the wound," he said just before puncturing a hole in the Father's sleeve.

"I've never met you before. Are you a friend of Mr. Booker and Sebasten?" The Father could have been the Catholic version of Mr. Rogers.

"I know them," he said, his eyes focused on tearing the sleeve all the way around, then slipping it off the arm, exposing a nasty gash.

Sean used his only two clean fingers to pry around the blood pool on the outer part of the arm. "It grazed the skin. Doesn't appear to be any muscle damage. Probably stings like hell. A good cleaning, maybe a few stitches. Might need to immobilize it for a day or two."

He sounded like an Army medic.

"A dirty back alley probably isn't the best place for putting him back together," Sean said.

Out of the corner of my eye, I noticed Julio up on his hands and knees. His amigos stirred on the ground, still moaning from their injuries.

"We can't let them go, and we can't call the cops," I said. "If they get word back to Amador, we're toast, and we'll have no chance of finding Esteban."

Sean dug a finger under his wig and scratched his head. "If Julio and his buddies are late getting back to camp, they might think something is up."

"But it's Saturday night. Party night." Bolt put a finger to his puffy lip, which had made him sound half his age. "No one will notice they're gone."

"That might buy us until sunrise tomorrow," Sean said.

"First things first," I said, jogging over to Julio. "On the ground."

"Fuck you!"

Slipping my foot just inside his knee, I flipped him off balance and jammed my knee into his back with a thud as he landed face first on the pavement.

"Who da fuck are you?" he said.

Ignoring him, I held up my hands as my knee applied about two hundred ten pounds of pressure into his left kidney. "We can turn him over to the authorities after we get Esteban out."

Bolt ran over. "Maybe we can force him to talk, to tell us where they have the kid."

"This lying sack of shit? I wouldn't believe a thing he said."

Julio jostled across the graveled pavement, and I shifted my weight, jabbing my knee even further into his back. "I only have two knees. Any ideas, at least temporarily?"

"Damn, I almost forgot I carried a few spare ones," Sean said, jumping out of his stance. He pulled out a zip tie. "Here, bring his hands back."

"I got this," I said, grabbing a tie and pulling it tight onto Julio's wrists.

"Ahh!" he grunted.

"Perfect," I said.

Sean hogtied the two others, although neither appeared to be much of a flight risk.

Pulling out my phone, I tapped the only other contact I knew on the island I could trust.

Fifteen minutes later a tan SUV rolled down the alley, squeaking to a stop just in front of Father Santiago.

"Father, Father please let us help you," Valdez said the moment his foot hit pavement. Behind him was another man with round, wire-rimmed glasses, thinning hair. Barely taller than Bolt, he waddled more than walked over to the priest, then kneeled down, his hands covered with blue rubber gloves.

"A friend of the family," Valdez said, shifting over to Sean and me, while appearing to study everything the doctor did.

"Can't have enough doctors in the extended family. I'm just glad he's okay working off the radar, so to speak."

"Radar?"

I recalled that English wasn't Valdez's first language. "Sorry. Not many doctors would agree to leave a hospital or office. This isn't a battlefield." I questioned my use of the phrase the moment it left my lips, but I didn't correct myself.

His rubbery face coiled a bit. "He's not a doctor, not exactly anyway."

My eyes shifted to Sean, then back to Valdez.

"He was a doctor up until five years ago. Well-respected even. But he got caught giving out more than prescriptions from his office." He arched a full eyebrow.

"How did you get to know him?"

"Just like Alejandro. I put him behind bars."

"Usually doesn't work that way in the states. Back there, they hunt you down after you put them away."

"He was an addict. Once he got clean, he knew what he did was wrong. Now he works as an accountant. Says it's boring. He's just itching to use his knowledge of medicine."

The doctor waddled to us, pulling off his rubber gloves. "I've stopped the bleeding. We can transport him back to my house. I have an area set up in my garage. I have everything I need there to treat the wound. He should be okay, but I want to make sure he doesn't get an infection."

We spent the next few minutes explaining how our hike across town was interrupted by Julio, and the ensuing brawl that left us bloodied and beaten, but not defeated.

Valdez scratched just above his mustache. "Let's put them in the car, tie them down somehow. I know of a warehouse where I can take them. I'll pay Manuel a few bucks to make sure they don't run off."

"Thanks, Valdez."

"Yeah, dude. Thanks, Tito Jackson. Woo hoo!" Bolt spun around and grabbed his crotch, à la Michael Jackson.

"That's messed up," I said.

"I can see why you have a fat lip," Valdez said, rolling his eyes.

"Sean and I will take Bolt with us. Still have to try to get to Amador tonight, if possible. Can you fit everyone in the SUV and make sure everything stays calm?"

Valdez pulled back his coat, revealing a handgun stuck in a holster. "The doctor will drive. I'll take care of the rest."

We rounded up everyone, put them in the SUV, with the wobbly doctor behind the wheel as Valdez sat in the back seat facing the cargo area with his gun drawn. Father Santiago extended his good arm out of the window.

"Mr. Booker, I hope you and your friends will be careful, whatever your plan is." His eyes caught Bolt walking by. "And watch out for that little guy."

I turned to Sean as the SUV drove off. "I hope you have a spare shamrock. Something tells me we're going to need all the luck we can get."

Thirteen

Her black stilettos clipped the tiled flooring with an even cadence, her shoulders and hips moving in perfect rhythm. Turning my head as she strutted through the kitchen, she caught me out of the corner of her eye, her blue sapphires creating a heat wave up my back.

"One more minute," Britney said, disappearing down a hallway.

Just as I realized I'd forgotten to breathe the last thirty seconds, Bolt ran right into me, his mouth hanging open.

"What you looking at?"

His hand was buried in a bag of popcorn.

"Mr. Booker, I'm almost fifteen. The same thing you were looking at."

"Whatever. She has nothing over me. She's just another pretty face," I said, looking for a magazine to sift through.

"Is that what you were looking at?" He winked while walking past me, then plopped into an overstuffed armchair.

Shaking my head, I ran my fingers down the nail heads on the back of the sofa, checking out Britney's apartment. She'd told me earlier that she'd kept her own place while she and Juan were engaged, mostly for appearances, given the mostly Catholic population. She only occasionally stayed over here, which was about two miles farther into the teeth of the city. It was a gated community, a nice skyline view on the fourth floor. The security was pretty stout. From a wall-mounted monitor off the main hallway, or off her main TV in the living room, she could punch up three camera positions, including one just outside her front door.

The décor was simple, yet elegant, like her the first time we met for lunch at a swanky café in Uptown almost nine months ago. A few days prior to our lunch, she'd witnessed her fiancé dangling off the Old Red Courthouse clock like a puppet. For a few agonizing minutes, everyone watched in horror as he flailed around, his arms and legs tied to rope. Suddenly, he disappeared. A massive bomb exploded, killing Ashton Cromwell, with thousands watching in person, and millions on TV.

Tonight, for the first time since I'd found her in the Dominican, the Britney of old had resurfaced in many ways, but not all.

She suddenly appeared back in the kitchen. I watched her walk toward the bar in the far corner. Her gait was unmistakable.

"You can close your jaw now." She smiled, knowing all four eyes in the room were on her. Sean had insisted on making a run by his place to pick up some equipment. I tapped my phone checking the time.

"While we wait on your mystical friend, I'm having a drink. Can I serve you one?" A decanter clinked against a glass tumbler. Looked like she was having rum, neat.

"You know my rule. No drinking while I'm on the job."

She held up her glass. "Sometimes rules are made to be broken." Arching an eyebrow, she sipped the liquor.

"Rules are one thing, laws are another. And for you, we're not talking about racking up a stack of traffic tickets."

"*Touché*. I guess I walked right into that one." Her chest lifted as she took in a deep breath and held her gaze at me an extra second.

Her leer was addictive, as thoughts of us rolling in the proverbial hay filtered my mind. I forced myself to look away.

"Thank you for agreeing to do this," I said staring at a woodcarving resting on a round table, trying to change the conversation back to the kidnapping of a helpless teenage boy.

"Seriously, Booker? I should be thanking you for finding out who kidnapped him," she said, prowling in my direction.

"We're not sure. But as I told you earlier, Amador is paranoid about this El Jefe group. By kidnapping the son of a famous, rich baseball player, he might be telling the world that he has all the power and there's nothing that anyone can do to stop him."

"He's sick and he needs to be stopped." Her body went stiff, and she downed the rest of her rum. "Given my mission tonight, I need another one," she said, raising her empty glass. "To be my best slutty self, I think it's necessary, don't you?"

I was tongue-tied, unsure how to answer that one. When we'd been fully immersed in our relationship, slutty was the last term I would have used on Britney. Classy, a lady of immense resolve and dignity were terms that had first come to mind, and it was hard not to share my thoughts with the world. She was intoxicating...up until the time she became oddly protective about me when there was never any competition.

I should have seen the signs.

Studying the wooden carving again, I finally was able to detect it was two people intertwined in some type of lovemaking position.

"You don't like me using that term, slutty, do you?"

Her voice caught me off guard. I turned, relieved to find Bolt engrossed in a Spanish cartoon.

"It doesn't matter what I think." I just didn't want to go there.

"So, Juan is okay with you putting your life at risk to try to find his son?" She'd agreed to be our bait, to try to seduce one of the most brutal men in the Caribbean, hoping to pull information about Esteban out of Amador. When I'd brought up the idea earlier on the phone, she didn't hesitate for a second. Despite all of her personality warts—murderer at the top of that list—she had a huge soft spot for Esteban, and apparently a bigger one for Juan, the man she would never marry.

"He's desperate to have his son back. When I told him the idea, tears bubbled in his eyes. It was tough to watch this larger-than-life man, a hero to so many, break down so easily. That's when I knew I had no other choice. I'd do anything to bring that boy home to his father. Anything." Her eyes stayed on me.

"But he still believes you're Ana Sofia, despite your ability to change your appearance so easily?"

Setting a taut arm against her granite countertop island, she popped her hip outward. Her black dress wrapped her body like cellophane. It cupped her derriere and hugged her upper thighs as if it had been molded exclusively for her frame. Almost uncontrollably, my eyes zipped up and down her legs, long and slender. They never stopped.

And neither did the fashion tease. Slits of velvety skin were exposed up the left side. If that wasn't enough to mesmerize the male population, the last slit exposed the side of her breast.

Damn, I needed a cold shower...or a kick in the crotch. She still had power over me like no one else. My lack of self-control, even if only in my mind, pissed me off.

"What's wrong?"

She must have been talking. "Sorry, didn't catch what you said."

"I didn't say anything. I could see that you're thinking...a lot. Something has upset you."

Not a fan of someone reading my body language, I could feel my face tighten a bit. "I'm fine. Just a lot that needs to go right tonight. And after today, it doesn't appear that luck is on our side."

She sauntered closer, moving within a couple of feet. I felt my butt hit the back of the sofa as she reached a hand to her face and licked a finger. She wiped the side of my cheek. I flinched a bit, which fired a spear of pain throughout my ribcage. I wondered if ribs were cracked or broken from the mugging just an hour or so earlier.

"You are quite jittery. I was just cleaning off a smidge of blood you missed earlier."

Her touch created the strangest sensation I could recall, a bipolar combination of revulsion and intimacy. Once again, I chastised myself for going there.

Then my eyes found her lips, and I had to force myself from not running my fingers across her face and pulling her closer. Her skin color was a shade lighter than just a day earlier. I studied her hair, long and flowing but with an extra kick of frizzy curls, enhanced by some type of product.

"Is this the wig, or was your short, choppy brown hair fake?"

Her neck coiled back a few inches. "Is that a question you should really be asking a lady?"

"No, that's why I'm asking you."

"Another dig. Whoa, you're getting good at this. Glad I don't take your jabs too personally," she said with a wink.

"You going to tell me, or do I have to pull your hair?"

She giggled. "I remember some hair pulling back when we were…an item."

I turned over my shoulder, checking on Bolt. His eyes were fixated on the TV as he shoveled in more popcorn.

Filtering my thoughts to the cold shower side of my head, I planted my hands at my waist. "I don't want to play games. It's just a question."

"A girl has to have some secrets, right?"

She quickly flipped on her heels, strutting back to the kitchen just as the alarm buzzed.

"That should be your friend, right, Booker? If it is, please let him in. If you don't recognize him, call for me. I need to visit the powder room."

Britney strolled down the far hallway as I made a beeline for the alarm panel in the foyer. The picture flipped between the three perspectives. On the third, I instantly recognized Sean, with his graying ponytail sticking out from his frayed Cubs cap. He actually tipped the cap, apparently knowing the location of the camera. I pressed a button, the iron gate clicked open, and Sean walked out of view off the bottom of the screen. About a minute later, the next camera shot showed him exiting the fourth-floor elevator. I counted to ten, and then the doorbell rang.

"Welcome," I said, as he walked inside pulling a plastic garbage bag out of his shirt.

"*Hola.*"

"*Hola*, Mr. Sean," Bolt said from the chair, his voice sounding tired.

"That kid's been through hell today," I said.

Sean walked over to the kitchen island and rifled through the bag. "I know, and it didn't happen in the camp. It happened under our watch while we walked along the street. I should have spotted Julio and his buddies before we were attacked."

"You really think you could have prevented that?" And here I thought my guilt factor was a tad on the high side.

"I was distracted, thinking ahead to all the possible scenarios with Amador tonight, as well as how this first conversation with...uh, what's her name might go."

I chortled. "You sound like me up until recently, unable or unwilling to say her name," I said, looking over my shoulder, checking for any sign of her. It was clear. "At times, I got so riled up just by the thought of her, of everything she did right under my nose. I could have chewed off the leg of a chair."

"Sounds like you were more pissed at yourself." He turned his head toward me.

"Just like you are now," I shot back.

"Yeah, maybe so." Sean picked up a round, black object, no bigger than the size of a dime, domed on one side, flat on the other.

"By the way, why were you thinking ahead to this discussion with...Britney?"

"For many reasons. I thought it would be obvious."

"For me, yes. You?"

He looked beyond my shoulder, keeping his voice low. "For one, we have to rely on an untrained citizen to be the main cog in this operation. It's up to her to get close to Amador, pull information from a man who's not only brutal, but likely paranoid. Secondly, can we really trust her? Look at her life the last year and her situation here in the Dominican. She's a pathological liar, it sounds like to me."

"I've used the same term," I said, biting the inside of my cheek.

Dropping his head a tad, Sean paused. He turned his sights back to me. "Most importantly, she fucked up your life. She almost killed your mother, and she hurt you. She's not on my top-ten list of favorite people. In fact, if it wasn't for Amador—"

"You must be the secret friend of Booker's."

Britney's voice from just behind me. I wondered how much she'd overheard. The last thing this operation could withstand was her vindictiveness rearing its ugly head.

She leaned her hands on the island, creating a cleavage wave.

"Hey," Sean responded, lifting his eyes for a quick second.

"A bottled water, or maybe something stronger?" Her eyes shifted between me and Sean.

"I could use a bottled water after my long walk, the humidity and all," Sean said.

She took a bottle from the fridge and set it a couple of feet in front of him, exchanging a few more glances in our direction. It seemed like she was about to speak, but instead she turned and ambled to the bar and poured herself another shot of rum.

"You sure you should have a third?"

She paused with the decanter halfway to the glass, a smirk at the corner of her mouth.

"Ever the protector, huh, Booker?"

"I want the mission to go well, and if you're stumbling all over yourself, we don't have a chance."

She turned and put a hand on her hip. "I'm not a machine, you know. I just need something to take the edge off," she said, swirling the brown liquid in her tumbler. "You do realize what you're asking me to do."

"Uh…yeah." Wasn't it obvious?

"I have to pretend to want a man who repulses me, who's hurt a member of my family."

"I get it."

"Do you? We don't know what it's going to take to get Amador to open up. What if I'm asked to…?" She brought a hand to her face.

While I could understand her anxiety, her preemptive drama seemed overblown. "We're not asking you to sleep with the guy. We just know he has a soft spot for women, especially American women. You said Juan is on board with you doing this, right?"

A stiff nod of her head, although my eyes were drawn to her straw-colored hair framing her face. Similar to the sensation of smelling rain in the air, my senses could recall the fragrance in her locks. It had been intoxicating.

"Despite what you might think, I don't welcome the opportunity to cheat on my fiancé."

She was right. I did think the opposite, but drawing her into an emotional tug of war wouldn't help us or Esteban. "Okay. I believe you."

Squinting ever so slightly, she said, "I can see it in your eyes. You think I'm nothing but a conniving, murderous slut."

Even after all these months, she could read my mind.

"Your words, not mine." I could see Sean hunched close to the counter, toying with his gadgets, obviously staying clear of the fray. "Does it really matter what I think? You hired me to find your fiancé's son and bring him home. This is only a means to an end. But if you don't want to do it, we'll see if we can come up with another idea."

She paused, her eyes wandering across the aqua and black granite. "I know how much danger Esteban is in. It crushes me to see Juan every day. He's wilting like a flower with no water." Her shoulder muscle rippled as she raised her hand. "I would screw that Amador asshole in the middle of the baseball field if it would bring that boy home to his father."

"Point made," I said casually, checking over my shoulder to ensure Bolt was preoccupied by the mindless TV program. Or was I only trying to divert my eyes and thoughts to anything other than Britney?

"Okay." Sean muttered one word, then cleared his throat. I could see Britney's neck coil back just a tad, her eyes again playing ping pong between Sean and me.

He continued. "We need to figure out a way to get this contraption here attached to your clothing."

Shuffling to the opposite side of the island, Sean held out his hands as if he were a high school kid trying to pin a corsage on the girl with a knockout figure. Britney just stood there, her lips turning up at the corners.

"Have at it, Sean." She looked my way and winked.

I just shook my head. She was the queen of making people feel awkward.

"Since this is black, it should blend in with your outfit," Sean said, his eyes looking for just the right place.

Britney brought a finger to the middle of her chest, the bottom of the V cut out of her dress. "How about there?" She beamed a Cheshire-cat grin.

Sean moved his hands closer to her chest, then paused. "Do you mind if I put it on? I'm not trying anything."

"A true gentleman. They're all yours."

His head did a double take on her answer, then he completed the task in about two minutes.

"That's not going anywhere. Let me test it."

Pulling out an iPad, he tapped a small box on the home screen, but not before I noticed a picture of a beach as his home-screen wallpaper. He plugged in a pair of earbuds and stuck one in his ear.

The screen went black for about five seconds. Suddenly, it flicked on, and it seemed like we were looking into a mirror since the camera was staring right at us.

"Cool."

"We need to test the audio and a bit of distance. Can you go into your bedroom, maybe even your bathroom and shut the door? Then speak quietly so I can set the volume levels."

Britney walked out of the room just as Bolt invaded our space.

"What's the plan, Mr. Booker?"

"Put your dance shoes on. We're going clubbing."

Fourteen

The scent of fresh St. Augustine grass clippings hung in the thick, nighttime air. I could hear a hooting owl perched in an overgrown tree off to our right while a muted thumping bass reverberated in my gut.

The odd combination of sensations actually seemed to match the pattern of experiences in Santo Domingo. Eclectic might fit. That's a term Britney, a would-be interior designer before she escaped and became an international fugitive, might use.

Sean put one earbud in his ear and handed me the other as we sat on a park bench, Club de Python just on the other side of a low bank of white-flowered shrubs across the street. The tablet was hidden behind a newspaper.

"When do I get to listen?"

Bolt leaned over the back in between both of us, a fat purple lip still impeding his ability to speak clearly—not that a fat lip would ever slow down his motor mouth.

"You'll have your chance once Booker heads into the club," Sean said.

"You do know that I'm really the best person to go into the club, right?"

Sean and I traded stares.

"You don't have trust in your little buddy? I'm hurt," he said with no conviction, his hands covering his heart.

"Trust isn't the issue, Bolt."

"I don't know the drinking age in the Dominican, but I doubt it's fourteen," Sean said.

I flicked a ladybug off my knee, feeling the linen texture of the gray pants I wore. At the last minute, Sean and I had decided it would be best if one of us could observe the scene from within the two-story club. As if she expected as much, Britney directed us to a closetful of clothes that fit me perfectly. She said they were for Juan, whenever they stayed closer into town. We seemed to be about the same height and weight, so it made sense. But why did my Britney radar go up?

Over my objection, Britney insisted on handpicking my outfit—the gray linen pants and jacket and a white collared shirt, untucked. She called it classy, understated, while telling everyone who saw me that I was a player and belonged in the trendy club. I considered making a statement and selecting any combination of clothes that she didn't want, but Sean used a hand signal to get me to back off. It was the right thing to do, given the alcohol buzz she was carrying and the related tension in the air.

We watched the video come alive on the tablet, the camera shaking at the same cadence I could imagine Britney striding across the floor—undoubtedly all eyes peeled to every inch of her skin.

"Looks like she's turning toward the bar," Sean said.

Her arms leaned forward, then one waved off to the left.

"You give me a fancy suit, and I'm sure I could pass for an eighteen-year-old. *No problemo*," Bolt said.

"First, it would take two Bolts to fill up this suit. Second, you still have a baby face. It would take a complete makeover to turn you into a young man."

"You've got to realize that's who these clubs cater to, guys and girls in their upper teens. At thirty-something, you're considered old."

I paused, looked at Sean. "How old is Miguel Amador?"

"Said in his dossier that he's forty-six."

I glanced back at Bolt.

"But he's the man who stirs *la bebida*. The flow of the whole club will revolve around the man with all the power and money."

"You seem like you know a lot about how things work."

He opened his arms. "I've been living in the adult world for a few years. I have to know if I'm going to survive."

"Something tells me you'll be visiting these clubs long before you should legally."

"I'm sure I could walk around to the back of the club building, convince the people to give me a job no one wants, like cleaning the restrooms?"

Shaking my head, I almost chuckled at his pestering insistence.

"Does he ever give up?" Sean asked.

"I'm not sure he's ever been told no," I said, remembering my Samantha and the critical role parents played in kids' lives, even those who thought they'd figured it all out—usually known as teenagers.

"I'm standing right here," Bolt said.

"We know," Sean and I said in tandem. A quick shift of our eyes, and all three of us nearly cracked up.

I pushed up from my sitting position and put on my jacket.

"You look like a cross between Lenny Kravitz, the American rocker, and the next James Bond."

"Thanks, Bolt. I guess that makes you Q." I nodded at Sean.

"Yeah, right," he said, typing in a password of some kind on his tablet. "You should be able to hear me in the earpiece right about...now. Testing, testing, one, two, three."

I gave him a thumbs-up. "It's all good."

"So I'll be able to hear what's going on around you. We can feed each other information verbally, although the loud music might make it tough for me to hear you."

"What the heck should I do while Mr. Booker is in there having all the fun?"

Sean pulled a device from his bag and motioned for Bolt to sit on the bench next to him.

"I'll give you an earbud to listen to both Mr. Booker and Britney as long as you do some research for me."

"Research? I don't do school."

Sean put the free earbud in his pocket.

Bolt quickly conceded. "Okay, okay. School is back in. Tell me what you need."

I gave my cohorts a two-finger salute, then turned and walked beyond the confines of the park, across the street, and up a set of stone stairs to the entrance of Club de Python.

My vision caught a bank of spotlights anchored to my right, randomly swirling across the dark sky.

"*Muévase a un lado para que otros clientes puedan entrar.*"

A man with greasy, slicked-back hair guided me to the side of the front door.

"Mr. Booker, he wants to frisk you," Bolt said in my ear.

I held up my arms while one man watched, and the other did the frisking. Once finished, the frisker turned to his colleague and said, "*No hay armas. Está limpio.*"

"He said you have no weapons and you can go inside."

I nodded and walked through the first of two sets of doors. The thumping music turned up a couple of notches, but I could tell that once I entered the last set of doors, my brain would struggle to function.

"I think that greasy frisker would win the gold medal at the TSA pat-down Olympics, if they had such a thing," I said to myself, knowing Sean and Bolt were on the other end.

"Trying to keep all weapons out of a club that attracts criminals can't be an easy job," Sean said. I felt the urge to press my earpiece to hear better, but I didn't want to draw any unwanted attention.

"Something tells me they won't be quite as strict when Amador shows up," I said off to the corner.

"Speak of the devil. Just spotted a line of black Hummers pulling up to the curb. I'm guessing he and his entourage slash security detail will be walking in shortly," Sean said.

"Roger that," I said.

"Roger. *Yo no soy*, Roger," a man said, glancing at me with confusion in his eyes.

Ignoring my own stumble, I flipped on my heels toward the club's inside doors, nearly running over a woman almost half my size.

"*Su chaqueta.*" A woman with a ponytail sticking straight up started pulling off my jacket. It felt like she was groping my chest.

"Mr. Booker, she's offering to take your jacket."

"*Chaqueta, no,*" I said, shaking my head.

"*Se pone muy caliente en la pista de baile,*" she said with a toothy grin.

"*Chaqueta, no,*" I repeated, not understanding why she continued to paw at me.

"Mr. Booker, she's saying it gets really hot on the dance floor. I think she's really wanting to check in your jacket so that you'll tip her later."

Having a translator in my ear gave me a little more confidence that I could navigate these waters.

"*Yo soy bueno*," I said, shifting toward the last gateway into the club proper.

The moment the door swung open, I was met with a furnace blast of warm air. It felt like someone had been running a humidifier.

Glancing around, the club could have been in Dallas or LA. It was large, had multiple levels, more lights flashing than at a five-alarm fire, and a set of cages perched from the ceiling, each containing one or more scantily clad women dancing their asses off.

Wait…was that a guy in the cage nearest me? Hard to see through a haze of lights. I only saw boots zipped just over the knee, leather straps crossing this way and that, what looked like a policeman's hat and a whistle. Suddenly a whip cracked the side of the cage, and the person stuck out his or her tongue.

I steered clear of the cage, then found a path around the main dance floor lined by columns on either side. While I could already feel the perspiration trickling down my spine, I kept a hand in my pocket, casually scanning the scene. The dance floor was filled with couples, most probably under thirty years of age, but heavy on the cool factor. Over the years, the dance moves had changed, but they all included a heavy dose of hip gyrations, just a different brand. This crowd had mastered the art of hip swivels.

Veering around a cluster of folks raising shot glasses to celebrate some important milestone, I kept my eyes open for Britney. After all, I was here, at least partially, to protect her. Or was it Amador I should be protecting from her? I showed teeth, laughing internally.

At the back end of the club, I noted a hallway with black walls and a single spotlight that led to the restroom. In another shorter inlet, a swivel door was in constant motion, wait staff and bartenders going in and out, balancing drinks as if the glasses were glued to the tray. I took a curved staircase up to the second floor. People hung over the railing, peering down to the main dance area below, swaying to the nonstop beat of the music with drinks in their hands.

I walked by one couple who had just toasted with two champagne glasses and proceeded to mug down, slobbering all over each other.

"*¡Consigan una habitación!*" A John Travolta lookalike, circa the *Saturday Night Fever* era, blew by me, barking something at the couple.

I could hear Bolt shouting in my ear. Turning my head, I said, "Say again?"

"Get. A. Room. That's what he said."

I rolled my eyes, then Sean spoke up. "Booker, I spotted Amador surrounded by a mob of bodyguards walking through the front door. Wearing a black short-sleeve T-shirt. Looks like he's been hitting the weights."

"Did they frisk him?" I asked for fun, as I moved to the stairs and nonchalantly ambled down the staircase.

"You kidding? You would have thought the Pope was approaching. They parted like the Red Sea, but still stuck out a hand hoping he'd touch it," Sean said.

Once downstairs, I positioned myself in the back, on the side of the bar, my eyes still searching for Britney.

"People know he's a drug smuggler."

"Hell, they know he's done far worse, including kill people. A lot of people. Innocent people. A few might even know about his latest venture," Sean said.

"What business venture is that, Mr. Sean?" Bolt asked.

"Nothing."

"That means it's something."

"Not for your ears."

"Right, only when I'm older. Shit."

With no one in my space, I said, "Cussing doesn't make you any older." I sounded like a parent. Thinking about Samantha ever speaking that way was mindboggling.

Suddenly, a ripple of heads turned toward the front. People kept dancing and drinking, but they were noticeably distracted. Excited smiles, "oohs" and "aahs" all around me. On the other side of the dance floor, I spotted a beehive of people moving across the floor. A smattering of applause and whistling, and people again trying to get a glimpse or, even better, touch his shirt or arm.

"It's the freaking Kardashian Effect," I murmured.

"What's that?" Sean asked.

"You know the game. These poor souls show up hoping to interact with a violent criminal, and for what? To try to join his group? To somehow find their fifteen minutes of fame latching on to a killer? They're either desperate, addicted to the drugs he's smuggling, or officially brain dead."

"Who's that, the Kardashians?" Sean asked, his sarcasm evident.

"Have you seen that Kim Kardashian?" Bolt asked with way too much fervor.

Damn, that kid needed a parent. If he was going to fall for a girl, why couldn't it be a member of the national soccer team?

Bolt couldn't let it go. "Have you seen her—?"

"Put a lid on it, Bolt," Sean said before I could.

Teenagers.

Just then, the DJ laid down a heavy scratch, momentarily taking the focus off Amador and his crew.

A thumping bass quickly morphed into a rhythmic horn riff.

"*Es Bruno*," a girl said running by me to the dance floor, a lanky boy lagging behind her.

Bruno Mars, I guessed. Following the girl to the floor, I finally spotted Britney.

Damn.

All I could see were legs as long as a python, and twice as deadly. Making it very apparent she was a solo act, she put on a display that would have brought shivers to a blind man. Using a pole in the middle of the floor as a seductive prop, she coiled around the floor as if she was trying to ensnare the Pope. Considering how people treated Amador, somehow it seemed necessary...in the most inappropriate way I could have ever imagined Britney prior to her betrayal.

But after everything I'd witnessed, I wasn't surprised she had it in her.

I ordered a drink, tonic water on ice, and joined dozens of others gawking at the sexy blonde, the men with their jaws hanging open and the women with their jaws clenched shut. Thankfully, a few brave souls ignored Britney's antics and joined her on the floor, trying to out-slut the queen slut, if that was possible.

"What do you see, Booker?" Sean asked. "We only see a lot of movement."

"It's almost making me seasick," Bolt added.

"Don't think you'd say that if you were in here."

"What? Tell me, Mr. Booker."

I ignored his hormonal response. "She's giving it her best effort, that much I'll say. Amador and his core group are moving to the opposite corner. He glanced at her, but didn't seem interested. Are you sure he's not gay?"

"Dammit, I knew we should have used Valdez," Bolt said.

"Bolt, you've got to let up on that poor guy."

"Just kidding," he said.

"According to the dossier, Amador is all about the women, and not in the most flattering way. Think about the story Julio told Bolt about that young girl. She killed two people just to show she was the biggest badass in the camp, and then that sonofabitch rapes her."

The club tune hit the chorus.

"Isn't that Uptown Funk?"

"Sure," I said, not really hearing Bolt's question. Britney reached straight down and pressed her head against her legs before popping back up and gyrating like she was dancing right alongside Bruno. I knew she was limber. My memory fought to tap the brakes on about twenty different visuals…and scents and textures. Back then, I never thought months later she'd be seducing a maniacal killer.

Out of nowhere, a girl at each arm started pulling me toward the dance floor. Each had huge smiles and wore body-hugging red-and-blue checkered miniskirts with white halter tops. Wait…they were twins.

My Dallas buddy, Justin, would be in hog heaven. Me, a curmudgeon at age thirty-two, saw beauty, but also annoyance.

Trying not to be forceful, I shifted my body weight back toward the bar.

"*No gracias. No gracias.*"

They kept tugging, and I started to feel eyes shift in my direction.

"Booker, what's going on? Everything cool?" Sean asked.

The girl on the left quickly leaned in, resting her lips against my ear. "We noticed you staring at us when you were upstairs."

She spoke English.

"Uh, well…that wasn't me." That was smooth. I didn't even recall seeing them.

She giggled, her breath brushing against my neck.

"My sister and I are actually from the Bronx. We're here as part of our post-doctoral studies in environmental science," she said, her deep brown eyes catching mine for a second.

I couldn't deny her beauty. And she had brains. And there were two of them. Justin would be egging me on, his bony shoulders jostling up and down from his incessant laughter. As for the reaction of the better half of Booker & Associates, Alisa, I couldn't say. Perhaps I didn't want to think about how she'd see this. Ever since we joined forces, we had interacted more like old friends. Now we were old friends who had crossed the line. Was there even a line anymore? With everything else going on, tiptoeing through that minefield of choices and expectations wasn't something I wanted to do right now.

"We've been studying our asses off, and now we just want to have some fun. I'm Evita, and my younger sister by ten minutes is Marisol."

Marisol winked in slow motion.

"*Lo siento mucho.*"

"Why are you speaking Spanish, Mr. Booker?" Bolt asked.

For a quick second, I'd forgotten about the device placed in my ear.

"I'm sorry, I'm just not up for…whatever you have planned," I said, still trying to use my leverage to touch home base, the bar. "No offense. You're both very pretty and apparently very smart."

I attempted to look beyond the Wonder Twins. I spotted a streak of blond hair, and I knew Britney was still in the middle of her routine. I just hoped Amador was taking notice.

"You sure we can't convince you? We've been known to…" Then, she whispered something in my ear that I couldn't understand.

"What?" Bolt exclaimed.

Apparently it was undecipherable through the mic.

Without warning, I was attacked by ten fingers, tickling at my rib cage.

Bullseye. Marisol pinched the exact spot that Julio's pal had used as a battering ram. My elbow clinched my side, and I flinched.

"Oh, did we hurt Mr. Tall, Dark and Handsome?"

The hand invasion continued, but was much softer. I still felt like a piece of meat. I was starting to wonder if Evita and Marisol had been home-schooled and never seen a grown man.

"Ladies."

Their intensity increased, and they rubbed me like they were kneading frozen dough.

"Laaadiessss." I attempted to pry their hands off my body.

"Mr. Booker, are you a crazy man?"

"Shut up, Bolt."

"I'm sorry?" Marisol said.

Good, I pissed off the Wonder Twins. But it didn't last long.

A shove from behind, and I practically fell into their arms. I turned over my shoulder. The bartender was smiling so wide I couldn't see his eyes.

"Thanks for the help," I said, and his facial expression didn't budge.

But I did.

"Okay, okay," I said, finally relenting. "One dance."

The girls grabbed my arms and pulled me faster than I wanted to move. We finally stepped up to the dance floor, and I felt the whole thing shaking. With all the drinking going on, I was shocked as hell not to see everyone tumbling over.

Marisol and Evita did their thing and I did mine, as subtly as I could, the Bruno Mars song now in about its eighth minute. Just as I thought they'd lost interest, they redirected their hip swivels my way, and I found myself stuck between two gyrating women.

"You go, Mr. Booker. You go, man," Bolt said.

How did he know what was going on?

A firm hand gripped my bicep and spun me out of the twin blender and into the waiting arms of Britney.

"Bitch!" I heard one of the twins say.

Before I'd taken a breath, Britney had placed my hands at her hips and locked her arms around my neck, and we were swaying slowly back and forth.

Something else had changed. The music, a slow song from John Legend.

"And the legend grows," she said, shifting her sights between my lips and eyes.

"Nice pun, but you're seducing the wrong person," I said, suddenly conspicuous of my hands.

"Am I?"

I noticed a twinkle.

"What if we could just get on a plane, shove all the lies and betrayal away, and just start over?"

I wouldn't have been more surprised if she had revealed she was actually a man. I did a quick scan of the most beautiful woman I'd ever known. Well, that sure as hell couldn't happen. But still.

"Can't happen, Britney. You screwed that up months ago. A little thing called murder. Three times. That I know of." I shifted my eyes slightly. "Have you forgotten about poor little Esteban, the innocent one in this sordid mess? He's going to die a disgusting death unless we, as in you, figure out where he is."

"I know. Why do you think I'm slow dancing with you?"

"Mr. Booker, Mr. Booker!" Bolt exclaimed.

I must have flinched.

"They can see you through the camera on my chest. Are they asking you what's going on?"

I nodded.

"Look, I know Amador noticed me. He tried to act like it was nothing, but I didn't get where I am by not noticing every subtle expression by a man."

I couldn't dispute that.

"And?'

"I'm guessing that he'll get jealous watching me turn my solo dance into a date, and then one of his brainless goons will come retrieve me like I'm a prostitute."

"You sure about that?" I asked.

"Believe me, no one can buy my body," she said defiantly.

"That's not what I meant," I said.

A beefy finger tapped Britney's shoulder. She shot me a wink and mouthed "Wish me luck." She then turned and strutted away with the goon watching her backside.

I left the floor and found a stool at a table between two larger columns off behind the bar, positioned diagonally from Amador's crew. Britney and her escort approached the main table. She gave him a stiff shake of the hand, as if it was a business introduction. Not very seductive.

"*¿Me puedo dar algo de beber, señor?*"

A woman in spandex startled me. She must have entered from the swivel door at my right.

"Um…" It was difficult to take my eyes off the scene across the club.

"You're asking me if I want something to drink." I said while realizing I'd left my tonic water at the bar. Glancing over her shoulder, I could see the bartender had already trashed it.

"Another tonic water and ice, *por favor.*"

"*Sí, un momento.*" She batted her eyelashes and padded away, which made me feel exposed. I surveyed my surroundings, on the lookout for Evita and Marisol, the twenty-something sisters who'd apparently just been introduced to the male species.

I felt like I'd been the focus of a test based upon one of their environmental science theories.

Wonder if I passed.

Thankfully, the Wonder Twins had disappeared or hitched their ménage wagon to one of the charming goons picking up Amador's trash.

It didn't take long to spot Britney again, her long legs crossed as she sat along a curved wall in a blue leather booth. There must have been ten guys standing or sitting within twenty feet of my ex. Even if their job was to keep an eye open for possible enemies invading their space, I found every head turned toward Britney. The school owner was positioned a couple of feet away from Amador, her arm draped on the side of the seat extending to the drug smuggler's shoulder. He seemed interested, but had yet to hit the smitten threshold.

"Haven't heard anything from the motley crew lately," I said while lowering my chin to my chest.

"Busy," Sean said.

"It's good to see that Amador didn't recognize Britney. At least that's how it appears from a distance," I said. "Have you guys heard anything yet to think otherwise?"

"Nothing. Just a lot of small talk about the beach, the history of the island. Bolt, take out your earbud and cover your ears," Sean said.

"That just means I'm going to miss something juicy."

"Bolt," I said.

"All right."

I heard the mic rustling against a shirt or something similar.

"I was going to say that up to this point, Amador seems rather calm and collected, as if Britney is just another groupie who would do anything to get in his pants. But he's given some subtle signals that he's the aggressor, like bragging about all his money and gadgets." Sean said, then to Bolt. "It's okay, you can listen in again."

"Mr. Booker, what did I miss? All I can see are a bunch of hairy men staring at the camera on Britney's chest. But we all know they're not really staring at the camera." He giggled, finishing with a snort.

"Glad to see you act your age some of the time, Bolt."

My drink arrived, and I sipped from the tall, thin glass.

"We're hungry and thirsty, and we have to listen to you have all the luxuries," Bolt said with an extra flare.

Just then, someone handed Amador a phone. Holding a finger, he smiled toward Britney as he stepped off to the side.

"What do you guys hear? Anything?" I leaned forward, but kept my shoes anchored to the crossbar of the stool. I couldn't read his lips.

"He apologized for the interruption in their conversation," Bolt said.

"Almost sounded too nice," Sean added. "But he's too far away from Britney. Maybe you could do a drive-by, and we can try to pick up a few words?"

Drink in hand, I lifted from the chair and strolled by the bar, seemingly with no place to go. The thickening haze in the rafters bent through the whirling lightshow that appeared to never end. I could hardly walk a straight line. The crowd must have doubled in the last thirty minutes.

Rounding my way to the other side, I lifted my glass just as I reached the perimeter of the goon patrol. "*Oye, Paco, mucho tiempo sin verte.*" I repeated a phrase I'd heard my old DPD partner utter on many occasions, showing off his exaggerated Spanish. Essentially, I'd called out for an imaginary friend at the other end of the dance floor, allowing me to scoot past guard number one with only a brief glance.

"Almost there," I said through a toothy smile, as if I was anticipating a joyous reunion with my old buddy just up ahead.

For just a second, I thought about how seamlessly Paco and I had worked together. We complimented each other's skills and, at times, finished each other's thoughts, occasionally in two languages. But he was the professional talker. I had been the closer. I missed that little guy, one of many people I looked forward to seeing when I got back to my home turf in Dallas.

A hand in my pocket, I pulled out my phone. Wadded up cash dropped just to the side of an animated Miguel Amador. Only a few feet from the dance floor, I leaned down to pick up the loose bills, straining to hear anything from the drug lord.

"*Tiempo…*" he said in a string of words. And then a "*mundo.*"

Time and world. His world? I struggled to understand what he was saying. I just prayed Sean or Bolt could hear and interpret what was being said through the noise pollution.

I spotted a boot sidling up next to Amador. Without looking that way, I scooped up the bills, stuffed them in my front pocket, and reengaged with my distant, make-believe friend.

"*¿Cómo estás grandote?*" I yelled, weaving through bodyguards and regular folks coming off the dance floor.

I withheld the urge to turn my head and glance at Britney for two reasons. Most importantly, I didn't want to blow her cover. Secondly, she reminded me of Medusa. Beautiful, almost irresistible on the outside, but seemingly poised at any moment to use her mystical blue eyes to put me in a lifelong curse, a granite statue notwithstanding.

Once safely past, I found another base, this time in the opposite corner, anchored near a group of folks busy playing drinking games. They didn't know that I was pretending to be part of their faction.

I took a quick sip of my drink. "So, did you guys catch any of that? I only heard a couple of words."

A few seconds ticked by.

"Sean, Bolt, you there?" My pulse jumped up a notch, and I couldn't help but bring a hand to my ear.

"Sean, Bolt, do—"

A shrill shot through my ear. I winced, as much as I tried not to show it.

"What the hell, guys?"

"Sorry, had to drop your connection for a second," Sean said. "I switched over to my audio analyzer application and replayed the little bit we picked up from Amador."

"Damn, you're definitely not the guy I thought you were when I woke up and saw you messing with that ancient phone."

"I was able to parse out most of the extraneous sound from Amador's voice."

"So, what did he say?"

Bolt responded with, *"No hay tiempo para jugar estos pequeños juegos tontos. En mi mundo, o estás conmigo o contra mí. Y todos sabemos que optan por jugar para el otro lado. ¿Estoy en lo cierto?"*

"That's a mouthful. I need some help in the translation, Bolt."

"You need to learn better Spanish, Mr. Booker."

"I'll add it to my priority list. What did he say?"

"No time to play these silly little games. In my world, you're either with me or against me. And we all know who chooses to play for the other side. Am I right?" Bolt said as if he actually was the legendary drug kingpin.

"Disturbing, but no surprise there," Sean said.

"No mention of Esteban or even of a generic kidnapping."

"It was a shot in the dark," Sean added.

"There is smog, Mr. Sean, but I can still see," Bolt said.

Sean chuckled. "It's another one of those American terms. Just means we took a chance and hoped to learn something about Esteban. But it wasn't likely to work. And it didn't."

"I don't recall you having that kind of patience," I said without thinking.

A pause on the other end. "We've all grown up over the years."

"I am confused. How do you two know each other?" Bolt asked.

The earpiece went silent.

"Hey, Amador just handed the cell phone back to his lackey and is now extending his hand to help Britney up to her feet."

"We got the visual here. They're going to the dance floor?" Sean's voiced pitched higher.

"Yep. It's time for another Britney tease show," I said.

"I hear jealousy in your voice, Mr. Booker. No?"

Nothing better than being outed by a teenager. "Hardly. That left when she whacked the side of my head with my own gun, after, of course, she'd already beaten up my mom and killed three innocent people."

It was a little easier to think like a PI hired to bring home a killer when I wasn't ensnared by Britney's legs or her web of guilt.

I watched the two of them ogle each other, amazed at how Britney could flip a switch so easily. Even with people gyrating all around them, the cute couple was locked together. Britney's arms draped over his shoulders, and he had his hands planted at her hips.

"We're not getting any audio," Sean said. "Just body movement."

"Doesn't look like they're saying much. They look like two lovebirds, oblivious to everyone around them."

I sipped my drink, forcing myself to look around, while hoping I wouldn't spot the Wonder Twins prowling nearby.

"Booker, I just received some intel from my…friend," Sean said.

Friend most likely meant his CIA handler, but I knew he couldn't outright share everything with Bolt sitting right next to him. "About what?"

"Yeah, about what?" Bolt said.

"Look, Bolt, I know you're more or less part of the team. But I have to pretend you're not really here. Do you understand what I'm saying?"

"If I get to listen in, then yes." He giggled.

"Booker, I think I know what's spooking Julio, Amador, the whole cartel from the sound of it."

"Spill it."

"El Jefe—The Chief. That was the nickname given to a dictator who ruled the Dominican for over thirty years, brutally killing anyone who dared to speak against him. He was merciless," Sean said.

"Yeah, I've heard people mention the name, El Jefe, but I never knew much about him. No one wanted to talk about him," Bolt said.

"Says here that Rafael Trujillo ruled the Dominican for thirty-one years, 1930-1961, until he was assassinated."

"Damn. Must be an all-time record in the category of ruthless dictators."

"Well, over time it states that he became paranoid, stopping anyone he considered an enemy of the state, whether it was someone standing up to his political party or a possible incursion from neighboring Haiti."

"Amazing. By not having a true education, I feel like I've missed out on so much involving my country." Even with all the racket around me, I could hear Bolt's somber tone. He wasn't the kind of person who sought sympathy—at least when he wasn't scamming an unsuspecting tourist. When this was all over, Esteban safe and at home and Britney in custody, I'd have to figure out a way to allow Bolt to be a normal kid for at least a few of his teenage years.

"Keep your head up, Bolt."

"*Servicio de Inteligencia Militar*," Sean interjected. "Known as SIM, Trujillo's secret police murdered and tortured anyone that threatened Trujillo's rule. They used a bunch of methods to kill those who dared to stand up to El Jefe: burning people alive, electrocution, hanging, a shot to the face, as well as kidnapping and rape, creating a climate of fear and intimidation."

"Holy mother of Jesus. I never heard about this, and I went to school, even have a college degree. Might need to rethink what they're leaving out of textbooks."

"Sounds like you're creating a platform. You going to run for office?"

"Yeah, right. My direct style would really win over the press."

"SIM also controlled the press. In addition, they extorted money to lobby American legislators, spread propaganda."

"I can't imagine living during that era. I may not have a home or family, but I consider myself lucky," Bolt added.

"Freedom. We all take it for granted," I said. "Until we don't have it."

"Apparently, the group patrolled the streets in Volkswagen Beetles. They called them *Cepillos*."

"It goes on to say that SIM was connected to the death of fifty thousand people over those years. Fifty thousand. Think about that."

"Messed up. No one knew, outside of the Dominican? Sounds nuts."

"The Dominican remained at peace with the US the entire time this was going on, through what, six or seven administrations?"

"Someone in the US government must have known we were backing a cold-blooded killer."

"Motivations of a few can dictate the actions of many," Sean said.

"What does that mean, Master Yoda?" I joked.

"Smartass. Once politics are involved, and analysts look at all the global parts, and how one domino holds up the others, then most of the people with skin in the game—the state department usually leading the way—almost can't stop their own machine. Justice is inexplicably replaced by the game of justification. And that's a slippery slope at best, trying to rationalize thousands of people dying just to ensure you have a friend of the state providing so-called stability in the region."

"Reminds me when the government used to back the Shah of Iran. Then the whole country blew up, and the Ayatollah marched in—"

"More like shuffled in."

"Yeah, that."

"The cries of an oppressed Iranian generation put the US in the crosshairs of the so-called revolution. Lots of shit happened behind the scenes, and don't get me started on how the radical Muslims manipulated the followers, brainwashing them to follow their doctrine of hate."

"Where were you when all of that went down?"

The earpiece went silent for a few seconds. I'd forgotten our little friend was still on the line. Sean wasn't about to break his cover for anyone—except me apparently.

"Yes, it's me. Bolt. I'm here and listening," he said.

I tapped my thumb off the frosted glass tabletop, as Britney and Amador continued their uncomfortable dance. It was obvious he had no rhythm. The old Britney would have left his ass on the floor or laughed hard enough to pee her pants.

"What?" Bolt asked.

I think Sean had given him the eye.

"Bottom line, though, Sean. Does your friend believe that a member of Trujillo's family has returned to the country and used a different tactic to rule the land?"

"Said it's possible."

"That's all he could tell you, it's possible?"

"He's awaiting more input."

"You mean the...uh, your old group doesn't have all the information at their disposal?"

"Uh, no. They never have. The new buzzword in that world is collaboration."

"They actually practice that? Good for them."

"I said buzzword. I didn't say they actually used that approach with their fellow agencies. It's still as cutthroat as ever. Everyone points the finger when something goes wrong in another agency, boasting they could have done it better, making a play to take ownership of an area they have little to no expertise in."

"Politics."

"Yeah, the dirtiest word in our language."

"*La política es una mierda*," Bolt added.

Sean laughed so hard, it turned into one of his hacking, gurgling coughs.

"You're right, Bolt. The bullshit is so deep it's hard to wade through it all."

"But you do, every day, for how many years?" I asked.

A silent pause.

"Another time, Booker," he said solemnly.

Two girls stumbled into my table, and I quickly picked up my drink.

"*Lo siento mucho*," they said through giggles.

They were obviously drunk. I just smiled and crunched some ice out of my glass.

I thought through everything I'd heard about Trujillo. "I'm not an expert on Caribbean politics or the drug-smuggling scene, but the presumption of a Trujillo relative even stepping foot back on this island would take a lot of—"

"*Testículos*," Bolt snickered.

"If Amador is viewed as the so-called new dictator of the island, then don't you think this El Jefe character knows that if he knocks Amador off the pedestal, then he would seize control of all the power and money associated with that position? El Jefe might even see it as the circle of life. Someone assassinates their father or uncle, whatever the relation, then they return and take down the man with all the clout—Amador."

"I like how your mind thinks," Sean said.

"Any data on Trujillo's relatives? Your friend needs to identify and locate every family member, and check out what they're doing, who they're in business with."

"He's already on it. I just received the first batch. The second one is in the oven as we speak."

"Hey guys, someone is on the move," Bolt said.

Shifting my eyes right through a sea of hard bodies, I saw the hardest being pulled along like a reluctant dog on a leash.

"Amador has Britney by the wrist. He's practically dragging her across the dance floor." I jumped to a standing position. "They're headed toward the kitchen."

"Shit," I heard Sean say, followed by rustling noises. "We lose the camera and sound after about two hundred yards."

Just as Britney vanished through the door, she seemed to turn her head my way, but we didn't make eye contact.

"Amador's goon squad is right on their heels. Something is up. I think they might have just kidnapped Britney."

Without giving a second thought, I lunged out of my stance, making a beeline toward the kitchen, the door still swiveling.

"Britney's been made," Sean said. "She's as good as dead."

Fifteen

Lifting an arm to plow through the swivel door, I popped the pad of my hand off the metal facing. A quick crack-back, the door nearly slamming against my nose. A woman screamed. Suddenly, my feet stumbled over something—or someone—and I saw a tray whizzing by my head just as I lost my balance. Trying to catch myself on the way down, my shoulder clipped another tray, larger, with something chocolate stacked sky high. A guy yelled out a Spanish cuss word. A knee popped my chin.

Was that my knee or that other guy's knee?

Whatever. I finished bouncing off body parts and tumbled to the tiled floor.

Moans all around me.

A quick assessment to determine if I was still put together. Twisting my torso, I felt a twinge. Well, more than a twinge. More like a dagger twisting between my third and fourth ribs.

"Are you guys okay?" I asked.

That was the wrong question apparently.

The woman I'd first mowed over got to her feet and ran off a string of cuss words that would put a ship of sailors to shame. Good thing I didn't understand a word she said.

"Are you hurt?" I asked the male waiter. Lifting to my feet, I noticed a wad of icing smeared down my shirt and onto my pants.

More cussing by the woman.

"Marta, she is a bit wacko when she thinks someone has done her wrong," the man said, scooping up the mess on the floor.

"Sorry about running you guys over."

"Everyone is in a hurry tonight."

"Did you see where a middle-aged man in a black T-shirt and a pretty—"

"Oh, the hot blonde and those guys? Yeah, we have a back door where they let some of the VIPs in and out. It's down this aisle, then go to the end of the hallway and turn right."

"*Gracias*."

"*De nada*."

I flipped on my heels and darted down the aisle, dodging two more would-be tacklers—rather, waiters—then cut left. I didn't see a soul, which was really not surprising given my graceful entrance into the kitchen. I hoofed it to the end, swung to my right, and then flew out the door.

The back parking lot. Twisting, I saw brake lights at the exit, turning right. A Hummer. Another already in the street moving in the same direction.

"Mr. Booker!" I put a hand to my ear as I picked up my pace.

"What?"

"Where are you?"

"Back parking lot, chasing after Amador," I said through heavy gasps.

"Hold tight. We're going to pick you up."

Pick me up? How? I didn't have time to debate logistics. Swinging my arms, I extended my stride, cars and windows and small bushes nothing more than a blur. I caught a waft of something foul, then whizzed by a dumpster and connected the thoughts.

The last Hummer completed its turn and motored down the street. I lost sight when it moved past neighboring buildings.

"Dammit!" I knew I'd never catch up, and my all-out sprint slowly pulled back a bit, reaching the edge of the cross street just in time to see the procession of black Hummers turning left about a quarter mile away.

"Mr. Booker!"

Jerking my head left, a motorcycle of some kind was skidding, trying to stop. Bolt's eyes were bigger than the full moon overhead. I leaped to the side, hitting the pavement, my own elbow stabbing my rib cage.

Just as I looked up, rubber squealed off the pavement, and the two-wheeler awkwardly pulled to a stop, nearly dropping to the ground.

"What the hell, Bolt? You said you knew how to drive one of these," Sean said, trying to keep the bike upright while holding his tablet in one hand.

I hadn't seen Sean since Bolt had been riding shotgun.

Peeling myself off the pavement, the scent of burning rubber lingering in the air, I placed a hand against my torso.

"You okay? It's your ribs again, isn't it?"

"They just turned left at that first intersection," I said, lifting to my feet.

"I know. I can't hear or see anything, but the device has a GPS signal attached to it."

I took another look at their ride.

"You're on a moped?" I rubbed my eyes in disbelief.

Bolt leaned his head one way. "What do you expect on short notice? It's all I could come up with."

"Get on," Sean ordered, his eyes studying the tablet.

"Where?" I asked moving toward the mini-motorcycle.

"Bolt can stand on the foot rest. I'll drive and you hold on behind me."

This was nuts, and not just dangerous nuts.

"I hate to be Captain Obvious, but why doesn't Bolt hang back here? We can pick him up later, or call Valdez and have him drop him off at the brownstone."

"Don't have time to debate it." Sean revved the tiny engine as he pulled Bolt into place. "Valdez called earlier and said Julio and his thugs out-tricked Manuel and escaped. Can't risk Bolt being alone."

"Shit," I said, straddling the small seat.

"Hold this." Sean gave me the tablet. "Tell me which way to go."

With the moped hovering just inches off the surface, Sean popped a small wheelie, the tires leaving a mousy squeal behind me.

"With all our weight, will this thing ever get to ten miles per hour?" I asked, only because our starting pace was slower than my light jog.

"This one has the hundred ten horsepower engine. Just takes a little time to get it up to speed," Sean said over his shoulder. "Hell, this is nothing. I once had to haul three hundred pounds of cash across the India border into Pakistan."

"Cash?" I said as wind finally started slapping my face.

"Can't get into details, but it was up and down hills and mountains. A two-hundred-mile trip. The engine was toast by the time I crossed at Wagah. So was my ass." He chuckled, then asked, "Still turn left here?"

"Uh…" I studied the GPS map. "Yeah. No, wait, keep going another street. Might be able to catch up."

I heard Bolt up front, yelling, his words lost in the wind-whipped air.

We whizzed past a car turning right and two couples who were dressed like they'd just left Club de Python. They pointed fingers and broke out in laughter.

I would have cracked up too, if I wasn't the one clinging to the back four inches of a moped seat.

"Turn left on Charles Sumner," I called out.

Sean slowed just slightly, leaning left. "Whoa!" To keep from sliding to the concrete and being trampled by the moped, Bolt leaned the opposite direction...which only caused Sean to lean harder.

The tiny two-wheeler scraped the bottom of its side carriage off the concrete, creating a quick spark.

"Whoa!" I yelled this time, trying to keep my shoe from clipping the street.

Sean righted the clown mobile and opened the throttle.

"Damn, you really know how to maneuver this piece of crap," I said.

"I've always had to improvise. You learn to do the best you can with what you got," he said, craning his neck around Bolt to see the road.

Studying the screen, it appeared we were about two blocks behind, but still losing ground. We had to take a chance to catch up.

"Go right on Defillo just ahead."

The team executed the turn like a well-oiled boat crew. "Now we're moving," I said, trying to steady the table as we picked up speed and crossed a swath of cobblestones.

"Hold on!" Sean shouted.

He locked the brakes, and we started fishtailing. I tried to lean against the violent thrust of energy pulling us off balance.

"Fuck!" he said.

I dropped my sandals, and instantly felt a flash of heat searing the bottom of my feet.

We finally came to a lurching stop, the moped just inches from dropping to the ground, Sean and I both on one knee, and Bolt draped over Sean's shoulder.

"I always wanted to visit Disney World. Check that off my wish list," Sean said, his face a tone lighter.

"Why the hell did we stop—"

I shut my mouth just as I glanced in front of us. A woman in a blue uniform holding a sign that read *Deténgase* planted a hand on her hip and shook her head, saying something under her breath. Just behind her, a line of four Segways glided across the road. A couple of the riders turned their heads. I knew what they were thinking. I was thinking the same thing.

The Segways whirred left and down a sidewalk as the guard shot us another condescending look and ambled off to the side.

"Let's roll," Sean said, squaring the bike and peeling less rubber than found on a pencil eraser.

"They're still in my sights," I said over the wind.

"If we get more than a half mile away, the accuracy of the GPS is less specific. Then if it goes away, turns off for whatever reason, finding her will be difficult, to say the least."

"Hang a left here then."

Sean made the turn smoothly. With nothing but flat concrete in front of us, he gunned it. Bolt held up his hands if he were at the bow of the Titanic—prior to crashing into a glacier.

"The road ends, but then turns into a small alley. We get through the alley, I think we'll be close enough to spit on them."

"Got it," Sean said.

Another hundred yards, and Sean hit the brakes hard...again.

"Damn, Mr. Sean, you almost sent me flying," Bolt said.

"Sorry, I couldn't see the opening to the alley."

We puttered a bit, then slowly picked up speed, whizzing by chain-link fences.

Dogs barked all around us.

"If the dogs weren't behind a fence, they could easily catch us," I said.

"If." Sean shrugged his shoulders.

With the moon hidden behind a bank of clouds, and buildings and homes on either side of us, it was difficult to see.

Suddenly, the moped hopped up and over a bottle, which exploded from the weight pressure.

"Shit. Hope we didn't puncture the tire," I said, watching the moving bubble. "Should be curving to the right soon."

"Now," Sean winced as we hugged a wooden fence while arching right.

I looked straight at the handle bar. No more than an inch separated the moped from clipping the fence, which would crash the bike, break us into a few pieces, and likely lose any signal from Britney.

A quick, distracting thought. Why had I immediately darted off to rescue Britney? Because she was our only link to Esteban. Right?

My teeth clanged off each other as Sean barreled through a pothole.

"I might have to get dentures."

"I can't see squat," he said.

"Get ready to hang a right onto Nunez."

We finished the turn.

"Where are the Hummers?" Sean asked, his head moving left and right.

I checked the map. "They must have sped up. Maybe they know we're chasing after them."

"Not likely. If needed, the Hummers can actually go faster than forty miles per hour. But that's our light speed."

"We're still within striking distance. Need to keep our same pace, try to run a light up ahead." Saying the words out loud was a mistake.

"Fuck!"

"What, Booker?"

"The frickin' GPS signal. We lost it."

Sean pulled the moped to the curb, a major intersection about a quarter mile in front of us. I lifted from the seat and held the tablet closer to his sights, as Bolt jumped from the bike and paced the area.

"Let me check something." Sean swiped the screen. "The Wi-Fi hotspot is still working. Five bars as a matter of fact. Show me where you last saw the signal."

I pointed to the map, then flipped my head back to the intersection in front of us. "That's Churchill Avenue up head. I last saw the icon about two blocks to the south."

Sean coiled his lips. "It just vanished. And I'm afraid so did our hopes of finding Esteban."

He got off the seat, walked a few steps toward the road, then turned to Bolt. "What's in the area where we lost Britney's GPS, do you know?"

"Financial district. Lots of glass office buildings, restaurants, and a couple of fancy hotels."

Sean jumped back on the moped, started the engine. Bolt and I hopped on, and we cruised to the end of the street and hooked a right.

"Keep an eye on the GPS. I'm going to drive slowly. I'm hoping they pulled into an underground garage or walked into an elevator and that the signal will pop back up again."

We puttered down the six-lane street, heavier traffic whizzing by us on the left.

"Anything yet?" Sean yelled just as an eighteen-wheeler motored by, spewing exhaust in our faces.

Bolt spit off to the side, but a trail of saliva lingered in the wind and glanced off my face.

"Hey!"

"*Lo siento*," he said with a quick chuckle.

Typical teen, I thought.

"We're at the point where the GPS disappeared, right?" Sean asked.

"Yep. And nothing shows up. You sure you weren't issued faulty equipment? Wouldn't be the first time our government scrimped on those who serve to save a few dimes."

"It works," he said with certainty. "At least I hope it does."

I glanced down at the screen for the twentieth time in the last five minutes. Lifting my eyes, I scanned the area around us, hoping to see Britney or Amador or one of his goons walking in a parking lot or out of a restaurant.

"They must have known we were following them. Maybe they found the device and destroyed it."

"I thought the same thing," Sean said, his head on a swivel.

"So you think it's possible?"

"Given how Julio sniffed out Bolt, it sounds like the whole group is on alert. They're freaked out by this El Jefe group, maybe the possible connection to Trujillo, the former dictator."

I took a quick peek at the screen. A blue dot came to life. "It's back."

"The GPS signal? Where?"

"We're almost on top of it. Stop."

Sean pulled into a parking lot and jumped off the moped before the engine completely shut off.

"I think it's coming from over there." I pointed at the tall glass building across the street.

"Columbus Hotel," Bolt said.

"As in Christopher?" I asked.

"I think it's named after his brother, who founded Santo Domingo."

"See, you do have a lot of knowledge in that head of yours."

"She must be in the hotel with Amador. If we can get close enough, we might be able to reestablish audio and video connectivity." Sean nudged Bolt and me, and we scooted across the busy street, a few horns blaring behind us.

We hit the front lawn of the high-rise, thick blades of grass rippling against my sandaled feet. "Strange place to bring someone if they're really kidnapping Britney," I said, craning my neck to the top. "We need to get inside, see if we can connect to her."

"Must be thirty floors or so," Sean said.

Bolt held up a knowing finger. "It's thirty-two."

"Good to see you can count."

"I'm connected, Mr. Booker. You should know that by now."

I could have made a snide remark. "Connected to who or what?"

"I've got an old friend who used to live…in my community."

"And?"

"He got a job at the hotel a little more than a year ago. He's already worked his way up to overnight assistant manager of the maid staff. A very prominent position."

"I think you need to introduce us, quickly," I said.

"Consider it done."

Sixteen

Ten minutes later I was pacing in a small office. Sean had just entered the room, sliding his phone into his pocket, a couple of veins snaking down the side of his neck.

"What's up?"

His eyes shifted to Bolt, who was playing hacky sack with a pouch of bath salts he'd found on a shelf.

"Nothing," he said, sliding his chair up to his tablet where he resumed trying to pick up the video and audio feed from Britney.

"Nothing, as in it was a direct marketing call asking you to buy a travel package to Belarus, or nothing as in you have a new assignment that will put you on the front lines of the latest terrorist struggle in Afghanistan?"

Now his eyes locked on mine. They were older, a few lines sprouting off the corners. Despite his corny disguise, he seemed a bit worn, maybe by the stress of what he was being asked to do again and again. Assassination couldn't be easy to deal with, even if you could rattle off twenty reasons why it saved lives in the long run.

"Nothing for you to worry about."

"I get it."

A few seconds later, he let out a disgusted breath. "I've frickin' tried everything." Placing his palms against his eyelids, Sean leaned back in his swivel chair.

"We might need to get hotel security involved and go door to door looking for Britney and Amador."

"Or, we could ask my friend, Fernando, and he could see if he can get access to the hotel directory."

"Thanks, Bolt, but if we do either of those things, word could get back to Amador's goon squad. Then we'd have a real mess on our hands. Hell, we're at risk just being in this office, even if it's in the basement," Sean said.

I picked up the tablet and tapped a few keys.

"What are you doing?" Sean asked.

"Turning it off. That's the first thing you do when a gadget isn't working. Reboot and cross our fingers we can pick up a good connection."

"Forest through the trees. Thanks, Booker."

Bolt dribbled the hacky sack twenty times off his knees without it hitting the floor, apparently in his own world, unaware of our conversation—all for the better. A blink on the tablet caught my eye. An image of a hotel room.

"We've got video."

Sean jumped out of his chair and peered over my shoulder.

"What are we looking at?" Bolt, suddenly interested, popped his head in between Sean and me.

Twisting my head, I said, "Think it's the ceiling."

Sean and Bolt mimicked my angled head, then they both nodded.

"What's that in this corner?" Bolt pointed.

"Hold on, let me make sure we've got audio." Sean adjusted the settings. "If you look at this bar, it shows audio is coming in, but at a real low decibel level. We'll have to be real quiet and see if we can pick up any conversation."

Sean brought the tablet closer. "Hey, I can hardly see now," Bolt whined.

"Shhh!" Sean and I said in tandem.

"I hear voices," I said. "Two people. A man and a woman. Sounds calm, casual even, but I can't tell what hell they're saying. Not sure they're close enough to the mic."

"Can't be sure others aren't in the room."

"Or what room they're in," I said.

Sean arched an eyebrow.

A quick flutter passed by the camera.

"Was that a hand?" Sean wondered.

I studied the angle of the camera, trying to guess at the distance to the corner of the ceiling we had on the screen.

Just then, Bolt put two and two together. "Wait, if the camera was attached to the front of her dress, then what are we looking at?" His eyes looked off to an award hanging on the office wall. "She took her dress off. It's probably lying on the floor or a chair."

Sean and I turned our heads in slightly, connecting our eyes. "It's possible," I said.

"Listen," Sean said.

I heard quick-paced thuds through the faint audio feed.

"What the hell?" My neck grew stiff wondering what we were hearing.

A wicked laugh, then Britney dashed by the camera and leaped onto something off-camera, presumably the bed. She was naked.

I jerked my hand over Bolt's face, blocking his vision.

"Holy shit!" he said, trying to squirm to get another view.

"Oh brother," Sean said.

"I knew Mr. Booker was a lucky man." He glanced at me and smiled.

I shot him a quick smirk. "You need to go over there and set your new personal record with the hacky sack."

"But how can I be expected to support this important operation if I'm not given the same access to the information at our disposal?" He inched backward, his shoulders scrunched above his ears.

"Have you heard the phrase children are to be seen but not heard?" I asked.

"Not sure you paid that much attention when you were a little rugrat," Sean said.

I almost shot back a snippy comment about how would he know one way or the other. I just ignored it and kept one eye on Bolt, the other on the screen.

"I've heard it, but it doesn't apply. I haven't been a child in a long time, Mr. Booker." His voice had a trace of sadness to it. He simply turned, walked over, and picked up his makeshift hacky sack. Then he leaned against the far wall, his eyes studying the little toy, or nothing at all.

I could see something existed in Bolt that had impacted his life. Underneath all of his sarcasm and endless quips targeting anyone he could needle, there was an inner lining of sadness. I could see it every so often, and a quick pat on his back or joke wouldn't allow him to forget. It seemed to be carved into his psyche. I knew he'd been on his own for years. But what event had triggered his life as a kid with no family and no home?

Sean nudged my arm. "You still with us?"

"Yeah, just thinking a few things through." I narrowed my eyes, moving my neck closer to the screen. "I think I see Britney's toes just at the edge of the screen."

"I guess you'd know."

"Uh, yeah."

A couple of seconds later, a man jogged past the camera and made a similar leap.

"Shirtless," I said.

"Looks like Chewbacca," Sean smirked.

"Chewy?" Bolt said, his voice sounding more alive. "He didn't say much, but he was a great sidekick."

"All the action heroes have a memorable sidekick," I said.

"True." He tossed the sack in the air and caught it on his forehead, keeping it balanced for a few seconds before thrusting it off and then dribbling it off his knees six times. "I connected with Han Solo. He had all the great lines."

"Why am I not surprised?" I thought more. "I'm kind of surprised you've seen those movies."

"Actually just had a marathon movie session a few months ago. Fernando snuck me and three of our old running buddies into the Presidential Suite, and we watched the first six *Star Wars* movies in one long night."

He grinned while nodding.

I brought my sights back to the screen.

"My favorite was the end of *Empire Strikes Back*. You know that movie is considered the best made, right?"

"Now you're a movie critic."

"I've actually seen quite a few movies. That's what I want to do when I grow up—direct movies, if I can't make it on the Dominican national soccer team and go to the World Cup."

"It's possible." I had no desire to throw a bucket of water on a kid who obviously needed to envision a better life, with goals and dreams, just like the rest of us at that age.

"Do you remember that scene?" Bolt asked, his eyes full of stars, and he washed a hand across his face like he was some type of Jedi master.

"What…" I shifted my eyes to the screen. Britney's toes had moved off-camera, and I could only hear a ruffling of some kind. I could feel a wave of heat slowly creep up my torso until it singed my neck. "…scene?"

"As smoke billows across the screen, storm troopers move a captured Han Solo into the carbonite machine. Darth Vader is going to freeze him and turn him over to Jabba the Hut." Bolt stretched out his arms and made his cheeks puffy with air. "Just before they lower Han into the machine, Princess Leia leans in and kisses him. She says, "I love you.""

"What did Han say?" Sean asked.

"You never saw *Star Wars*? And you call yourself an American?" I joked.

"I saw the last three, not the first three. I was in college when the first came out. Too interested in other things."

I could have guessed at girls or guns, but I refrained.

"So, what did Han say?" Sean asked again.

""I know."" Bolt said solemnly.

"That's it? I know? Lame," he said.

"You're kidding me, Mr. Sean. It's iconic."

"For English as a second language, you seem to have an incredible dictionary in that mind of yours."

He stood a little straighter. "I suppose I could use my multi-language skills to navigate the dangerous waters of being a...*CIA operative*." A straight face coiled into a devilish grin.

I think Sean's face turned red.

Tension filled the air, and Bolt quickly dropped his head. It's obvious he'd overhead some conversations and made some assumptions.

The silence only lasted a few ticks. A man shouted. Amador.

"What's he saying?" Sean asked.

"Sounds angry." I struggled to understand what he was saying.

More barking from Amador. Just then, I could see Britney's shoulders in the right part of the screen.

More yelling, but I couldn't make out a single word.

Sean shook his head, his eyes focused on the screen. "Crap."

Amador's hairy mitts had just grabbed Britney's arms. He moved her back and forth, and then finally shook her twice.

"We can't let him beat her up. Or worse," I said.

Just then, the door swung open.

"*¿Bolt, cuánto tiempo más que ustedes van a estar aqui?*"

A tall kid leaned inside, donning a slick uniform, black pants, and vest with a starched white shirt.

"Fernando?" I asked.

He nodded, as I shifted my eyes to Bolt then back to Fernando.

"Wants to know how much longer we're going to be," Bolt said.

"Hard to say. It might be quicker if he was to help us. Can you ask him if he has a uniform that might fit a guy about six-three, two hundred ten pounds or so?"

"Why, do you know someone looking for a job?"

Fernando.

"You speak English?"

"I've had to learn. We host many people from the states at this hotel."

"What about the uniform?"

"I can check. We might have something. Will this expedite your stay with us?"

"It might."

Sean took a step in his direction. "Bolt told us that if anyone in this world could be trusted, it was Fernando."

The gangly youngster walked in and shut the door behind him, arching his back as if standing at attention.

"This matter might impact the national security of the Dominican Republic and the United States of America. Can we rely on you to ensure our presence remains a secret?"

He gave a quick nod. "Of course, but what could involve—"

"No questions. Now, can you get Mr. Booker here what he was asking for?"

I took another glance at the screen. Britney had turned forty-five degrees. The back of her bare torso was all that was visible, but Amador still had her by both arms.

Fernando plowed through door and handed me a stack of clothes.

"*Gracias.*"

On his way out, he turned back around at the door. "Just let me know if there's anything else you need."

More movement on the screen. Suddenly, Britney twisted away, drew back her arm and swatted the man in front of her.

"Fernando, I need to know Miguel Amador's room number. Quick."

The flute glasses on the tray wobbled just slightly as I plodded out of the elevator on floor thirty. Two penthouse suites occupied the entire floor. As I moved west down the long hallway, I caught a quick glance of my sandals. Not exactly a perfect fit with my formal black and white uniform. Hopefully, they would go unnoticed.

Turning a corner, I spotted one of the men from Club de Python sitting in a chair next to a set of double doors. I assumed his buddies were nearby, in a side room next door maybe. I tried to maintain a ho-hum expression, act as if this was just another task in another day of drudgery.

"*Hola,*" I said.

"*Hola.*" He lifted from his chair.

As I raised a fist to knock on the mahogany door, I listened for any voices from inside the room. I heard nothing. Just before my knuckles bounced off the wooden door, the bodyguard held up his hand. It was missing the ring finger.

"What do you think you're doing?" He asked like I hadn't received the company memo regarding Never Disturb Señor Amador.

"Oh, I thought you knew?"

He paused, looking away for a second, perhaps replaying all the instructions given to him in the last few hours.

"It's okay. Every time a VIP stays at our hotel, our general manager insists we go the extra mile and provide the finest bottle of champagne we have. Complimentary, of course."

He curled his lip inward, exposing a set of gnarled teeth. "I...I don't think Señor Amador wants to be bothered, even for a fancy bottle of champagne."

I lowered the tray to show him the bowl of chocolate-covered strawberries and whipped cream. I leaned in a bit, keeping my voice low.

"Our general manager caught a glimpse of Señor Amador's girlfriend." I cleared my throat. "He knew Señor Amador would want to make tonight...special. I think we'll both look good if we give this to him and his girlfriend."

He looked at the tray. "Can I have a strawberry? I haven't had a thing to eat all night."

I moved the tray toward him. "No one will know." He picked one off the top, then flicked his head toward the entrance and took a step back.

I gave the door three quick knocks. "Room service."

No answer. I tried a double-knock. "Room service, Señor Amador."

The door flew open, and Amador nearly stumbled over himself.

"Compliments of our general manager, sir." Before Amador could react, I walked right in, scanning the condo-sized hotel room for Britney, or any signs of blood.

I found a round table off to the right, Britney's black heels about ten feet from it.

"What the hell is zat man zooing in here?" Amador barked at his guard behind me, slurring his words slightly.

The guard stuttered, unable to formulate a response.

"Compliments of our general manager, sir. Only for our most special VIPs," I called out.

I heard his bare feet shuffle against the plush carpet behind me as I tried to catch a glimpse of movement through a small crack in a set of double doors off to the left.

Just then, a sweaty hand touched the back of my neck. A flood of adrenaline shot through my body, my instincts poised to spin and drive a fist into the man's larynx. Somehow, I managed to pause an extra second.

"Well, I can't turn down a good bottle of champagne. And I think my woman will enjoy zese strawberries." He patted my back, then stepped in front of me while rubbing his prickly face. I picked up a stench that pinched my nostrils—a cross between rotten eggs and ammonia—matching his beastly appearance.

A soft, feminine hand reached through the door. The other room was nearly pitch black. As the door opened slowly, I could see a bare arm, then a shoulder.

"Alisa, my dear, come on out and enjoy a late night drink," Amador said while plucking a strawberry off the top of the heap.

Britney actually used the name Alisa? My partner and friend, maybe something more. For some reason, Amador's words lingered in my mind like a room full of smoke.

Taking my eyes off Amador, Britney was in the process of slipping on a fluffy, white robe as she entered the room. I think I stopped breathing for a split second. She'd forgotten to tie off the belt, creating a gap in the front. Using both hands, she flipped her golden locks over the collar, while locking eyes with me, almost daring me to look down. It was obvious she was naked underneath, but I kept my sights at eye level, wondering what she was trying to prove.

"This is wonderful. I'm starving," she said with a bit of an accent.

Wait. Was she trying to pull off a British accent?

"Here my precious, Alisa, try one of these decadent chocolate-covered strawberries." Britney opened her mouth and slid out her tongue. He moaned when he placed the fruit in her mouth. She followed suit. They made me want to puke.

Taking in a breath, I studied Britney's face. No noticeable marks. I still wondered what had provoked her swat at Amador, and how he had retaliated. Right now the pair appeared to act like any loving couple—with more personal issues than a full-time psychiatrist could keep up with.

"You just going to drool over my pretty lady, or are you going to uncork the champagne?" His eyelids acted as if they were being pulled down by weights, or some other inducement.

"What kind is it, Miguel?" she asked, taking the bottle off the tray just as I put a hand on it.

"Uh, ask the bellman. I don't know shit about champagne."

I paused for a quick read of Britney, but picked up no signals. "It's a special edition Dom Perignon Champagne Brut produced by Moët and Chandon. It was released in 1998 and designed by German fashion designer Karl Lagerfeld."

"I've met Karl, the creative direction at Chanel in France, but I don't recall him ever mentioning his champagne. I'm sure he didn't want to boast," she said more to herself, it appeared, than to Amador or me.

The lilt in her voice was no accident. It sounded like she'd been born in Liverpool. It was that authentic. Even the way she carried herself seemed different, her chin a tad higher than normal. It appeared she had this special Lady Diana-type persona tucked away in her bag of identities, just waiting to share at the most opportune moment. It was bizarre interacting with my third Britney, and disturbing.

Any way she could have a touch of schizophrenia? And how would that impact her ability to deal with everyday emotions, including jealousy?

"You may have the honors to pop my cork." Britney put the bottle in my face, her eyebrows arching toward the ceiling as Amador fiddled with a tablet of some kind near the sofa. He brought a hand to his nose and sniffed.

"Uh, yes, ma'am." Leave it to Britney to play with fire right in front of the arsonist.

What she was trying to accomplish with this Downton Abbey act I couldn't figure out, let alone her constant attempts at trying to seduce me in front of other people. How I wasn't able to see right through her bullshit girl-next-door attitude months ago, I had no idea. I had actually begun to wonder if she was *the one*. Damn, I must have had my head up my ass.

"Now that's the kind of respect I'm used to receiving." Amador stabbed a finger at me, as if he was proving a point to his crowd of just Britney.

Check that. I noticed the four-fingered bodyguard still lingering near the entryway, his arms extended like he was walking a tightrope. Perhaps he wasn't sure where to go, in or out.

"Yes sir, Señor Amador. The best service for our most cherished clients." I laid it on thick.

I untwisted the metal tied around the cork as Amador came up to Britney and smacked her right on the ass. She released a playful chirp, bouncing up on her toes. Turning into him, Britney closed her eyes as Amador slurped a kiss. His free hand found a crevice in the robe and he began massaging her chest with me standing right there.

I glanced over at Four Fingers, and his mouth was agape, although his nose twitched, as if he was repulsed.

I matched that sentiment.

Pop.

"Oh!" Britney jumped out of Amador's arms, clapping slightly.

"I haven't had champagne this nice since I was in London for the Summer Olympics and I was a guest at Sir Elton John's party," she said.

Amador beamed a smile, his eyes half closed and his body rocking a bit. It seemed like he might crumple to the floor and start snoring.

"I'll hold the glasses, and you pour," Britney ordered.

I wanted to give her a mocking salute, but I instead bowed my head slightly. Amador grabbed the first glass from Britney and walked over to the bodyguard.

"Here. You've been working hard tonight, and you deserve it."

Just as Four Fingers reached for the flute, Amador tossed the entire glass of bubbly on Four Fingers. He just froze.

"You might think you deserve a taste of the sweet life, but I assure you that is not going to happen when you make such a stupid decision as to let this hotel employee into my room without asking me first."

"I thought it was our room, dear Miguel," Britney said casually while wrapping her lips around a strawberry, one eye on me.

Dear?

I think my eyebrow arched higher.

"Uh…I'm very sorry, Señor Amador. It will not happen again." Four Fingers marched toward me, his hands moving up as if he was about to grab me by the collar and drag me out.

"Stop where you are, dumbass," Amador said. "He's harmless. But you didn't know that, did you? Of course you didn't, because you're nothing but a four-fingered dumbass."

Amador chased him from the room like he was herding cattle. "I hope you'll learn from the error. If you don't, you will suffer the same fate as all others who have failed me." He slammed the door shut.

Ambling back to Britney and me, Amador wobbled, and his hand grabbed the top of the Queen Anne chair.

"Here you go, Miguel." Britney held up a flute of bubbly, acting as if Amador's life-threatening rant had been nothing more than a learning moment for Four Fingers. Maybe that was why he was missing a digit.

"I gotta pee." Chewy snorted again, then cut toward a hallway.

Britney casually looked over her shoulder, waiting until he wobbled out of sight, then turned and spoke in a hushed tone. "Thank you for checking up on me, Booker. It means a lot. It really does."

I placed the cork on the tray. "It's nothing. Just making sure the operation doesn't crater. What happened earlier?"

"He's high as a kite. Was snorting coke like it was oxygen. He started raving about someone. I couldn't understand who he was talking about. But his eyes turned red, and then he started shaking me."

"Did he hurt you?"

"Not really. When I smacked him, I thought he might retaliate. But it woke him out of his trance. It's like he respected me more for fighting back, standing up for myself."

"Have you had to—?"

"What?" Her lips turned up at the corners, a twinkle in her eye.

I tried to ignore...everything. "What have you learned? Anything about Esteban?"

"Nothing yet. But I think he might share it with me if I spend the night. He's already sharing information about his drug-smuggling operation. I guess you and Sean have heard that?"

"Can't hear much with your dress sitting over on the side." I peered over her shoulder to ensure Amador wouldn't surprise us.

"Are you jealous?" She leaned her neck forward, her smirking face no more than six inches from mine. She slowly brushed her tongue across a pair of lips that couldn't have been any more perfect.

I felt like an addict being tempted with the very same drug that had nearly killed me. In this case, it—Britney/Ana Sofia/Alisa—had killed other people. I wasn't about to be added to her resume of death.

"Are you fucking serious? We've got a madman in the other room. The same guy who holds the life of a fourteen-year-old boy in his hand. The son of your fiancé. And you want to play verbal foreplay? If I didn't give a damn about Esteban seeing his father again, I might just leave you here to be devoured by that animal."

Her eyelashes flickered a couple of times, and the corners of her mouth dropped. "I'm trying to cope with all of this the best I know how. I told you before at my place, this isn't my comfort zone. Booker, you are someone familiar, someone I've loved with all my heart. It's natural for me to reach out to you with all of this tension in the air. And yes, I smell Amador's foul stench. It makes me want to vomit, just like him feeling me up. It's all disgusting and sordid. But I cope with it the best I can, hoping that I can coerce him into telling me where Esteban is, praying we can return him to his father, Juan. Just because I don't follow some script of how you think a woman should react in a situation like this doesn't mean I'm some type of black widow. I'm human, just like you. I bleed, just like you. I want love, just like you."

Her chest rose with each panting breath, as her eyes filled with water.

"Sorry. Didn't mean to question your motives." I shifted my eyes away, cleaning up the tray.

"Don't tell me ze both of you have downed the entire bottle of champagne?"

Amador stopped at the entrance from the hallway. I could see his blood-rimmed eyes from twenty feet away. He rested a hand against the wall, his belt was dangling from one loop.

Keeping her sights on me an extra tick, Britney's eyes seemed to reach out for me. For the first time in forever, I could sense fear in the leggy blonde, as if she wanted to jump into my arms and never let go. Instead, she inhaled, shot me a quick wink, then turned and pranced right up next to Amador.

"How could we do that? You're the life the party." She took his head in her hand and gave him an open-mouthed kiss, finishing with a nibble of his lip.

Damn, there goes another flip of her personality switch.

He wobbled a bit more, as if she'd just injected him with a lethal dose of Britney pheromones.

Been there, done that.

"A drink?" He snapped his finger, and I jumped out of my stance, handing him a frothy glass of champagne in quick order.

"A toast to the most lovely woman I believe I've ever met."

Pressing my lips against my teeth, I stood there with my hands clasped behind my back.

He turned his head and bit her lip until it bled. She didn't blink.

"What are you doing? This is a festive occasion. You must drink," he said, raising his glass as if it were loaded with a full magazine of bullets.

I brought a hand to my chest. "Me?"

"Who else?" He chuckled, turning to Britney. "Can you believe this guy, Alisa? *Los campesinos están tan jodidamente patéticos.*"

She whispered to him. "Remember, Miguel, I don't know Spanish all that well."

He shifted his bloodshot eyes toward me, then grabbed Britney by the waist and shoved her midsection into his crotch. "I know I have a....a short fuse." He pulled her hair back, his lips brushing against her ear. "But it's because of your beauty and remarkably cultured mind that I have the strength to not let the pathetic peasants turn my mood sour." He cleared his raspy voice.

"You may go. Just leave the tray where it is." He flicked a wrist in my direction, his eyes still trained on Britney. She held her gaze, as if enthralled by his very presence.

I nodded and scooted toward the door.

"Now, are you ready to have some real fun?" I heard Amador say.

Turning back as I reached for the knob, Amador stripped off Britney's robe and tossed it aside with the single-minded vigor of a bull plowing up dirt, preparing for a stampede. I could already hear his lecherous grunts.

The last visual I got was Britney putting her arms around the hairy beast, her eyes just visible over his shoulder. She looked into my eyes, then gave me a quick thumbs-up.

"I've got a special bag in my coat in the bedroom. It's time to get fucked up." Amador chuckled just as I shut the door behind me.

I wondered if I'd just seen the last of Britney Love—alive.

Seventeen

"**F**ooood," I heard someone say. I wrestled awake, nearly falling out of my stiff office chair and quickly saw Bolt hovering over me, waving the scent of something sweet and spicy under my nose.

"How long have I been asleep?" I rubbed my eyes and reached into my pocket for my phone.

"Oh, just long enough for me to ask Fernando to put in three breakfast orders before his overnight shift ended."

My eyes zeroed in on the plate. "Smells great. What is it?"

"*Mangú* seasoned with tons of onions and dices of green and red bell pepper, and olive oil. With it are juicy roasted Roma tomatoes and boiled banana, what we call *guineo,* in a sweet and musky thick sauce, topped with chunks of different fruit."

My stomach growled. I looked to my right and found Sean also waking out of a slumber, rubbing the back of his neck, then flipping his gray ponytail like an old horse.

He crouched down to the level of the tablet propped on the desk in between us. "Looks like it's still quiet."

Taking a quick peek, the angle of the camera had been lowered, but something was covering the right side of the lens. I could see a bedpost and what appeared to be Britney's bare feet.

She looked stiff and pointed, as if she was in a perfect diving position.

Swinging my phone around, I noticed the time: 6:45 am.

I brought a hand to my head. A throbbing sensation had started in my temples. "Thanks for the breakfast, Bolt. Any water around here?"

He pointed at the tray in the corner perched on a metal stand. "Mr. Booker, you should know by now that I will take care of you and your friend. When it comes to my country, I'm still a prideful man."

"Man?"

He shrugged his shoulders.

I turned to Sean. "The last thing I recall was Amador snorting so much coke he started tossing glasses at the wall, while trying to convince Britney to participate."

I lifted out of the chair, padded over to the tray, and held up a bottled water. "Want one?"

"Sure," Sean said, taking the water bottle, cracking the top, and chugging at least a third of it. I followed suit.

"Just to confirm, no one heard anything about Esteban, or even a kidnapping in a general sense?"

They both shook their heads.

"But we really don't know," Sean said, walking over and picking up a plate of *mangú*. "Since Britney wasn't wearing the mic, they could have easily had a conversation out of earshot. We need to talk to her."

He stuffed a full fork in his mouth and nodded. "Great stuff, Bolt. Make sure you tell your buddy thanks."

"He believes he's doing this for the national security of our two countries," he said, a smirk forming on his face.

"We might have embellished slightly," I said.

"Em-be-llish?"

"Overstating the truth so that he would help us out."

A long nod of the head. "I think I've done that before."

"You could teach a course on it," I said with a grin.

"Actually, I think I could convince you otherwise, Booker. That this was…is a threat of national security." Sean twisted his head. I think he was attempting to communicate that he would have no other reason to be given this assignment unless it involved national security of the US. Extending that premise to the Dominican Republic wasn't difficult, given how Amador's cartel controlled so much of the drug trade. Add in his connection to the L-FARC terrorist group, and this island might be the number one hotspot for the CIA in the Western Hemisphere.

I traded a stare with Sean, and he could see that I'd come around on his national security claim without me having to say another word.

Trying to clear the cobwebs and mute the stomach growls, I ate from a plate of *mangú* and downed three bites before taking a breath.

"Where's your plate, Bolt?"

"Couldn't wait. I finished everything before I brought in the tray." He flashed a quick grin.

Resuming my position just right of the screen, I stared at Britney's feet. They were so still. Was she asleep, or had something happened in the last hour, maybe from ingesting too much coke? Perhaps Amador had killed her in her sleep. Strangling seemed like a possible method that would fall in his wheelhouse. A knot of anxiety mixed with my spicy breakfast.

"We don't know enough to draw a conclusion one way or the other," Sean said.

"How do you know what I'm thinking?"

"Saw you staring. I'm wondering the same thing." Sean chewed a mouthful of banana and *mangú*, his eyes fixated on the screen.

Bolt picked up his makeshift hacky sack and started kicking it around near the layered towels that had served as his bed for the night.

"Make sure you don't knock over the tablet."

"I'd have a lot more room if I wasn't crammed in this corner." He caught the sack of bath salt in his hand. "If you treated me like an adult and allowed me to actually help you on this operation, we could have found Esteban by now."

A fork loaded with *mangú* stopped just before entering my mouth. "Really?"

"Okay, I might have embellished slightly."

"Thank you, Mr. Obvious."

"Ha. I get your sarcasm, Mr. Booker. Very clever, I must say."

He resumed bouncing the bath-salt pouch off his knees.

"Okay, you can come take a quick look. There's really nothing to see right now."

Dribbling the sack off his ankle then back to his knee, Bolt made his way around Sean and me.

"Any thoughts on our next steps if Britney doesn't get anything out of Amador?" I asked Sean, each of us scarfing down our food.

He looked off to the corner for a second. "First, we make sure she's alive and well."

I nodded, glad to hear him agree with another internal thought. "Then?"

"Remember, we have multiple goals here. I might need to try a more direct method. Not something you should be involved with."

Starting at his food, he forked in the last bit of *mangú*, then set the empty plate on the desk.

"What if I said I wanted to help?"

"Too dangerous."

I glanced back at Bolt, his eyes focused on his own impressive dribbling skills.

"That's for me to decide. But you do know my number one goal. Returning a kid back to his dad."

"I get it."

"Hairy beast on the move," Bolt said, pointing at the screen.

Shifting my vision to the tablet, I caught a quick flash moving right to left.

Sean said, "It's Amador. Looks like he's walking out of the bedroom."

"He's shouting, but I can't make out what he's saying," I said.

The screen went still like a photograph again. Not wanting to interrupt any dialogue, I pointed at Britney's feet. Despite Amador jumping out of bed and racing out of the room, she hadn't moved an inch.

"Not a good sign," Sean said.

I leaned on my knees, hoping she would wake out of her slumber, but knowing the more seconds that ticked by, the more likely her body had turned cold. Perhaps Amador had awakened, made a call, and was arranging to have the body removed.

"Dammit!" I finally said, scratching the back of my head.

With Bolt leaning on the desk, the three of us stared at a blank, motionless screen. The only sounds came from outside our small office, hotel employees unpacking boxes of goods, discussing the morning weather. I was able to glean that it was already another humid day in Santo Domingo.

"Do you think he just left the body—Britney—there for now? Maybe something else urgent came up," I said, looking at Sean.

"Could be something going down with this El Jefe character."

"He is running a multimillion dollar business with a multimillion dollar target on his head. He's got a lot to worry about," I said.

The noise outside our room dropped to a couple of low-key voices. "We can't just sit here. We've got to know if Britney is okay." I smacked my hand off the desk.

Sean nodded, responding with a calm tone. "I understand." Sean lifted from his seat, adjusted something in the back of his waistband. "First we need to find out if Amador is still in there."

"I know, dammit. We need a bigger team."

"Hello. I know you think I'm a gullible kid who's afraid of his own shadow, but that is not the case. I can find out if Amador is in the room. Leave it up to Bolt." He thumped his chest, then marched to the door.

I held up my arm, stopping him in his tracks. "Not so fast."

"I'm going up there," Sean said, ensuring his wig was on securely.

I instantly wondered what Sean would do if he ran into Amador. End his life right there? But would we ever know where Esteban was being held? And would Sean survive?

"But—"

"This isn't the time or place to take this to the next level, I realize that," Sean said.

"Wait, are you wearing a disguise?" Bolt held out a finger, then shifted his eyes back to me.

"I knew something was screwy. You are undercover, aren't you?" Bolt's face lit up, as if he'd just figured out the real identify of Santa Claus. Then again, he may not have ever been visited by Santa during his childhood years.

Sean's lips drew a straight line. I could sense his radar going up, the kind that detected risk. I couldn't blame him. Just a couple of days back he'd run into me trying to navigate through the cloak of darkness to a drug cartel and terrorist training camp.

He used it as an opportunity to finally open up and share his life's secrets with the one person who had resented him most in the world—me. I could tell taking that step was monumental for him.

But sharing it beyond a blood relative? He had probably killed for less.

"Bolt," I said, rising from my chair. "It's complicated, that's all I can say...we can say. Up to now, I've entrusted you with far too much for a kid your age. In turn, it's gotten you injured, almost killed."

"How many times do I have to tell you, I'm not a kid. I'm a young adult." His voice carried an extra edge of agitation. Perhaps not enough sleep, like the rest of us.

"Okay. You've experienced more than most any other kid....uh, person, your age. But right now, it's not safe for us to share anything more about who Sean is and why he's wearing a disguise."

He nodded, his lips tight.

"That means you can't share this with Fernando, or any other friend."

Another head nod.

I tried to recall what it felt like to be a teenager. "You can't even share that you know something they don't."

"*Entiendo*."

"You understand?" He and I locked eyes, then Sean put his hand on the doorknob.

"*Gracias*," Sean said to Bolt, turning his eyes to me. "As soon as I know something I'll call you."

He swung open the door, stepped into the adjoining room.

Turning my head back to the tablet, nothing had changed. I kneeled down and touched the screen. "Are you still with us, Britney Love?" Staring into a blue maze of industrial carpet squares, my mind pulled me back in time for a brief second, disconnecting me from reality.

Bolt came back around the desk. "Mr. Booker, you're sad about Britney, no?"

"No," I said, pushing up to my feet. "I'm sad for Esteban, who had no control over what these insane adults did to his life. I hope like hell we can find him before it's too late...if it's not already."

A moment passed, and I took in a fortifying breath, knowing we still had hope.

"Alisa!"

Jerking my head to the screen, Amador marched into the bedroom while slipping on a shirt. After seeing him barely able to stand on his own two feet late last night, it was a small miracle he could function any time before noon. But something had infused his body with a jolt of energy. He walked off camera to Britney's side of the bed.

"Alisa. You must wake up."

Bolt pointed at the same moment I noticed—Britney's toes wiggled.

"She's alive, Mr. Booker. She's alive."

"Try to catch Sean," I yelled out, my eyes peeled to the screen.

Out of the corner of my eye, I could see Bolt run out the door and cut left.

Britney moved a foot up and down her opposite shin. Why did every movement have to be so damn sexual with her? Or was it just me? Hell, she was a sexual dynamo, a pheromone magnet.

Her legs moved up, as if she was bringing her knees to her chest. I listened closely.

"Oh, I...I feel so loopy," she said. "I feel like I've been trying to wake up, but I couldn't for some reason."

She still had her British accent, which told me she was either quick on her feet or had been in character while she lay in bed.

He chuckled. "I think I know why."

She giggled, but it sounded forced, her lilt not as convincing. She sounded tired as hell. I'm not sure Amador noticed.

"My dear Alisa, I have urgent business I must attend to. I didn't want to just run out on you. Last night was one of those magical nights," he said.

Her foot moved, rustling the sheets at end of the bed. I heard lips smacking.

Gross.

Amador walked back into camera, turning back to Britney at the door. "When all of this settles down, we must get back together. You're not going back to England any time soon are you?"

"I was due to leave a couple of days from now. But I suppose I could extend my stay."

"Until then," he said.

"*Señor Amador, tenemos que darnos prisa antes de que sea demasiado tarde.*"

Another man's voice. He must be standing near Amador, and it wasn't Four Fingers. This voice was deeper and croaky, as if he hadn't slept in the last two days. I thought he said something about leaving before it's too late? I wasn't sure. Where was Bolt and his translation skills when I needed him?

I heard a low growl, then Amador paced back in the room, a hand to his scraggily chin. "*Mi tiempo con la bella dama se ha interrumpido. Esto es una mierda. Miguel Amador le enseñará a esta persona una lección que nunca olvidarán.*"

I said aloud to myself, "He used his name in the third person. Not a good sign. Dammit, where the hell is Bolt?"

"Right...here." Bolt burst into the room gasping for air, holding up a finger. "I...I think I heard Amador. He said..."

"What happened?"

"Your friend Sean decided to take the stairs. Probably a smart move, but he'd already made it up twelve floors. I...I came back as fast as possible."

I glanced back at the screen. Amador's heels bit the carpet with each pacing step.

"So?"

"He's angry that his time with the beautiful lady was interrupted. He said it was bullshit." Bolt shrugged his shoulders. "I am just the messenger, don't forget."

I nodded, urging him to continue.

"He said that Miguel Amador will teach this person a lesson they will never forget."

My accelerated pulse just downshifted and punched the gas. "I wonder if there's any way this is connected to Esteban and his kidnapping."

"Doubtful," Sean said, turning into the open office, his face lined with sweat.

"By the way, you're quick," he said to Bolt.

"It's required for my job," Bolt said.

"How could I forget?"

"You were saying?" I looked at Sean, who picked up his bottled water and downed a swig.

"I can't see Amador making that kind of statement about some teenage kid. He doesn't seem easily intimidated. This is about something much bigger, or someone more threatening, I'm guessing."

Suddenly, Amador picked up a glass from a table and hurled it against the wall, the sound of shattering glass penetrating my pores.

"He's got anger management issues," I said.

"On steroids," Sean added, arching an eyebrow.

"*Vamos*. Goodbye, my sweet Alisa. We will talk soon."

Amador walked off camera, and I turned back to Sean. "We need—"

"Wait, Miguel."

My eyes almost did a double take. Britney ambled out of bed dragging a sheet. She jogged straight at the camera, most of her torso uncovered. And she didn't seem to care.

Sean stepped in front of Bolt.

"What am I missing now? The natural beauty of a woman?"

"Deal with it," I said.

Britney leaned directly in front of our view, her eyes narrowed while she chewed on her lower lip. Suddenly, the picture went dark, and the device sounded like it had been tossed into a garbage disposal.

"What the hell?"

"She plucked the device off her dress," Sean said.

Seconds ticked by, then I heard, "And don't forget to call," Britney said. That was followed by a return of the garbled sounds, drowning out any conversation. Then the irritating noise quickly dissipated. But the screen remained dark, only a faint bit of audio coming through, as if someone was moving.

"Did something happen to Britney?" Bolt called out from behind Sean.

"Shit, I don't know," I said.

Sean added, "He sounded smitten by her, but he's been taking a lot of drugs and he's volatile. It's possible he could have seen her with the bugging device and responded by killing her."

My phone rattled off the metal desk.

I punched the green button while looking at Sean. "Britney?"

"He's gone, finally," she said releasing an audible breath. "Pardon me. What do you think you're looking at, asshole?"

I held the phone away from my ear, and Sean's eyes grew wide with confusion.

"Britney, I don't know what you're thinking—"

"Just because your boss fucked me last night doesn't give you the right to stand there and get your jollies. I'll leave when I'm ready to leave. ¿*Comprende?*"

I heard a door slam.

"Britney, you there?"

"Yes. This fucking asshole thinks he can screw me? Thinks I'm nothing but a whore? Fuck you."

I realized my jaw hung open. Even with all of her flaws, and they were plentiful, I'd never witnessed Britney so raw and direct.

"One of Amador's bodyguards?"

"Hell yes."

I could hear her nostrils pumping air into the phone.

"Is he threatening you?" I didn't want to ask, but it spilled out.

"Doesn't matter. I can handle myself. He's in the other room, or left the suite altogether. I'm fine. Give me a second."

By the time I locked eyes with Sean, she came back.

"Had to throw my dress back on. I don't think last night will be one I want to share with Mom or Dad." She tried laughing at herself. Or was her sarcasm replacing a round of tears?

"Booker, you there?"

"Yes, I'm here. Sean too."

"And me," Bolt said. "Am I allowed to leave timeout?"

"Shhh. Yes," I said with my hand covering the phone. "Britney, what happened in there?"

"It doesn't matter. But you need to follow him."

"What? Why doesn't it matter?"

"Because I placed the bug in Amador's coat pocket without him seeing me. You should be able to track him."

I turned to Sean, who had already reached for the tablet and was tapping icons.

"We're on it. That was smart." The words lingered too long, neither of us filling the dead air. Finally, I continued my line of thinking. "Anything on Esteban?"

"I tried every trick in the book. And yes, that's a loaded answer." She giggled, sounding as if she was rubbing her mouth. "I stroked his ego and everything else I could find, but he just didn't go there."

I forced out a breath. "Dammit. Now I'm starting to question if he even has Esteban?"

"You sound like me, with the trash mouth."

"Whatever."

A couple of seconds passed, then I thought I heard a sniffle.

"I have no idea what to tell Juan," she said. "I...I rubbed all over that...fucking animal, made him feel like he was all that. And what do I have in return for whoring myself out? I don't have Esteban, that's all I know. Juan will be even more devastated, if that's possible."

Another sniffle.

"I know it won't be an easy conversation," I said.

Sean thumped my shoulder and motioned for me to follow him and Bolt.

"By the way, I...I wondered if he had...hurt you earlier."

Weaving through countless shelves of supplies, I stayed close to Bolt, who followed Sean.

"I had to act like I was unconscious. Too much drugs," she said.

"Did you?"

"What, snort the coke? First line of the night, then nothing after that. He was like an anteater, just sucking it up his nose. It was vile, just like him."

"How did you avoid taking any more?"

"I literally tossed it off the bed, let it blend in with the carpet. He was so whacked out, I could have turned into Godzilla and he wouldn't have known better."

A brief chuckle.

"I like hearing your laugh. It reminds me of the good times."

"Britney…"

"I know. I can't undo the past. I have to be accountable for what I've done. I understand that. I want to do the right thing."

Her words, the authenticity behind them, caught me off guard. I could still feel a longing for her, for us. But it couldn't be. She had taken it too far.

"I'm going to hold you to that."

"I'm sure you will. But that's a good thing, right?"

I noticed the back door up ahead.

"Look, we're about to start trailing Amador. You sure he didn't hurt you?"

"He's a lunatic. Whether it's the drugs or his natural personality, he's paranoid, volatile, and he smells like a pig."

"We heard him tossing glasses last night, during his first outburst."

"You know, during his rant, he literally sounded crazy, as if someone should fit him for a coat that ties in the back. But during all that, he was wondering if a member of the Trujillo family had come back to the island and was attempting to seize control of the drug-smuggling business."

I recalled Sean's history lesson about El Jefe and his thirty-year reign of terror. I began to wonder if the real or imagined return of the Trujillo clan had to do with Amador's outburst and quick exit.

"Thanks for the info. I'll run it by my friend."

"Your friend."

"Was that a question?"

"It was nothing. I'm headed home, talk to Juan. I need a shower, some way to wash this night off my body and out of my mind. Call me if you guys find out anything about Esteban, a sign of hope to lift Juan's spirits."

I tapped the red button just as the door opened and a blistering sun scorched my eyes.

Eighteen

"**Y**ou don't carry a portable battery for situations just like this?" Bolt toyed with the tablet, pushing buttons, tapping the screen. It was dead.

We'd lost the GPS signal about a mile down the road. We hadn't seen a soul in the last ten minutes, let alone a procession of Hummers.

Sean gave him the eye as we stood next to the moped, five-foot weeds nearly rising above Bolt's head.

"Given your experience and background, I would think you'd have every gadget. Don't you have a P or a V?"

"You mean Q?" I asked, my eyes scanning the exterior of a dilapidated building. Bolt felt certain that Amador and his team could be holding Esteban in that building. He said he'd once been held here against his will many years ago, when he refused to be a drug runner for the gang of addicts who'd basically taken over one of the factory floors. He was certain most of them had died, given their chosen lifestyle of using tainted needles.

"I'm no James Bond. This is the real world. And we might find that out real quick." Sean removed a pistol from his waistband, checked the chamber, then handed me the weapon.

"Never seen one like this."

"It's Russian-made from back in the 1990s, called the Makarov. It's the best I could do for a backup that isn't traceable."

I nodded, wrapping my hand around the grip. "I like the weight."

Sean took out another handgun and prepped it.

"That doesn't look familiar either," I said, my eyes still on the lookout for Amador or anyone who might be associated with him.

"Not used in America much. But they're missing out. Called the Glock Killer. It's a Steyr M-A1. Feels like it's glued to my hand, which helps if I get pulled into a skirmish."

"Which way?" I asked Bolt.

"What, you have nothing for me to protect myself?"

"We'll protect you," I said.

"These aren't just for defensive purposes," Sean said. "Isn't there some place we can hide Bolt? I know Julio escaped and would do some real damage if he caught Bolt again, but if we find Amador, shit is going to hit the fan."

Glancing around, I spotted a tiny wooden shack, barely larger than a phone booth, surrounded by more weeds. "Outdoor bathroom. Want to hang out in there?"

"You'll have to use that gun on me if you expect me to step inside that shithole."

"Didn't think you would." I gazed left and right, but still couldn't see the end of the massive building.

"Down here," Bolt said. "This door has always been open, and then we can wind our way through, moving toward the front."

"Sounds like a plan," Sean said, his handgun by his thigh.

We approached a metal door, about ninety percent of the yellow paint chipped off, similar to the entire façade of the building.

I leaned forward, peered through a small, foggy window with what appeared to be a bullet hole at the center of a spider web of cracks.

"Looks like we're not the only ones to carry guns into this place," I said.

"That's an entry hole. Someone was shooting inside," Sean said, his body stiff and his eyes still scanning the exterior to ensure we weren't ambushed for the second time in two days.

I reached for the handle, but only found a hole. Leaning my shoulder against the door, it didn't budge.

"Must be rusted shut." I stepped back then popped the door a little harder. Nothing.

"Bolt, you got another way into this place?" Sean asked.

"There are many ways, but this is the most concealed," he said.

Leaning down, I peered through the open hole. "Metal pole angled against the door. Obviously someone put that here to keep people out." I rose up and clapped my hands. "Bolt, we need another way in, some place where we wouldn't be noticed."

Bolt stuck an eye in the opening and held up a knowing finger. He darted away from the building, toward a row of shorter, bushy trees laced with wiry weeds. He plodded around in the weeds, looking for something.

"Bolt, keep your head down. Amador's thugs could see you." I waved an arm to no avail.

"He's ignoring you," Sean said.

"Would you expect anything more?"

A few seconds later, the resourceful teen hopped back next to us, holding what looked like a small baton from my old track and field days, but just thin enough to fit through the door's hole.

"Nice. Did you know it was out there?"

He inserted the steel pole into the hole. "The area around this building used to be called the killing fields," he said, pulling the pole so hard that veins bulged through his neck.

"Do I want to ask?" Tapping him on the shoulder, I took another peek through the opening, readjusting the placement of the foot-long lever.

"You can find anything around this place, including dead bodies. I got lucky I didn't trip over one."

"So we know this place doesn't attract the opera crowd," Sean deadpanned, as he wiped his brow dripping with sweat.

With one hand on top, I swung the side of a closed fist horizontally. Metal clanged off a concrete slab, and I nudged the door open with the tip of my sandal.

"Ladies first," I said just as Bolt took a foot inside.

He paused, shaking his head, releasing a teenaged chuckle. "I owe you one."

The room was deep and wide, pillars situated every thirty feet or so. Oddly, the ceiling and columns had been encased by beadboard and painted fluorescent yellow sometime in the past. Bolt led us across the enormous space. It was nearly impossible not to step on half-empty bags of trash or longer metal poles, creating unwanted noise.

"I'm afraid they're going to hear us coming," Sean said.

"If they're here."

"Trust me," Bolt said. "If they're in this place, it's not in this section. We called this section the swamp."

Taking a few more steps, rotted wood with nails sticking up dotted the floor.

"Careful. Q didn't load me up with any tetanus shots this morning," Sean said.

Glancing up, they saw the ceiling had caved in. A leafy, dense vine engulfed the entire space and had extended its fingers along the ceiling that was still intact.

"Looks like something out of a Harry Potter movie," I said.

"You watched those?" Sean asked.

"Samantha's obsessed over Hermione lately, so I've sat through a few minutes here and there. Her mom would rather see her infatuation center on someone with a little more…uh, cultural diversity."

"Sounds like a spitfire."

"Who, Samantha?"

"No, your ex-fiancée."

"You couldn't imagine," I said with a straight face.

"Your mother is pretty much the same way," Sean said, tiptoeing over every board and nail, joining Bolt near the edge of another doorway.

I paused for a second. I didn't know how protective of Momma I'd become, at least when it came to the man who she believed had simply abandoned her, us. She wasn't all wrong, but I'd learned a great deal about Sean the last few days. He was no longer a target in my mind.

Bolt guided us through a narrow hallway, and then up two darkened flights of concrete steps no wider than four feet.

"Hope no one is claustrophobic," I said, my hands pressed against the unmovable walls.

"I'm good," Bolt said, all business.

At the top, it opened into a wide hallway, windows on both sides and an object sitting in the middle. "What the hell is a gurney doing in the middle of a factory?" The gurney's cushion was covered with a gooey, orange stain.

"The story told to me was that the owners wanted to have everything onsite so the workers would have no reason to leave. Probably came from a medical room and some homeless person or addict took it for a spin."

I avoided the stained gurney and walked down the hallway, noticing mushrooms growing from the window sills. Leaning closer, I tried to peer through a cracked window.

"No sign of the Hummers."

Sean nodded and followed suit on the other side. "Clear on this side too."

Toward the end of the hallway, spears of light found their way into the hall, and I could see the dust and grit floating through the air.

Suddenly, Sean choked, then released a flurry of rapid coughs before finally clearing his throat. The echo lasted a good ten seconds.

"You okay?"

"Something about bad air that gets me going."

"There's got to be asbestos throughout this entire facility," I said, following Bolt into a dark room, the door lying on the ground next to a load of crumpled bricks.

"Where the hell you taking us?" If I looked away from the door, I couldn't see my hand.

"Could be a trap," Sean said.

"Chill, my man," Bolt said. "I know where I'm going, I just don't want to—"

I flipped on my phone flashlight. "What the—?"

All I saw were dozens, if not hundreds, of beady eyes hanging off the ceiling and walls, encasing us like a shadow.

Just then, Sean tripped over an empty glass bottle, and the room erupted.

"Hit the floor," I yelled, shutting off my flashlight on the way down. Wings fluttered all around us, mixing in with a symphony of screeches. Crouching over, I felt sharp pokes into my back and neck, a few peppering my head and arms as I tried to cover my face.

Moments later, the sounds died back, and I lifted to my feet. Bolt had already opened another door, and light spilled into the room. We stepped out of the cave, and Bolt took one look at me and cracked up.

"I guess the bats were full of *mierda*."

Shifting my eyes, I could see stains on my shoulders.

"Do you think Britney's going to want her clothes back?" Sean asked as we marched behind Bolt down a barren hallway, a few office doors on both sides. I peered in each one as we passed.

"She said they were for Juan," I said.

"You don't believe her?"

"Believing her will put your life at risk," I said, wondering if she'd grown on me a bit in the last day.

"I've been around a few women like that in my line of work." Sean poked his head into a vacant office.

"And what line of work is that?" Bolt asked.

Sean stopped in his tracks. "I thought we made it clear?"

"Kids are to be seen, not heard. A wise man once told me that when I was a kid."

"Your Uncle Charlie?" Sean asked.

"Probably."

"He knew what he was talking about."

"Who is this Uncle Charlie? I need to meet him and explain that this is not the world of Christopher Columbus."

I nearly stepped on something hairy and overstuffed. "You're right, this is the world of bat caves, asbestos, and dead rats the size of dogs."

Bolt lurched, as if he might puke. "I'm not a fan of rats. Been around far too many in my life."

Just then, off to my left, I noticed a set of double doors missing. Turning, I spotted stained glass at the far end of the room.

"A sanctuary?" I stepped into a room with arching ceilings, stone columns, and mounds of rubble. One pew near the front was still intact and upright, although it leaned heavily to the right.

"A heavy Catholic population. Owners wanted *everything* onsite. A one-stop shop, I think I've heard people call it," Bolt said.

"Looks like someone set off an explosive," Sean said, leaning down and picking up tiny pieces of wood and debris.

We continued our trek, shifting through a large foyer that faced what must have been management meeting rooms. We passed a kitchen that still had ceramic bowls sitting on the counter.

"You don't want to look in those," Bolt warned.

I respected his counsel and steered clear of the bowls to look through a tiny hole in a bank of fogged up windows.

"Off to my right, three black Hummers parked in a triangle."

Sean glanced up and down the hallway. "I've seen that before. Usually cartels or organized crime creating a barricade. Serves as a safe zone, creates confusion with all the cars looking the same. These guys are smart."

"Wait," I said. "I see one of Amador's thugs. Holding what looks like an Uzi sub-machine. I think he's supposed to be the welcome party."

Sean nodded, and I could see his neck grow tense.

"We need to be careful from here on out," Bolt said, stepping down the hallway. He paused, put a finger to his head. "I think they could be in one of two places."

"Remember, we don't want to just walk right in. We need to observe first," I said.

He gave me a frustrated shake of the head. "I watch the Bourne movies. I know how this is done."

"Except people die in real life, Bolt. Just need to be extra cautious," Sean said, moving to within three feet of our little sidekick.

Twenty feet farther in, I found a dead snake.

"You can make a pair of boots, Mr. Booker. Something to remember from your stay in the Dominican."

Just as I nodded, the floor vibrated ever so slightly. I held up an arm, then moved a finger to my mouth. Padding closer to a pair of swivel doors, I began to hear a man's voice.

I turned back to my team and mouthed *Amador*. Suddenly, the voice seemed like it was almost on top of us. Not knowing how many or their weapons, I turned to Bolt and threw up my arms, as if I was asking him where to go. I turned and fell into a Weaver stance, my Makarov aimed in the middle of the two doors.

"Mr. Booker," he whispered, turning down a hallway off to my right, Sean at his heels waving me on. I lunged out of my position on the balls of my feet. Just as I hit cover, I heard hands smack the door and enter the hallway.

"*¿Dónde está ese gilipollas? Julio dijo que lo había traído aquí hace treinta minutos.*"

Walking as if his feet were on fire, Bolt scooted into a room and out the other side, then cut down another hallway before turning back around to Sean and me.

"Amador asked where the little prick was, Julio. His words, not mine." He rubbed his face and glanced over my shoulder. Sean was already looking that way.

"Apparently, he's waiting on Julio. He expected Julio to bring *him* thirty minutes ago."

"We need access to the room they're in without them seeing us. Can you do that?"

"Esteban could be in there," Bolt said, staring at the wall, his chest rising with every breath. Flipping on his heels, he waved us onward. I moved up next to him, my eyes shifting constantly, more trash around one bend, the next a dam of discarded desks. The structure was a frickin' obstacle course.

Sean barely made a noise walking in reverse with his back to us, both hands gripping his Glock Killer.

"Hold on," Bolt whispered.

We'd stopped just inches shy of a hallway intersection. We'd passed two others before going down another hallway, both vacant of anything living that I could see, just more debris and filth. I pointed at my chest and moved Bolt behind me. His radar was up, for what reason I didn't have the luxury to ask. Pressing my back against the wall, I glanced down the right side of the perpendicular hallway without exposing a body part. It was a dead-end wall.

I swallowed and heard a crackle in my ear, but nothing else. I even held my breath for a moment. I had no idea if there were two drugged-out hoodlums waiting for us, aiming Uzis at the open space, or if it was nothing more than a rat sniffing around for more food.

But Bolt sensed something was there. I wasn't going to question it.

A quick glance over my shoulder, and I gave Sean a tilt of my head. Kneeling lower, I picked up two clumps of dried mud and a small rock. Squeezing the clumps in my fist, I inched forward. I took in a breath, then angled my arm away from the wall and lofted the rock high into the hallway.

Ping-ping, ping, ping!

Four quick shots. I chunked the clumps of dirt down the hall, hoping to distract, possibly blind the shooter, then I dove headfirst into the open space, spinning once, my body bouncing off the far wall. I got off one shot, clipping the asshole's shoulder. His gun dropped just as Sean lunged into the space, ramming an elbow into the guy's chin. His head bounced off concrete and he didn't move.

I jumped off the ground. "Is he alive?"

Sean rested two fingers against his neck. "Faint pulse. Unconscious. Bullet wound won't kill him, for now."

Bolt ran up next to me. "Fucking A," he said, his eyes unblinking.

"We've got to move. They probably heard the gunfire."

"This place is huge. I highly doubt—"

"This isn't a debate. You going to lead or me?"

Bolt hoofed it past me, cutting down a hallway. Sean and I followed right behind, the three of us in a steady jog, our feet low to the surface. We turned right at a dead end, then stopped in our tracks.

"Looks like the ceiling puked," Sean said.

A hairball of mangled wires and vines spewed out of the ceiling, taking up the entire path.

"Not sure if the wires are live," I said, glancing over my shoulder.

"No other way for us to get access to that room, unless we turn around and walk through those double doors," Bolt said, both hands to his head.

Out of the corner of my eye, I spotted a metal grill that had been used to cover a ventilation hole. Locating the end of an exposed wire, I tossed the plate against the wire. It fell harmlessly to the floor

"We're going through," I said, pressing my back against the wall.

Sean helped peel back the thick curtain of prickly limbs and wires. Covering my face, I leaned my body forward and pumped my legs, reminding me of pushing a tackling sled at football practice many years before.

Finally in the clear, I could feel tiny stings all over my arms and neck, a few on my face.

"You next, Bolt. Be careful. The vines are covered with tiny thorns that will cut you."

A moment later, his head bumped my shin. "I found a quicker path, one that wouldn't damage my Hollywood face."

"Okay, Hollywood, help me pull back some of these vines for Sean to get through."

Sean pushed through, but his foot got tangled in the maze of wires, and he nearly toppled into Bolt.

"What happened to your neck?" Bolt inched backward.

"You never stop asking questions," Sean said, urging us to keep moving down the hallway.

"Samantha's in the same phase, but she's six," I said.

"I just..." Bolt didn't know what to say.

"You already know too much." Sean paused, then hacked up a guttural cough. "This," he pointed to the mangled flesh on his neck, "is why I sound like my larynx was diced in a food processor."

Bolt winced, showing a grill of white and yellow teeth. I doubted he'd seen a dentist his entire life.

"Where now?" I asked.

Bolt darted down the hall, finally turning right at a dead end. He brought his finger to his mouth. "This is where we must be very quiet," he whispered.

Sean and I both moved like we were featherweights, instead of the two-hundred-plus pounds that we each carried. For being just south of sixty years of age, Sean's level of fitness was phenomenal. Then again, if my life was on the line every day like his was, the motivational factor would be automatic—at least up until the time I quit.

He can quit, can't he?

Just before I was about to trip over a small set of stairs, Sean nudged me. Long, black curtains hung from a higher ceiling. Some were ripped, all were coated with a thick film of dust, and a few had fallen to the floor around us, gray-squared linoleum.

Bolt held up a hand, moving to his hands and knees. I heard more voices, muffled, but close by. Sean and I crawled along the floor, moving around another thick curtain, and then the space opened up, aside from looking squarely at the backside of an upright piano.

Looking up, I noticed a metal rod of spotlights, or where they used to be.

"Are we on a stage?" I whispered to Bolt.

He nodded, pointing a finger toward the piano.

"*¿fue la última vez que alguien trató de llamar a Julio?*"

I traded stares with Sean as Bolt whispered to me. "Amador is asking when someone last tried calling Julio."

Scooting on my elbows, I peeked around the ancient piano, which appeared to be missing three of its four wheels. No sign of Esteban. Amador paced back and forth across a floor covered by a shredded carpet. A card table was set up off to the side, two empty fold-out chairs facing each other. Five of Amador's closest thugs were facing the opposite wall with the doors. One appeared to be Four Fingers. He must have arrived since we'd entered the back door, after he'd tried to ogle Britney back at the hotel. Either he and his hooligan friends hadn't heard the earlier shooting, or one of their colleagues had run off to check on their wounded friend. Given Amador's anger about Julio's delay in arriving with someone else, his focus wasn't on who was in the rundown building, but rather who was about to show up—that much was obvious.

A quick scan of the rectangular room, and it looked like an elementary auditorium. The stage was no more than three feet off the ground. A bank of offices with glass windows rimmed the left side of the expansive space. They appeared mostly dark. A section of the ceiling in the far right corner had caved in, just as we'd seen in the hallway and, earlier, downstairs. Vines and wires spewed into the room, giving the room an Amazon rain forest vibe. Just the thought produced more sweat.

Curling back to our little safe zone, I explained the setup. Sean asked if all five had weapons.

"Must have had a special sale at Walmart. All are carrying Uzis."

"Do you think they're waiting for Julio to bring Esteban?" Bolt asked.

Shaking my head, I said, "Doubtful. You don't need five guys with Uzis to take custody of a kid you abducted."

Sean chewed the inside of his cheek a quick moment. Twisting on the balls of his feet, he poked an eye around the piano, then angled his head upward.

"This is a setup. I'll be back." Sean crawled around the curtains before I could stop him.

"Fuck," I said.

"Where is Mr. Sean going?" Bolt splayed his arms.

"He's going to get himself killed. Us too, dammit."

I inhaled, ensuring oxygen was reaching my brain. I had no idea where Esteban was and wondered if we'd just interrupted some type of high-level drug-smuggling convention. We were outmanned and outgunned, and I couldn't let this fourteen-year-old, smartass kid to my right die, regardless of Sean's ultimate mission.

I cursed silently this time, trying to figure out a plan that wouldn't get us all killed, yet somehow would provide us an opportunity to find Esteban alive. I realized it might take something severe, somehow taking out the henchmen, then threatening Amador with his life. Hard to imagine success. I moved back to the side of the piano just as the double doors swung open.

Father Santiago, flanked by Julio and one of his buddies that we'd corralled in the alley.

I forced my eyes shut for a couple of seconds, not believing what I was seeing.

Amador spun on his heels. He twisted his head and held out his arms, every action stiff.

"Father...I, uh...what brings you to this morbid building?" Amador glanced back at Four Fingers, then to Julio, and then back to the priest.

Had that fucker, Julio, abducted Father Santiago to continue to show his allegiance to the Amador cartel? He was absolute scum.

Bolt crawled around the piano next to me. He started to mouth something I couldn't understand, all the while lifting his shoulders and shaking his head.

"I come in peace," the Father said, approaching Amador with his arm in a sling from the earlier scrap.

"He's naïve if he thinks he's going to convince Amador to stop the killing and tell him where Esteban is," I whispered to Bolt.

I pulled my pistol out of my waistband, still pissed at Sean for leaving us. We couldn't let the priest get killed. I knew Amador wouldn't hesitate in making him another example that he could use to flaunt his power and intimidation.

The Father stopped about six feet in front of Amador, who studied him. "Why are you here?" He truly seemed puzzled, if not confused.

"To hold a calm discussion," the Father said in his normal pleasant tone.

I braced for a violent reprisal. Lifting up to my forearms, I prepped my body to lunge off the stage and take out as many of the bad guys as possible before I got hit. I could only hope that Sean would jump in and cover me.

"Where is this so-called El Jefe?" Amador asked, turning his head to Julio.

The Father meandered to his right, glancing at the rubble around him. "I understand that the L-FARC group has been using this facility as part of their training."

What did he just say? Wondering where this was going, I traded a quick glace with Bolt, his face turning paler every second.

Amador clapped his hands twice, and no one moved. "What has this world come to?" He turned to his minions, then twirled to face the priest, who ambled about like he was window shopping.

"I'd been thinking all along that a member of the Trujillo family had returned to the Dominican, seeking vengeance, vying to gain control of this country, stealing from me, killing my people." Amador thumped his chest.

"You, Father Santiago, you are El Jefe!" His voice bounced off the walls.

Bolt grabbed my shoulder. Shifting my eyes, I could see his jaw hanging open. I knew he must be devastated. It was hard to imagine. Impossible.

Silence for a few seconds. I could see Amador's chest rise and fall with each breath. His men traded stares, nervously shuffling their feet. Four Fingers crossed himself, then aimed his gun toward the Father.

The Father cast a gaze on Amador, holding up a finger. "There are consequences for every action that is taken."

"Do you hear this, gentlemen?" Amador glanced behind him. I ducked my head lower, hoping he didn't spot me.

"I am going to Hell. That is a fact, and I cannot reverse it," Amador said, his hands clasped behind his back. "So your spiritual threats won't work on me. But you...you are nothing more than a fucking hypocrite. Are there no more good people left in this world?" He released a chuckle, then brought his fist to his nose and sniffed twice.

Suddenly, the swivel doors popped open. Britney!

"What the—?" Bolt said.

Instinctively, I pushed up from the floor, but Bolt pulled me back.

"Alisa, my dear, what bring you to the outskirts of Santo Domingo?" Amador wandered a few steps, his face coiled in confusion.

Wearing tight jeans and heels that sounded more solid than a baseball bat bouncing off the linoleum, Britney marched across the floor like a woman possessed, her eyes focused on one man in the room. Without slowing her pace one bit, she walked up to Amador and smacked his face, then jerked her knee into his crotch.

Four Fingers started laughing, until he got the cold stare from his boss. Amador twisted his head, adjusting his jaw. As he coiled his arm back to hit her, I rose from my stance, ready to jump into the fray—feeling protective of the woman who'd once loved me and almost killed me.

No one looked in my direction as I took a step, unsure if I should fire a warning shot or simply try to take out thug number one. Amador swung his arm—but it was blocked by the muzzle of Julio's rifle.

"No," Julio said.

"You dare to stand up to Miguel Amador? You have just signed your death certificate, *mi amigo*. Kill him. Now!" he shouted toward his guards.

Britney lifted a gun at his forehead. "I'm El Jefe, mother fucker."

He chuckled once.

I crouched down, trying to process what I'd just heard. The schoolteacher, who had professed her love to Juan, her desire to save his son…how could she be the person everyone feared?

"You think it's funny. So do I," she said in her normal accent.

"What happened to your British accent?"

"It was an act. I fooled you and everyone else on this island. I funneled money through the school and used it to fund a business that competes against yours. The profit margins are just insane. But you couldn't deal with a little competition."

"You stole from me," he said, his face sweating bullets.

"I took advantage of opportunities given to me in the marketplace, just like any other entrepreneur. But you had to make it personal," she said.

I could feel my teeth grinding, as flames of air spewed through my nostrils. She'd fooled me. Again.

"Now, your thugs over there are going to put down their guns and lie on the ground face down."

"Julio, why?" Amador asked.

"El Jefe has true power and she respects me. That is why."

Suddenly, the ceiling collapsed near the vines and wires, Sean falling on top of another man. They both grunted as they bounced off the surface.

Ping.

Someone fired, people hit the ground, and Uzis went off everywhere.

Nineteen

Pushing Bolt back behind the piano, I could hear a cacophony of bullets bouncing wildly all over the expansive room. I led with my gun, my head on a swivel. At ten o'clock, I spotted Four Fingers. I took aim and a bullet pierced his temple just before I fired. He crumpled to the ground.

Screaming to my right. I flipped, saw a man on the floor slapping and pawing at Sean. The CIA operative connected with a jab to his nose, stunning the man. Sean then wedged a knife into the chest, yanking it downward. The man twitched, then fell from his knees onto the floor, digging the blade deeper.

I leaped off the stage as one of Amador's thugs took aim at the Father, who held up his arms. I fired a single shot, and it punctured his shoulder, blood pouring like a water fountain. The bodyguard flailed, then fell to the ground, groaning and holding his arm.

Out of the corner of my eye, I saw Bolt racing into one of the offices. *Dammit, he's going to get hit by a wayward bullet.*

Another Amador thug rushed the defenseless Father and bounced the butt of his gun off his head. The Father fell straight back to the ground. He didn't budge. He was lifeless.

In a dead run, I got to the pair before the thug looked up and swung my gun into his jaw. He fell like a tree. I heard wicked laughter and flipped my head right. Amador had somehow wrestled the gun away from Britney and now held it against her head. Over his shoulder, as both sides took each other down, Sean bull-rushed Julio. The pair slammed into the card table.

I raised my gun and fired. Amador fell into Britney, who looked up at me as Amador's blood smeared down her white shirt.

A man growled, and I turned to see Julio's buddy coming right at me, firing round after round from his handgun. Bullets whizzed by my head. No time to raise my gun, I lunged for the thug's arm as he ran right into me. We went to ground hard, but I refused to let go. He kicked and kneed me, then dug his teeth into my shoulder.

"Mother—" I started to yell.

Throwing my arm downward, I felt one of his teeth penetrate my skin. Blood went everywhere as I reached for his jaw. His tooth was embedded in my skin. I got off four body shots and an uppercut to his glass jaw, and he was out.

Looking over my shoulder, a ham-sized fist slammed into my eye before I knew what hit me.

"Stop!" Bolt yelled, running straight for the thug.

The man turned his gun toward my little friend. I lunged at him just as bullets fired. I landed on top of the man and saw blood oozing down my chest. I forced out a breath and pushed off his body. His eyes rolled into the back of his head, and I knew he'd been hit, not me. Sean must have killed him.

Turning back around, Britney used a roundhouse kick to send Sean's gun flying to the floor, then she grabbed Bolt around the neck in one smooth move.

Her eyes had an evil, almost possessed sparkle. "Britney, it's over. Everyone is dead, or halfway there. Stop and put your gun down."

"Booker, you more than anyone should know that it's never over. Do you hear the fat lady singing?" She put a hand to her ear then released a wicked laugh. "I didn't think so."

"It's Bolt. You can't hurt him."

"For me and my survival, I will hurt anyone I need to."

Sean took a step in her direction.

"That wouldn't be wise, dear old Dad." She laughed again. "You don't think I know? I have contacts, more than you'll ever know."

"Dammit, Britney, you promised!" I eyed Bolt, who looked up at Britney, his infatuation with her now nothing more than pure fear.

"Booker, Sean, think about what we could do together. We could rule this entire island. No one could stop us."

"You've already soiled the mind of a priest, and now you think you can brainwash us?"

"Father Santiago was nothing more than a pawn. He thinks he was leading me, but I led him like a dog on a leash, like every other male whose tongue licks the ground I walk on."

Suddenly, just below Britney's feet, the Father leaped upward, a gun in his hand, and jabbed it at the base of her skull.

"The queen bitch even turns on a man of God. Well, I don't die so easily. Your punishment for betraying me will be death. What's the saying? Let it be written, let it be said."

She winced.

"No más. No más. No más!"

A teenage boy, covered with bruises and bloody cuts, yelled from behind Sean. Just then, Bolt swung his left leg upward and cracked the Father right between the legs. Britney pulled away as I jumped for both of them. As we hit the ground, a gun fired.

Britney rolled onto her chest, while the father curled into a ball.

I scooted over to Britney and turned her over. Both hands covered her face. She was in tears. Looking over my shoulder, blood pooled around the priest.

Valdez ran through the double doors as sirens blared in the distance. "Mr. Booker, Bolt, are you okay?"

"Esteban...he saved our lives."

I watched Bolt run over to his new friend and hug him.

Beneath me, Britney cried uncontrollably.

I said, "We've got El Jefe. No more killing. No more."

Twenty

Booker,

As you might have guessed, I'm not great at doing goodbyes. I feel guilty, and it just doesn't go well. But I didn't want you to feel what you've felt the last thirty years. I'm not running away from you or your mother. I'm just doing my job. The agency is sending me on another assignment. It's better if I don't tell you where.

The last few days have been gut-wrenching, trying to reunite an abducted kid with his father. Through this experience, I got to know the real Booker Truman Adams, who's driven by a higher calling to do what's right. I'll never forget this time we spent together. You are a great man and a great father.

I love you, son.

Sean (Dad)

Looking out on to the Belo Garden across Commerce Street in downtown Dallas, a dog broke away from its owner and chased a frantic squirrel toward a tree. I stuffed the mangled piece of paper back in my pocket. I'd originally found the note slipped under my door at Lupe's brownstone the day after we'd found Esteban. I wasn't surprised, given his nomadic existence and job demands. I knew he'd made his life choices. No one had held him hostage or coerced him into continuing his work as a CIA operative, an assassin for hire nonetheless. But knowing, after all these years of resentment and anger, meant everything to me. Knowing that he cared. Knowing what kind of man he was. Knowing the sacrifices he'd made to make the world a safer place. Not just for me, but for thousands…no, millions of people.

And, yes, for me too.

A hand patted my back.

"Are you nervous?

Turning to face Henry, as assistant district attorney for Dallas County, his power red tie made him look like he was running for office. Not just any office, but something at the federal level. The suit fit my old college buddy quite well, considering we were hunkered down in the corner meeting room of the Earle Cabell Courthouse. The federal building housed, among other agencies, Health and Human Services, US Court of Appeals Fifth Circuit, and the US Attorney's Office.

"Doing okay. Much better than he is." I gestured toward Bolt, the only person sitting at a twelve-person table, his hands glued together while his thumbs twirled. The nearly-fifteen-year-old Dominican Republic native looked straight ahead, a solemn expression covering his face.

"Looks like he just lost his best friend. Strange not to see him happy, given everything you're doing for him. Teens. Hard to predict, huh?"

I nodded. Henry's version of "everything" related to strings being pulled to expedite Bolt's immigration to the US and eventual citizenship, as well as his guardianship, at least until he turned eighteen. Of course, I knew who'd pulled the strings, but I couldn't tell my secret to anyone.

I recalled our recent flight back to Dallas, Bolt's first-ever plane trip. He finally had a chance to explain at least some of his early life.

Bolt had no memories of his parents. He'd been told that they left him when he was just two years old, although his dad tried to sell him to a dealer just to get his daily fix in. As the story goes, the dealer wouldn't take him, said he wasn't worth that much to his business. Bolt was tossed around like a runaway pet up until he was seven, at which time he decided to take ownership of his life, everything from how to feed himself, where to sleep, how to survive the scam artists and perverts, to how to make it in this world.

"It's really not that big of a deal," I said as my partner, Alisa, approached us in the corner. "The kid needed a home, an education, a chance to make something of his life. If I didn't do this, I'm not sure he would have lived to see his eighteenth birthday."

Alisa squeezed my upper arm, her amber eyes contrasting with her dirty-blond, curly locks. I could feel an awkward sense of attraction with her. Before I'd left, we'd shared a...moment. It had been unpredictable, yet not totally unexpected, if those two could coexist in a relationship.

Relationships.

That term usually lit a firecracker under me. I dated pretty well, but I failed miserably at relationships.

"After everything we went through with my little sister, I'm surprised the teenager thing didn't scare you away."

"I thought about it. Hell, I've thought about what life will be like when Samantha hits that age. But that's more about me dealing with it. Growing up in those years is awkward at best. Speaking of..."

Samantha, dressed in her purple and white polka dot Sunday dress and matching shoes and headband, barreled into me, then squeezed my waist. I winced slightly, my ribs still on the mend, but I didn't want her to know that she'd hurt me. "Dad, what does it mean to be a legal guard? I couldn't understand

everything G-Nan and Uncle Charlie were talking about."
Missing teeth still created a hissing sound every so often.

I glanced over at Momma and Uncle Charlie, who had just
been interrupted by Henry's girlfriend and my former stalker,
Cindy. That girl had never met a person, or a fence post, she
couldn't force to listen to her nonsensical babbling. But she was
Henry's significant other, becoming more significant every day,
so I suppressed my natural instincts to put a bag over her head
and tried to be friendly.

Kneeling down, I let Samantha lean against my leg. She
crossed her arms while tapping the toe of her shoe to the floor.
"Legal guardian. It just means that I'm responsible for making
sure Sebasten is safe, has a roof over his head, and is being taken
care of."

"So you don't have to guard him?"

I looked up at Alisa and Henry, smiling. "No, Mittens, I don't
need to be his guard, although I'm hoping he feels secure for the
first time in his young life. I just want to make sure he gets to
school every day and help him figure out what he wants to do
with his life."

"Daddy, I think being in the BeginAgain Republic has hurt
your memory," she whispered, glancing around with no idea her
volume was just as loud as before. "You can't call me Mittens
anymore. I'm not a baby."

I nodded, but let her see some disappointment in my
expression.

"Okay, you can call me that in private. Deal?"

We swatted a high five.

"So, does all this formal stuff mean I'm going to have a big
brother?"

I wondered if this would come up, knowing her mother
would surely share her opinion.

"Kind of, yes. You know, Samantha, families are formed more by who really cares about you the most. Like Aunt Alisa and Uncle J."

She nodded, biting her lower lip, then darted off, running up to Bolt.

"I hope you get to be my brother. That would be cool for you. Me too."

The massive door opened and Justin, my best friend since high school, peeked his head inside. "Fooled ya, didn't I?"

He was met with a few moans. We'd been in wait mode since we arrived at the courthouse almost three hours earlier.

"So, the authorities in the Dominican haven't been able to find this nomad who helped you find Esteban and take down Amador and Britney," Henry said, as Justin joined our conversation.

"Not surprising. He seemed like a loner."

"So we're supposed to believe some homeless guy randomly steps in and puts his life on the line against a bunch of lethal drug smugglers? Seriously, Booker, we're not naïve. There is more to this story."

Sadly, I couldn't share the details of our dramatic search and rescue of Esteban with my friends, even those I'd known for over half my life. Even worse, I couldn't share what I'd learned with Momma, to give her a peace that I finally felt. But as I'd been told, I couldn't put more people at risk.

"Have you gone to visit...uh, *her* in jail?" Justin asked as he flopped his ponytail over his collared shirt.

"I can say her name. Britney. See?"

"So, have you?" Justin asked with a bit too much enthusiasm.

"She's put in a formal request to meet with you seven times," Henry added. "That just doesn't happen. Do you guys have some unfinished business?"

A quick glance at Alisa. "I—"

"Don't tell me, what happens in DR, stays in DR?" A wrinkled smile covered Justin's face.

He was partially right, although I couldn't admit it. "Hardly. It was sickening to see the lies and betrayal, not to mention the brutal violence. We're lucky to be alive," I said. "I'm just glad that Esteban was reunited with his father, and I was able to meet my clients' objective—to catch their son's killer. She just happened to be my ex-girlfriend."

Alisa balled up a fist and punched me lightly in the ball of my shoulder socket. Six months ago, it would have sent splintering pain throughout my throwing arm. This time, she purposely held back.

"It's been kind of strange not having you around."

"Is that your way of saying you missed me?" I couldn't help but grin.

Curling a lock of hair around her ear, she shuffled her shoes off the carpet. "I...well, it's just been different."

"Sorry I didn't call. I had a lot going on."

"No problem. Nothing I couldn't handle."

I touched my hand to the side of her face, brushing a loose curl out of her eyes. "You think we need to hold a Booker & Associates offsite meeting? You know, just to review our cases, billing, potential clients?"

A warm smile washed across Alisa's face. "Anywhere except The Jewel," she said, referring to Justin's bar, of which the second floor was home to our small office.

"How about I find a special place? Just the two of us." The words spilled out before I knew better. I didn't want to cross that line. Or had I already?

"I'll bring my computer. A working dinner," she said with a wink. She'd just bailed me out, knowing how I handled these types of things. Not well.

A few seconds later, the bailiff came in and said, "He's made his decision. He'd like to speak with you. All of you, apparently." The old guy grimaced, as if we were wild animals and he'd be left to clean up our collective mess.

An hour later, our procession exited the judge's chambers, but not before he gave us one piece of advice. "Borders are nothing more than imaginary lines." The silver-haired man lowered his readers, leaning forward. "We're all human, no better or worse than anyone else. All of you here before me have taken an oath to help this young man, Sebasten, adjust to his new life, help him grow into a productive member of society. Be mindful that he will always be part of your family. And family always trumps everything else."

Laughter and hugs all around, as our large group spilled into the open space, a bank of windows ahead of us that highlighted the downtown skyline on a warm, muggy July day.

"Booker, darlin'," Momma split through Henry and Cindy, finding me and Bolt leaning on the railing, just staring outside. "I wanted you and Sebasten—"

"It's Bolt, G-Nan. That's the name given to me by Mr. Booker. Bolt."

"Okay, Bolt it is. I spoke to my old boss at your namesake high school—"

Bolt scrunched his eyes.

"I'm not that important. I'll fill you in later," I assured him, and then to Momma, "You were saying?"

"I think I can get Bolt a scholarship if he's interested in an education centered around the arts."

Bolt splayed his arms wide and hugged her. "You are so kind. That means so much that you would go to the trouble."

I tried to imagine Bolt hanging out with the Bohemian crowd. He seemed more like a budding entrepreneur type, but then again, I didn't want to pigeonhole his life at age fourteen.

"Mr. Booker, have I shared my thoughts about some opportunities that could...how do you say...complement your business at Booker & Associates?" He stuck a hand inside his khaki pants.

Here comes the sales pitch.

Alisa and Justin pulled up next to us as Bolt continued his diatribe about how he could help us add to our bottom line.

I finally broke in. "You might be the next Perot or Vanderbilt, but for now you're going to start learning about Faulkner and Poe, and the periodic table, and the Pythagorean theorem."

"Oh joy. Sounds like fun," he said, raising an eyebrow.

I peered out the windows, thinking about everything I'd experienced in the last few weeks. Exhaling, my lungs emptied like never before. I felt different, possibly more settled.

I realized today probably wouldn't have happened had Dad not reentered my life. Dissolving the chip on my shoulder had helped me open my eyes and my heart. While I couldn't tell anyone else, I finally allowed an emerging thought to permeate my soul.

I love you, Dad.

Excerpt from BOOKER – Dead Heat (Volume 6)

One

The scent of urine clawed at his nostrils, as if his face had been encased in a used litter box. Ignoring the putrid stench, he lifted his chest, inhaling a deep dose of air. His breathing cadence didn't slow down a bit. In fact, it was on the rise. He couldn't stop it, even if he wanted to.

The pitter-patter of raindrops bouncing nearby off three plastic garbage bags was the only thing that drowned out the timpani of his thumping heart. A line of ugly trees, nothing more than overgrown weeds from thirty-odd years ago, cast jagged shadows across his face. A few matted leaves fluttered downward, instantly pasted to the pavement. A yellow bug-zapping light five doors away in the back alley provided the only illumination on a night where the dark October skies, thick with a wet fog, hugged the tops of buildings.

The morbid setting only made the man feel that much more restricted. He took in another gulp of air, his chest suddenly feeling like four cinder blocks were crushing his lungs.

Was the oxygen deprivation brought on by anxiety? He was about to cross a line that couldn't be uncrossed. By taking this step, his life would forever change.

The more he thought about what he was about to do, the more his breathing increased, and he became lightheaded. Wobbling slightly, he braced himself against the smooth bark of a wet tree. He reached down and tore open one of the garbage bags, found a filthy paper sack, and inhaled until his eyes refocused and the dizzying sensation subsided.

Steadying himself, his size-eleven shoe shuffled against the pebbled surface, kicking a garbage bag, the overflow from a stuffed dumpster to his right. A black cat and three tiny kittens jumped out from behind the bags. He could just make out their annoyed whines as they scurried between his legs and through the cluster of trees and grass, heading toward a building that was going through a refurbishment.

Halloween was less than a week away, but the irony of seeing a throng of black cats on this night—a night when the shadow of bad luck would engulf an unsuspecting victim—did not go unnoticed. Brushing a fist across his nose that dripped with water, he had a second thought, a more advanced thought. All of...*this* had nothing to do with luck. He only stood in the cold rain, a soaked, gray hoodie drooping across his forehead, for one reason. Redemption. An appropriate response to the acts carried out by others—and there were so many out there.

He sniffled, focusing his gaze at the metal door with the black number thirty-seven painted over a layer of rust. Checking his phone, the time approached midnight. Just then, the back door burst open, the metal knob smacking the white cinder-block wall. The man's body tensed. Keeping his head bowed, he raised his eyes. Live music and hollers invaded the empty alley as a woman with tight curls and even tighter stretch pants waddled in his direction.

Realizing she wasn't his intended prey, he eased his torso back slightly, hoping she wouldn't spot him.

"Eh," she said.

Was that directed at me? he wondered. His ears perked up, and his body prepared to launch forward.

"Nobody does a fucking thing around this bar, except me," the woman said, slinging a small bag of trash on top of the heap.

He could see her bending over, picking up a larger bag of trash, then grunting out loud as she heaved it with everything she had. Slowly, it rolled off the perch and fell to the wet pavement at her feet.

"Screw this shit. Someone else can deal with this smelly garbage."

He heard her shiver out loud, followed her rubber-sole shoes crunching gravel in a quick pace. Then the door slammed shut, taking with it a screaming rendition of "Big Balls" by AC/DC.

Wiping dripping water off his face, he released an annoyed breath. Had his research and preparation gone awry? He'd planned this event for weeks. He could feel his jaw tighten, his lips pressed against his teeth.

He closed his eyes for a moment, allowing the popping sounds of the rain to calm his frayed nerves. He knew that no one could match his tenacity, his incessant ability to push through adversity and reach his intended goal. Nodding, he'd figure out what happened—or didn't. He contemplated shifting his focus, possibly teaching a lesson to the person who screwed him over.

But it didn't feel right. He wasn't a vindictive person. He was honorable and could deal with the asshole another way.

Bam!

The back door smacked the building again, but twice as hard as last time, and then it closed. The man heard shuffling steps.

"Who the hell shuts down a bathroom for maintenance on a Saturday night?" a young man's voice said, slurring his last couple of words.

It was the voice he'd been waiting for. An off-duty police officer, actually *the* off-duty police officer. The man in the hoodie felt his pulse sprint. He had to dig his nails into the soft bark of the soaked tree just to keep himself from jostling around.

He heard a zipper and then a stream of pee echoing off the metal dumpster.

"Ahh, that's more like it," the officer said to himself.

The man in the hoodie eased his neck forward and saw the athletic twenty-something officer with cropped hair and a red sweater turn back to the building. Creeping two quiet steps, the man lunged over the back of the younger person, immediately gripping him in a headlock. The officer gagged while flailing his arms. One of his thrashing hands snagged the man's hood, pulling it over his face, momentarily blocking his vision.

"You don't know when to give up," the man grunted.

He rammed his knee into the officer's kidney, and the officer's body crumpled, his arms now swatting air. The man dragged him back under the cover of the trees, ensuring no one would interrupt this officer's final few seconds of life. Knowing he probably had just a few moments before one of the officer's buddies came out to check on him, the man in the hoodie set his feet, reestablished his grip, and then snapped the officer's neck, killing him instantly.

He let go and watched the dead body fall to the trashy pavement.

"Officer Miller, I think your crew is going to have a hard time putting you back together. You and your do-gooder fudge buddies act like the Avengers, thinking you're taking down all evil, but all you really do is let evil slip right through your fingers. Not anymore. I won't take it."

The man looked over his shoulder before taking two steps toward his escape route through the other side of the trees. He stopped in his tracks and turned to glance at the dead officer. It had been too easy, not as fulfilling as he'd envisioned. Suddenly, a torrent of fury overtook his body, and he kicked the officer in the face, the toe of his metal-plated boot connecting with the cadaver's chin and nose. He continued the relentless assault, moving down the body, slamming the officer's ribs and back. Repeatedly, the man in the hoodie punished the lifeless body until he finally broke out in a sweat.

Standing over his first victim, his breath pumped out smoke like an old-fashioned train. But he finally felt a sense of accomplishment.

The journey to emancipation had begun—freeing his spirit from the shackled, misguided culture that surrounded him every day.

Two

Leaping a good three feet off the ground, the fifteen-year-old soccer phenom headed the black and white ball away from his opponent. He chased the ball down, juked two defenders—nearly breaking their ankles—then unleashed a frozen rope toward the net.

I would have been pumping my fist in the air had I not noticed Samantha, my curious six-year-old, meandering onto the field, chasing bubbles that she'd just blown into the air. Darting forward, I snatched her off the field just in front of a diving goalie. Thankfully, the hooking laser beam, coming off the foot of the best teenage soccer play I'd ever seen play in person, just missed Samantha and the outstretched arms of the goalie.

I heard the ripple of twine behind me as I jogged off the playing field with Samantha hooked under my arm.

"What's the big deal, Daddy?" Samantha, her feet now standing on the grass, opened the purple bottle and blew out more bubbles, the breeze blowing the suds directly into my face.

"Way to go, Bolt! Whoop, whoop!" My business partner and new date mate, Alisa, whirled her fist in the air, cheering on the kid who'd only been in the states for four months, but had already established a nice foundation of friends while also excelling in his favorite sport.

I released a quick chuckle while swatting away the soapy bubbles and leaned down to my little girl. She was decked out in purple sweats and chomping purple bubble gum. I tried to be stern. "You could have gotten hurt out there. Those kids are big."

She stopped what she was doing and rested her cute hand on my shoulder. I noticed her nails half-covered in chipped, pink polish. "Daddy, I know you might not be prepared for this yet, but I'm kind of growing up, you know. So, I know what's around me. You don't need to worry so much."

"Heads up!" someone yelled from the field, and I turned to see the ball whizzing over my shoulder.

"I'll get it." Samantha darted away, chasing the ball through Edsall Park, just down the street from my condo off Bryan in North Dallas.

Rising to my feet, I nudged Alisa. "Can you believe Eva wasting money on manicures with Samantha?"

Just as a gust of wind lifted her blond curls, she made a fist and punched my shoulder joint. I think it was her way of flirting. "Come on, Booker. It's one of those women bonding things that you just don't question."

Extending my arms, I couldn't help myself. "Samantha's not a woman. She's only a first-grader, for Christ's sake," I said with a bit of attitude.

"Don't look now, but your little girl is growing up fast. In case you haven't noticed—"

Wham!

The soccer ball had just bounced off the back of my head. I heard an infectious giggle as I glanced over my shoulder.

"Sorry, Daddy. I was trying to kick it over you. You're just too tall," she said, unable to corral her laughter.

"Hey, Sammy, can you kick the ball over here? I need to set up a corner kick," Bolt called out.

Biting her lower hip, my not-so-little girl hopped once, then booted the ball as hard as she could.

"You got air," Alisa said, jogging over to high-five Samantha.

"I got air," Samantha responded, zooming over to the edge of the soccer field. She smacked hands with Bolt and then steered her airplane arms toward the swing set.

Bolt was known as Sebasten when our lives first collided in Santo Domingo, Dominican Republic, a few months back. After barely surviving a cab ride from the airport into the city, I had stood on the sidewalk and watched a cabbie peel away from the curb with far too much of my money, considering the back door had flown off mid-ride and nearly took me with it.

Sebasten must have thought I was a naïve tourist—who wouldn't have, given my initial island experience?—and then engaged me in some type of pity story, just long enough for me to take my eyes off my duffel bag. The little shyster snatched my bag and took off running faster than I could say "Dominican Republic scam." I chased after him and was fortunate to have the kid glance over his shoulder toward me just as a bellman crossed his path with a full load of luggage.

With his ego bruised more than his body, the homeless, smooth-talking teenager made it his life's mission to help me and someone very close to me take down a drug-smuggling killer and my ex-girlfriend, who was an even more dangerous killer hiding in plain sight on the Caribbean island.

Given the speed in which Sebasten's legs and mouth moved, it was natural for me to nickname him Bolt—as in "fast as a lightning bolt," or better yet, Usain Bolt.

In the end, I was unsure that Bolt would live to see his eighteenth birthday on that island, and I knew in my heart I couldn't just leave him there. With the help of someone special, I became his legal guardian and he began the process of becoming a US citizen.

"No puedes dejar que el cuadro de defender. Debes ser fuerte," Bolt pointed toward the middle of the field just before he kicked the ball.

"What did he say?" Alisa whispered into my ear, her hands clutching my biceps. Her Spanish was worse than mine.

"Something about a box and strong."

"Ah."

The pick-up game, which included Bolt, a number of friends from his new school—North Dallas High School—and his club soccer team, moved to the opposite end of the field.

With just a few spotty clouds dotting a blue sky on a cool Sunday morning, I scratched my goatee and took in the whole scene. I was a lucky guy. Our little private investigation firm, Booker & Associates, had just celebrated its one-year anniversary, and we were actually solvent and growing. We, of course, included Alisa, whose verve to dig in and sift through mounds of research had been the key cog in our little machine. We'd come a long way since we first met in Austin twelve years ago. But here in the last few months, we'd actually taken a step I never thought would happen. We were dating, although many of the dates usually turned into case discussions. Still, it had been easy, like the cool breeze blowing across the field. No strings and no pressure. Just my kind of relationship.

"Coach move Bolt up to varsity yet?" Despite her lime green sunglasses, Alisa used her hand as a visor to block the sun, staring down the soccer field.

"Just last week."

"Why didn't you tell me?"

Another faux punch to the shoulder joint.

"You're getting frisky," I said, turning slightly her way.

"I'm not a horse." She snorted out loud as soon as the words left her mouth, then shoved me as the laughter continued between both of us.

This was the side of Alisa that jazzed me the most. Carefree, silly even, yet a heart of gold. Not to say she didn't have an intensity about her...well, more like a don't-fuck-with-me attitude. Frankly, it made her more attractive. I didn't view her as a fragile little butterfly, and she never asked me to be her Mr. Perfect.

Fortunately, she'd rolled with the punches when I returned from the Dominican Republic, instantly taking a liking to my multilingual sidekick. It wasn't hard to do, given Bolt's effervescent personality. She had joined Momma, Uncle Charlie, and other friends in the collective effort to care for and raise Bolt. And I soon realized I needed every one of them.

Who would have thought that raising a fifteen-year-old boy would take so much effort? Well, probably any adult in the free world who was responsible for the well-being of a teenager. But most of them got there gradually. I made the giant leap in one day at the Federal Building in downtown Dallas. Not that I had any regrets. I just didn't fully comprehend what it took to raise a teenage boy.

My little Samantha hadn't prepared me for the endless number of things that required my time and input. Outside of the countless rides to and from soccer practice and school events, the biggest and most important revolved around Bolt's education. I had to work with school administrators and each of his seven teachers to ensure they had a solid plan to catch Bolt up with the rest of the kids his age. I knew once he caught up, he'd blow right by them, just like he was doing this morning on the soccer field. But that required a time-intensive effort to convince him it was a building-block process. He couldn't master the fun stuff—which was, in his opinion, anything that got him closer to understanding how to run a business—until he mastered the basics. While he grudgingly accepted the concept, the execution of the plan became more like pulling a mule with a tattered rope...on a weekly basis.

"Heads up!" I heard someone yell.

I ducked without looking, pulling Alisa down with me.

"That wasn't a surface-to-air missile, you know?" She tugged at the knees of her jeans, damp and darkened from the patch of mud, a result of the overnight rain. She tilted her head, her lips drawing a straight line.

"Oops. It was just instinct." I gave her a half-smile and raised my hands as if her stare fired a lethal laser directly into my chest.

Alisa rolled up her sleeves, curling her full lips together. With no warning, she jabbed her fingers into my ribcage, attempting to tickle me. Her hand lingered for a moment.

"Damn, I forgot what good shape you are in," she said, leaning closer while arching her eyebrows.

"Eh. I guess I work at it, but I've been in better shape."

"Not with me." She looked away for a brief second. "Did I just say that?"

She was referring to my torrid relationship with Britney, the ex-girlfriend-turned-killer, who had the looks of an international model and the venom of a snake.

"You did," I said, watching Samantha and one of Bolt's friends chase down the loose ball. Alisa and I hadn't crossed that magical intimacy line, mostly because I knew it came with unspoken expectations. Hell, after watching Britney morph into Jack the Ripper, I knew my psyche had been scarred. Alisa, though, had grown on me, like a long-time friend. We could rib each other and still share a fun night out, ending it with kiss.

A few seconds of awkward silence was interrupted by a charging Samantha, who was running from Bolt's female bestie, Rio.

"I'm gonna get ya, Samantha," the tomboy said with a smile, as Samantha whirled around my legs and headed toward Bolt.

"My big brother will protect me." Her giggle bounced to the cadence of each step.

Samantha had insisted on calling Bolt her brother since day one of our new family arrangement. He only thought it was the coolest thing in the world.

"We gonna play soccer or patty cake?" another boy asked from inside the goal box.

As opposed to kicking the ball over to Bolt, who was standing at the corner of the field, Rio ran the ball over and handed it to him, as if it were a personal gift. She jostled his hair that nearly covered his eyes, then shot him a wink before running back into position on the field.

I felt an elbow jab my ribcage, and I turned toward my partner. "You really like beating me up, don't you?"

As usual, she ignored me. "Do you think Rio likes Bolt...you know, as more than just a friend?"

Suddenly, a Bruno Mars song filled the air. "Bolt's been playing with my phone," I said, as I pulled it out of my pocket and viewed the screen. "Not on my contact list."

"Get it. Might be a new client," Alisa said.

I nodded. "This is Booker," I said, hoping it wasn't another random solicitation call from Pocatello, Idaho.

"Booker, Scott Ligon."

Covering the phone, I whispered, "Ligon, DPD Police Chief" to Alisa, then turned away from the game.

Scratching the back of my head, I could only think of two reasons why I would receive a phone call from the top dog at the Dallas Police Department. Either I'd pissed off one of his star detectives on a case I was working and he wanted to warn me to stay clear of his treasured employees, or he called to let me know someone I'd known when I worked on the force had died.

"Scott," I said, refusing to address him with a formal title. "What can I do for you?"

"I need your services, Booker. I want to hire you."

Three

Downshifting my Saab into second gear, I motored up the fourth-floor ramp in a parking garage at the corner of North Akard and Ross. Being Sunday, I wasn't surprised to see the entire level empty. As instructed by the chief, I coasted to the southwest corner and turned the car into the second spot from the end. I sat there with my engine running, contemplating why he would want to hire me, someone who'd been excommunicated from the rank and file, all because of the *incident*.

While working as a DPD beat officer a little more than a year ago, my partner Paco and I responded to a call around midnight behind a bar off lower Greenville. What ensued over the next half hour altered the course of my life. I witnessed a fellow cop abuse a homeless guy for no reason. When I stepped in to stop it and learn more information, the veteran officer, a smart-mouthed redneck shaped like a bulldozer, sucker-punched me, then attempted to kill me and the homeless guy. Somehow, I was able to fight and claw my way out of the conflict.

The next day had felt like an even worse beating. I sat in the office of my superior officer, Sergeant Kenny Young, and listened to him try to convince me that my interpretation of the events was simply a misplaced opinion. In what appeared to be nothing more than protecting some bullshit good ol' boy code, he was essentially treating it like Ernie Sims had merely called me a name on the elementary school playground.

I couldn't let it pass, even after KY—Young's nickname—first tried to bait me by offering a future promotion to detective. After that failed to turn me, he then threatened to take away my badge. In the end, I didn't give him the satisfaction. I quit.

But as one door closed, another opened, and thus, the birth of Booker & Associates, and along with it, a freedom to pursue my dream in a way I'd never envisioned, as a private investigator.

Checking the rearview mirror, I chewed the inside of my cheek, recalling that sense of "me against the world" and the irony of Ligon now soliciting my services.

Moments later, a white SUV with extra-dark tinted windows backed into the space three spots over. The driver's window slid down, and a young guy in uniform nodded, his eyes shifting toward the back seat. I took that as my cue, and I got out of my car and opened the SUV's back door. Ligon sat on the far side.

"Booker, thank you for meeting me here. Please come in. James, you can take a walk."

The kid left the engine running and did as his boss asked, with no response.

Ligon, in khakis and a blue sweater that zipped in the front, angled his body toward me. In his early sixties, he had a chiseled chin, but my eyes gravitated to his oversized schnoz. I'd never met him in person, but he looked like he'd put on a few pounds since I last saw him on TV.

Maintaining an even gaze, I let him initiate our discussion.

Just as it appeared he was opening his jaw to talk, he pulled out a package of gum and folded a piece into his mouth. He held out the pack to me. "Want one?"

"No thanks. I kicked the habit a long time ago."

One corner of his mouth edged upward briefly as he pocketed his gum. "There's some serious shit going down out there, and I need you to find out who's behind it."

I had a million questions, so I started with the most obvious. "Describe serious shit."

"Two cops dead in the last week. Murdered." He held his gaze and didn't blink.

"Wait...I recall hearing about an officer committing suicide about a week or so ago. What was the name? Douglas?"

"Donley. Walt Donley. Fourteen-year man. But he didn't shoot himself."

"Media got it wrong, I guess." Saying it out loud, the possibility didn't seem feasible, not for such a basic fact.

"The media reported what we told them. In fact, that was the initial belief at the crime scene. Gunshot to his temple behind the wheel of his car in a field east of Dallas."

"But something changed?"

"Coroner and CSI did a full investigation. Turns out Donley had broken his finger on his right hand a few years back, but never reported the injury, since he hurt if off duty. So, he learned to shoot with his left hand. No one knew...at least not in management. Once the investigators found out and did some digging, there was no way he could have pulled the trigger with his right hand, the hand where the gun was found."

"Sounds like your team has done a thorough job of investigating. Why do you need me?"

He continued chomping his gum. "Only a few people are aware of the final, official cause of death. Me, the lead coroner, a detective, and the head of our CSI unit. We're hoping to keep it contained."

"I get it. You don't want the killer to know you're on his trail. Good strategy, if you can keep it under wraps."

The chief rubbed a thumb across his wingtips, never missing a beat on his gum-chewing exercise. I couldn't ignore the obnoxious odor—it was grape.

"Everything blew up in our face last night."

I looked away, trying to recall if I'd heard any salacious news during my morning jog. "I guess I missed it."

"We didn't get a call until after midnight. News is just now trickling out. Another cop was killed. And this one wasn't set up to look like a suicide."

"Who?"

"Younger guy, off duty. Fourth-year officer named Derrick Miller. Good kid. Just got engaged."

"Damn." Shaking my head, I could sense there was more. "Your team believes these two murders are connected."

Ligon turned and looked straight ahead, appearing to watch James walk aimlessly around the garage. His gum chewing even ceased for a second.

Swinging his head back my way, led by his nose, he calmly said, "It's complicated. Everyone still believes the first death was a suicide."

"And you can't tell them because you're worried it will be leaked to the press and the public will believe we have a cop killer on the loose."

He nodded. "Cops are people too. Some will be really frazzled by this."

I was shocked to hear him admit that.

"We'll have every acronym of the press corps descending on Dallas in less than twelve hours. Live shots around the clock with eye-candy reporters acting like every crazy-ass rumor came from a 'high-ranking' source with knowledge of the investigation. It's all bullshit."

I nodded. "And you'll never catch the guy. He'll go underground. People, especially officers, will live in constant fear because the guy would never be caught. It would die down a bit, but everyone would be on edge."

"The city would be held hostage for…" He just shook his head and spread his arms.

Ligon's response made sense, but it was odd seeing the chief of police flustered.

Shifting in my seat, I still wasn't sure this felt right…on many levels.

"You're either thinking through questions about the case or whether you should take the case at all. Am I right?" Ligon asked.

"On both accounts."

Ligon cleared his throat. "I knew this would come up, and I'm glad it did. Look, I'm not happy with the situation around your…resignation from the department. I had no knowledge of it when it went down. I hope you know that."

"Some would say the problem was institutional. You know, a cultural thing throughout the department."

"Sims is serving twenty to life of hard time in Huntsville. And I'm sure you've heard how they treat cops in prison. He's paying the price, like he should."

"That's just one man. There are others, like my former superior officer."

"Everyone has a right to their opinion, but I can sit here and stare you in the face and tell you we have a few bad seeds. A few. Just like any other group out there: priests, teachers, doctors, business people. We can't escape society, but we do our damn best to clean it up when we see it."

I thought about what I might ask in return, but after a year it all seemed pointless. Water under the proverbial bridge.

"I'm not going to ask for a public apology. I've moved on."

"Yes, you have. And you've turned out to be one hell of an investigator."

I twisted my neck. "How would you know?"

He released a quick chuckle, and his man boobs jiggled. "How would I not? You've done more for this city—saving lives, taking down bad buys—than most of my detectives combined. We owe you a debt of gratitude. *I* owe you a huge thank you…whether you take this case or not."

I thought about all of my former colleagues. My old partner, Paco, one of the most sincere guys out there, and Eva, my ex. Both were damn good cops, who did it for the right reason. There were more like them than not.

"Let's say I'm on the fence. How would this work? I typically have clients sign contracts. Not sure you want this to go through the DPD procurement process."

"I'll sign it personally, but it's got to go through my personal email account. That's one of the reasons I'm reaching out to you. We have to do everything we can to keep this under the radar."

"You don't want to negotiate a rate?"

He smirked. "I trust you. I have to. You're my best option."

Peering out the front window, I watched the driver walk heel to toe, following the straight line of a crack in the concrete parking lot. He seemed so young, probably closer to Bolt's age than mine.

"Do we have a deal?"

"Still thinking. How do I get access to information? As a PI firm, we're used to working through other means to get what we need, but sometimes that can take longer. Given the speed in which cops are dying, we don't have much time."

He held up a finger. "Glad you asked. One of our assistant DAs, Henry Cho, is a good friend of yours from college, right?"

"You ought to apply for a job at the NSA," I said with a slight grin.

"I'm thorough. I have to be," he said, still chomping the purple gum. "Cho's been authorized to provide every bit of information he has access to."

My eyes narrowed. "Henry is a good guy, a great prosecutor. I like that idea. But I thought you were trying to keep this on the down low. By including the DA's office, you just opened the door more than a crack."

"I can see why you'd think that." He paused and fixed the pleat in his khakis. "I have a special arrangement with the US Attorney's office. Gives me full authority to get what I need to find the cop killer."

"Didn't that interaction just create a bigger net? Every interaction at your level involved admins and calendar appointments." I extended a hand to the young kid walking around outside the SUV. "And drivers. And others who need to know or want to know every movement of the chief of police and the lead US Attorney out of the North Texas office."

"I thought I was thorough. But this is good, you drilling me. That's why I need you to take this case."

My forehead creased higher. "And?"

"Me and Craig—"

"Craig?"

"Sorry. The US Attorney, Craig Collins. We go way back. Went to undergrad together at A&M. Then he betrayed every Aggie out there and got his law degree at UT-Austin."

"My school," I said.

"I know. I could write your biography."

"That's disturbing."

He didn't get the sarcasm, and continued, "I ran into Craig at the downtown YMCA. We both work out there a few times a week."

I wondered how he could achieve that body by working out any more than three times a year, but I kept my thoughts to myself.

"Did you share a nice game of handball?"

"Uh…no. But he gave me the green light to bypass all formal channels."

"But—"

"That includes the DA."

"Why?"

"Like you said, when you formalize things, information—misinformation even—spreads like a west Texas wildfire."

I turned to ask him another question, and he'd just pulled something out of the side door pocket. "Here. Don't want you to use it. But at some point, you might need a Get Out of Jail Free card."

I froze for a second, then he nodded and said, "Take it."

Taking the leather-encased badge, I flipped it around, rubbing my thumb across the words written across the front. "Special Assistant to the Chief of Police, Dallas Police Department," I read out loud.

I couldn't help but feel somewhat vindicated. The leader of the department that had turned a blind eye to one of its officers attempting to murder two people was now asking me to hunt down a cop killer. Apparently, human decency was still alive, at least when it became personal. But as my Uncle Charles would say, "That and a dime might buy you a cup of coffee."

I shoved the badge into my coat pocket.

"You'll take the case?"

"Strongly considering it. What's your best guess about this cop killer? I know you have one."

"I've tossed a lot of theories around in my head. I didn't sleep at all after I got the call last night."

"I can see why."

"On the surface, I can't help but wonder if it's race related. The two guys killed were white. I'm wondering if someone is making a statement, getting back at the 'white establishment' for some type of perceived abuse, maybe to him personally."

A quick thought pinged my mind. "Are you selling me on this because you think I might be able to tap into my black roots and find out who's killing white Dallas cops?"

He closed his red-rimmed eyes briefly while shaking his head. "Chill out, Booker. You're the best out there, and you know Dallas. All of it. The good, the bad, and the ugly. You know people, and you can be discreet. That's why I hired you."

"This may not be a killing spree based upon some racial vendetta, you know. Could be someone who was falsely convicted or had run-ins with both officers, or even just a guy who's getting his jollies by killing cops, regardless of what color they are."

"You didn't let me finish earlier. I don't give a damn what color they are. I only care about one color. Blue."

"You passed," I said, grabbing the door handle.

"You were testing me?"

I ignored the question, since he already knew the answer.

I opened the door, then turned back inside. "I'll be in touch."

Four

"**H**ey, man, can I get another?" Henry raised a hand toward the owner and chief bartender at The Jewel. He tapped the hardwood next to his empty glass, his eyes apparently lost in the melted ice.

Justin, my running buddy since we both stepped onto the football field at Madison High School in South Dallas, gave a knowing nod on the other side of the bar while filling two draft beers.

A cascade of cheers came from the TV mounted on the wall in front of us, a grudge match between the Patriots and Jets. I'm not sure Henry noticed.

"You think the Jets can pull off the upset?" I asked, sipping tonic water over ice.

He picked up the tumbler, tipped it to one side, his somber expression making it seem like he'd lost his best buddy.

He didn't hear a word I said. I tried another angle. "You and Cindy still cool?"

Blinking his eyes, he snapped back into real time. "Uh...sorry. Cindy? She's cool."

Wearing jeans and a gray shirt that looked like it cost three hundred bucks, the assistant district attorney hadn't said much of anything since he'd walked into Justin's long-time watering hole an hour earlier. Over the last few years, I was more used to seeing him in a dark suit, starched white shirt, and a red power tie. But he'd always had a vivacious energy about him, not only as a prosecutor, but also as a friend. We were an unlikely pair when we first crossed paths on the campus at the University of Texas in Austin. On the surface, we looked like polar opposites.

I was the son of a proud black mother, who raised me as a single mom while she put herself through nursing school. Then she traveled the earth, nursing sick babies and wounded souls. Aside from a few sightings, my father was basically AWOL throughout most of my life...until he ambushed me in the murky woods in the Dominican Republic four months ago. I wouldn't have been any more surprised if the president of the United States had been cooking me breakfast when I awoke from my drug-induced sleep at the time. But over the next week, I got to know the man I used to call Sean, if not a less flattering term. But these days, I can proudly call him Dad, although I'm not at liberty to share anything about him or his role in life to anyone in the world.

Henry had a much more rigid upbringing than I did. The son of Chinese and Filipino parents, education overruled every other priority in his house. His mom was a lifelong educator, his dad a successful attorney who once sat on the Board of Regents at Texas Tech University.

Henry was the nerdy type, especially in college, before he'd even taken an advanced course, let alone passed the bar exam. For the first two years, I was on the roster of the Longhorns football team. I can't say I played for the Burnt Orange, because I never took the field in an actual game. I moved up to second-string quarterback when we started summer camp in my third year, but I never got any further. I was kicked off the team, my scholarship revoked, all for taking up for a geeky kid who'd been bullied by a fellow UT offensive lineman.

Realizing I couldn't afford to stay in school, I was mad as hell at my coach, the athletic director, and even myself for pissing away the opportunity.

But Henry refused to let it rest. He researched everything he could find about similar cases and situations, then he demanded a meeting with the coach and AD. That's when I saw the future Henry Cho in action, the one who'd go on to finish in the top five of his law school class, the one who would be recruited to join the Dallas County DA's office. He'd presented a remarkably convincing case that not only should I have my scholarship back, but I should also be allowed back on the team in the same spot I had before the run-in with the ogre. Henry owned that room like no one I'd seen before.

We only won half the bounty, but it was the most important half. My scholarship was reinstated, but they wouldn't let me back on the team. I still felt like the luckiest guy in Texas. Henry and I bonded through that experience, and we'd remained friends over the years.

I took another slurp of my drink just as the Jets punched in a touchdown from five yards out. "You going to tell me who peed in your corn flakes?"

"Booker, let's turn down the volume on the urine references," Justin jumped in, setting down the refreshed drink. "Here you go, Henry. Gin and tonic."

I gave Justin one of those looks, knowing he was the poster child for childish humor. "Where'd Alisa run off to?" My better half not only worked for me—actually, we'd agreed it was a partnership—but she also waited tables for Justin. The bar work helped pay her bills, and it was fairly easy to juggle the two jobs since the Booker & Associates office was fourteen steps above the main bar area.

"No need to worry about her. She'll only fire off a zinger at me," Justin said, picking up the tip from the two guys who'd just moved from the bar to a table when their dates arrived.

"Right, that's why I want to find her. Her timing is usually just as priceless as her content."

We both chuckled, and then I turned to the staircase when I heard the familiar clip of Alisa's platform shoes off the wooden steps.

Flipping back around, Justin gave me the eye, tilting his head toward Henry, whose mind appeared to be occupied with distant thoughts. I had my theories as to why, but I had to get him engaged, talking like the regular Henry.

Alisa meandered by, brushing a hand along my shoulder. I gave her a wink, then leaned in closer to Henry.

"Hey, dude, it's me. What's going on?"

Blowing out an audible breath, his eyes finally raised. "I think you know."

"Ligon?"

"It's more than that."

"Look, I know it's complicated. But frankly, I thought you'd be jazzed to work with me...in an official capacity finally."

"This is messy. On many fronts," he said, lifting his drink and taking a swig.

"As of now, I'm on the clock for Ligon and the US Attorney, so let's talk through it."

"That's part of the mess. The US Attorney, Craig Collins, is in the know, but not the district attorney, my actual boss." Henry sat up in his bar stool, his hand speaking louder than his mouth. "Do you know what's going to happen once Rick Newsome finds out?"

"I can see your concern. I had the same questions for Ligon."

"Booker, no offense, but you're in the private sector. You could have told Ligon to shove his little job offer up his ass. In fact, given how they handled the *incident*, you probably should have. But me, I've got no choice. People are lining up around the block to be my boss. It's the most popular job in the city."

He arched an eyebrow to emphasize his heavy dose of sarcasm.

Usually the one with the level head, Henry's anxiety had caught me off guard.

I sipped more of my non-alcoholic beverage, glancing at the game.

"I've never seen Ligon so rattled. He seemed almost desperate," I said, noticing Alisa's watchful eye from across the bar. "And the fact he'd already reached out to you just hours after the second *event* tells me he's not screwing around. Neither is the US Attorney."

Henry popped his fingers off my arm. "I know I took this job to put bad people behind bars. And from what Ligon told me, the guy who's...you know..." His eyes shifted left and right, then back to me. "It doesn't get much worse."

I nodded, thinking about all the questions swirling in my mind. But first I had to make sure Henry was right in the head.

"Look, I can't promise that once Newsome finds out, he won't figure out a way to fire your ass. It's how the real world works. I've learned that I can't control the assholes. But I get to choose if I work with them."

Henry looked up at me, and he huffed out a smile. "Working in the private sector has been good for you."

"Damn straight it has. Be the man, don't work for the man. I think that's how the saying goes."

"The one from a fictional drug kingpin?" Henry chuckled.

"Yeah, that one." I slurped my drink, then held it up where Justin could see an empty glass. Using one hand as a shield, he shot me the finger with the other. "Prick."

"You must be talking about Justin." Alisa had just sidled up next to me.

"Who else? You know how he can get."

"One Nut's man period? Believe me, I know," Alisa said, patting my shoulder.

Justin probably never envisioned that a helmet to his groin in the last college football game of his life would create such a lifelong opportunity for derision. It was obvious that Alisa enjoyed reminding him of his deficiency.

"Hey, Henry, just know that I've got your back. And I know you've got mine."

His lips drew a straight line. "I know, but…"

I knew the feeling, all wrapped up in the politics of the job, losing focus on the purpose of the job.

"If something happens—" I started.

"My mom and dad envisioned me being the district attorney someday. You can't do that with even a minor blemish on your record."

"What does *Henry* want to do?" Alisa asked him, picking up my glass and downing one of my pieces of ice.

We'd learned to share pretty well in the last few months.

Henry looked at me and Alisa. "You guys seem pretty happy doing the PI thing. And you're damn good at it. Maybe I'm destined to do my thing on the other side of the aisle."

"It's contagious."

"What is?" Justin said, sticking his nose in while using his towel to wipe down a wet counter.

"The One Nut disease," Alisa said with a bit of attitude.

"Really? How many times can you—"

"Crack a nut?" Alisa snorted at her quick wit.

Justin raised his towel, as if he might try to sling it at Alisa's face, but he could feel eyes on him—paying customers—and he simply walked away.

I watched Alisa circle the bar and refill my drink. I gave her a quick smile, then shifted my eyes to Henry. "You all in, or do I need to get Bolt to convince you?"

"Hey, maybe we can steer him toward the lawyer profession...put some of those compelling argument skills to work in a courtroom. He might be able to save someone's life." Alisa arched an eyebrow.

"Or win over an unsuspecting jury so his client can walk away with millions. I think his current desire of entering the entrepreneurial ranks is best for him."

"Don't forget, not all lawyers are scum," Henry said with a grin on his face. "Well, not until they turn into politicians."

It was a relief to see Henry engaged. "So, you're not going to take a month-long vacation in Belize?"

"Where have you been? I'm already thinking through our next steps," Henry said.

"Cool. Here's my first question. Remember, I start with the most obvious ones, then work my way down."

Henry leaned forward, apparently eager to get the investigative ball rolling.

I said, "Ligon is connecting the two murders because—"

"From what he told me, the first one was initially ruled a suicide. Then, after further investigation, changed to a homicide."

"Right. So, he's basing his serial cop killer theory on two murders. I'm guessing the second one wasn't made to look like a suicide?"

"Nothing close. It was a brutal mugging behind some bar. The officer's neck was broken."

I winced, reminded of the constant danger men and women in uniform lived with each and every day.

I continued. "So the two officers were killed using completely different methods. In fact, it's hard to fathom that the mental mindset of the killer would even be the same. Think about it—one is set up to look like a suicide; the other was more of a surprise attack."

"But it still sounds like the second one was planned," Henry said, a couple of blue veins snaking across each temple. "To know you're going after an officer, the killer had to know who it was ahead of time."

"Or maybe the killer just had a run-in with Miller in the bar? May not have even known he was a cop. Again, I think it's too easy to assume that we're dealing with a serial cop killer."

Henry nodded.

A few seconds of silence had us gravitating back to the football game. The Jets were pounding the Patriots, 24-3, still in the second quarter.

But my brain continued to churn in the background. "Which leads me back to my first thought. Why is Ligon so damn paranoid that he thinks sharing this information would turn the city upside down? Put aside the point that if it's a serial cop killer, then sharing information would scare the killer off."

"Hmm. Maybe we're overcomplicating it," Henry said. "I hang around people who think their title means their opinions are fact. They're put on a pedestal. They're all about controlling the situation. I think it consumes them, because the alternative can really impact their lives."

"And career opportunities," I said, nodding.

"So, Ligon gets news that the first death is ruled a homicide, and the hair stands up on his neck. Then, the second killing last night. He's blinded by two bright objects, both with *cop* and *murder* painted on them. In that position, it's probably easy to make that connection. Worst-case scenario."

"So bad that he shuts down all communication on where the case is really going and then, essentially, goes outside the department to find someone to lead it?"

"Sounds like he doesn't trust anyone."

"But he trusts me, a guy who was essentially kicked off the force for not being a team player."

"If he was going outside of the department, hiring you was the right choice."

"I think he's trying to avoid some type of racial explosion," I said.

Henry pulled his neck back. "Because of two white cops?"

"He thinks it's a possibility the perp might be some black guy who's got a beef against cops. Or maybe just white cops. Or maybe cops who only go to church when their mother-in-law is in town."

We both chuckled, drawing the attention of a pair of guys off to my left. Bringing a hand to the side of my face, I turned the volume down.

"Like I tell Alisa—"

"Tell me what?" She snuck up behind me, leaning an elbow on my shoulder.

"After we're hired for a case, what's our number one rule?"

"Don't rule out anyone, including the client."

"Isn't that Detective 101?" Henry said, gulping the last of his gin and tonic.

"In the public sector, yes...usually, anyway. On this side, it can be easy to see the world through the lens of the person who's paying your tab. Most of the time, there's nothing there. But, on a rare occasion, people in our position are set up to be played."

Those words hung in the air for a few seconds.

I suggested, "From now on, I think we need to be careful about meeting in public. Ligon's paranoia might be reality. We don't want to start a rumor and then have the leak point back to us."

"Good point," Henry said. "That means no meetings at my office. Lots of nosy people there, starting with my boss,

Newsome. I'll have to figure out a way to funnel information to you without people reading anything into it."

"No emails either. At least not from your work account," I added.

Henry smirked. "Look at you. Did you go through CIA training in Langley?"

I thought about Dad and his possible influence on me—the first in my life.

"Is your cell work-issued, or do they just reimburse you?" I asked.

"It's reimbursed."

"Good. We should be okay on that front, although that doesn't mean someone couldn't tap your phone."

"You really think someone would do that?"

"One possible angle we haven't discussed? A fellow government employee, another cop even."

"I guess so. Just who would think—?"

"We can't rule anyone out now. The net is wide. We just need to narrow down the school of fish to a small number of psychos."

Alisa whispered something in my ear. I turned and nodded. "I realize you only know part of the story. I'll fill you in later. Basically, we've got some digging to do on two cops. Henry here is going to start feeding us data to analyze."

"That would be me," he said, raising a hand, lifting from his chair, tossing a few bills on the bar. "By the way, you do know Newsome is running for mayor?"

I paused for a brief second. "I forgot, or the countless political signs littering the sides of roads and public lawns have created a red and blue blur."

I let that nugget of information swirl in the moat of data consuming most of my brain cells.

John W. Mefford Bibliography

The Greed Series

FATAL GREED (Greed Series #1)
LETHAL GREED (Greed Series #2)
WICKED GREED (Greed Series #3)
GREED MANIFESTO (Greed Series #4)

The Booker Series

BOOKER – Streets of Mayhem (Volume 1)
BOOKER – Tap That (Volume 2)
BOILERMAKER – A Lt. Jack Daniels / Booker Mystery
(Volume 2.5)
BOOKER – Hate City (Volume 3)
BOOKER – Blood Ring (Volume 4)
BOOKER – No Más (Volume 5)
BOOKER – Dead Heat (Volume 6)

The Alex Troutt Series

Coming Soon

To stay updated on John's latest releases, visit:
JohnWMefford.com/readers-group

Made in the USA
Middletown, DE
31 May 2018